YELLOWBEARD

YELLOWBEARD

High jinks on the high seas

BY MONTY PYTHON'S

GRAHAM CHAPMAN

CARROLL & GRAF PUBLISHERS

New York

Carroll & Graf Publishers
An imprint of Avalon Publishing Group, Inc.
245 W. 17th Street
New York
NY 10011–5300
www.carrollandgraf.com

AVALON
publishing group incorporated

First published in the UK by Robinson,
an imprint of Constable & Robinson Ltd 2005

First Carroll & Graf edition 2005

ISBN-13 978-0-78671-662-3
ISBN-10 0-7867-1662-2

Printed and bound in the EU

CONTENTS

About the Author   vii

Yellowbeard: Pirate without Penance –
   Introduction by Jim Yoakum   1
About the Screenplay   37
Biography of Yellowbeard   39
Cast & Crew of Yellowbeard   41
Film Trailers   45
El Nebuloso's Song   51
Screenplay   53
Novel   237

ABOUT THE AUTHOR

Graham Chapman studied medicine at Emmanuel College, Cambridge. After mounting his own cabaret show, he was invited to join the Cambridge Footlight Dramatic Society at the same time as first-year student John Cleese. Eric Idle joined them one year later. (David Frost was secretary at that time.) He qualified as a doctor at St Bartholomew's hospital in London.

Chapman put his medical career on hold and joined John Cleese on his tour with *Cambridge Circus*, which ran on Broadway in October 1964. In England, he wrote for the *Doctor in the House* series (together with Bernard McKenna, Barry Cryer, David Sherlock, and sometimes John Cleese). He Met Michael Palin and Terry Jones while writing for *The Frost Report*, but he also worked with Marty Feldman, Peter Sellers and Ringo Starr. At one time he was writing for Monty Python, Ronnie Corbett and the Doctor series at the same time. Later he worked with (a then unknown) Douglas Adams on a BBC special titled *Out of the Trees*. Graham met long-time companion David Sherlock in Ibiza in 1966, and became one of the first celebrities to openly declare his homosexuality. In the early 1970s he helped co-found the *Gay News* paper.

Chapman had the lead role in the films *Monty Python and the Holy Grail* and *Monty Python's Life of Brian*. After he stopped drinking in 1978, he wrote his life story titled *A Liar's Autobiography, Volume VI*. After Monty Python, he wrote, acted in and produced the film *Yellowbeard* (a pirate spoof), with cast consisting of John Cleese, Peter Cook, Cheech and Chong, Peter Boyle, Madeline Kahn, Eric Idle and Kenneth Mars.

Graham Chapman died of cancer on 4 October 1989, just one day before the twentieth anniversary of Monty Python. Fellow Python Terry Jones called it 'The worst case of party-pooping I've ever seen.'

IN MEMORY OF

Peter Bull, Graham Chapman, Peter Cook, Marty Feldman, Sir Michael Hordern, Madeline Kahn, Ronald Lacey, Monte Landis, James Mason, Ferdy Mayne, Spike Milligan, Keith Moon, Harry Nilsson, Beryl Reid, Nigel Stock, Tony Stratton-Smith

THANKS TO

Cheech & Chong, Chris Chesser, John Daly, Carter De Haven, Martin Hewitt, Bernard McKenna and Michael Medavoy for all of their help in bringing the saga of *Yellowbeard* back to life.

Additional material taken from
The Graham Chapman Archives.

YELLOWBEARD:
PIRATE WITHOUT PENANCE

by Jim Yoakum
Director, The Graham Chapman Archives

'**G**raham and I were in a pub with Keith Moon one day and he said, "Look, I'd like you guys to write me a mad movie . . ."' Thus began the odd odyssey that was to become *Yellowbeard*. The pub was most likely Graham's local, the Angel Inn in Highgate, London. The time was 1975-ish. Sitting at the table were Keith Moon, the late and notorious drummer for The Who, Graham Chapman, the mad Monty Python, and comedy writer Bernard McKenna. 'So Keith goes, "You can do me a treatment or something,"' says McKenna, ' "how much would you charge for a treatment?" So we said, "About a thousand pounds." Then he promptly produced a thousand pounds from his briefcase, in cash, and just handed it to us in a pub! I mean, you just don't do that. We had to stuff this money into our pockets . . .'

Perhaps it needs explaining why Keith Moon would be asking two of the top British comedy writers of the day to 'write a mad movie' for him. Although well-regarded then, and well-remembered today, as one of rock's pre-eminent drummers, by the mid-seventies Moon had reached both a personal and professional plateau. Musically, he was bored. Keith Moon didn't so much play the drums as unleash the hounds of hell. There simply were no other drummers like

1

him, and no comers on the horizon brave (or stupid) enough to try and unseat him. While his drumming style guaranteed him a place in the history of rock, by the mid-seventies it had also left him on a very lonely rock; boxed-in and bored, endlessly repeating himself. Personally, he was bottoming out. His wife (and the love of his life) Kim had recently left him, taking their daughter with her, leaving Keith alone to fend for himself. He was open and looking for new adventures and, as he'd always been as much a personality as a percussionist – possessing natural charisma, a mad sense of humour and boyish good-looks – it was just a jump to the left for him to pursue a career in movies.

Aside from the filmed promos that Keith had done with The Who (what would now be considered music videos), Moon's film life proper began with cameo appearances in films such as *200 Motels* (a Frank Zappa extravaganza, 1971), *Stardust* (starring David Essex, 1974) and *Tommy* (the outrageous Ken Russell film of The Who's classic rock opera, 1975). Moon possessed true comic talent and, with discipline, could have become a decent comedic actor. But he didn't know discipline from dysentery. More often than not Keith resorted to the sort of over-the-top eyebrow wriggling and baggy-pants mugging better suited to the music hall. Still, he loved to make people laugh (which he did) and was actively searching for a film role that could excite and expand his creative muscles.

The type of film that he was interested in having Chapman and McKenna create involved superheroes. 'He said, "I want to do *Superman*, *Spiderman*, *Incredible Hulk . . .*"' While Bernard hated to put a damper on things he knew that getting the rights to do any of those characters would cripple the project before it even got started. But they had accepted Moon's money, so the idea of 'a mad movie' drifted around for about another two years, often put aside for more immediate projects. For Graham that meant a round of meet-and-greets for *Monty Python and the Holy Grail*, work on a stage play titled *Oh Happy Day* (with writer Barry Cryer), writing for the *Doctor in the House* television series and preliminary work with the other Pythons for a UK tour. For Moon it meant promotion for the films he had just completed, rehearsals for the upcoming Who record (*The Who By Numbers*), his own solo record (*Two Sides of the Moon*), as well as playing drums on dozens of tracks for other people and, well, simply playing. Keith even had Graham perform lead-on duties when The Who played the Hammersmith Odeon. His 'act' mainly consisted of leading the crowd in a silly Pythonic singalong (funnily enough, a vaguely piratical sea shanty called 'Ya De Bucketty') and then asking them for thirty seconds of abuse – something they were more than happy to dish out. And, of course, Graham and Keith always found the time to get together for their regular booze-ups.

In 1977 Graham moved on to another film project titled *The Odd Job* which was the tale of a man so devastated by his wife leaving him that he hires a passing odd-job man to kill him. The character of the raving odd-job man could not have been more perfect for Moon. In fact, Keith poured several thousand pounds' seed money into the project and was promised the role. But Moon was in bad shape. His years of drug abuse were beginning to take their toll and he was spending a great deal of time in a hospital or drying-out clinics. 'He actually auditioned,' says McKenna. 'And he was terrible. He was just sort of grotesque.' The producers of the film, and its director, Peter Medak, didn't believe the lead role could be trusted to Moon and relayed their concerns to Graham. Graham didn't agree – he thought Keith would be fine – but the producers said they were unwilling to continue with the film if Moon was the lead. They wanted Moon out, and they wanted Graham to tell him. While Keith pretended to take it well, Graham didn't.

In fact, he spent the rest of his life regretting that he had listened to his producers and hurt his friend.

Eventually, Keith asked how the 'mad movie' was going. 'Keith said, "Well, I gave you guys a grand, what have you got to show for it?"' McKenna recalls. What Bernard and Graham had to show for it were a few broad ideas, one of which, about a pirate, caught Keith's attention. ('Keith behaved rather piratically, with no thought to the consequences of his actions, which is an admirable trait for a pirate,' said Graham at the time.) In fact, Moon had a life-long obsession with *Treasure Island*, especially the 1954 film starring British actor Robert Newton as Long John Silver. Moon's impersonation of Newton as Silver was uncanny and was a role he would frequently fall into during the course of an evening's night of Moonish mayhem. 'We had all sorts of mad meetings with Keith about the story,' says McKenna, 'and he was very taken with the idea of playing a pirate. And then Keith died.'

On 7 September 1978, Keith Moon died in his sleep from an overdose of liquor mixed with Heminevrin, a prescription drug used to help people get off booze.[1] The news of Keith's death hit Graham hard, learning of it just as he was preparing to leave for Tunisia for several weeks to film *Life of Brian*. Graham had even worked in a role for Keith in *Brian*.

Although Monty Python were riding the crest of their critical and commercial success in the late seventies with the films *Monty Python and the Holy Grail* (with Graham in the lead role as King Arthur), and now *Life of Brian*

---

1 It was largely thanks to Keith that Graham had weaned himself off booze in the first place. He'd seen the horrors first-hand as Moon had tried to quit alcohol again and again, only to fall back into the abyss. Graham was determined that he would not succumb to the same fate and successfully managed to give up drink in 1978. He remained sober the rest of his life.

(again with Graham in the lead role), things inside the Python team, especially between the writing team of Graham Chapman and John Cleese, were a bit unstable. So with *Brian* in the can, a newly sober and invigorated Graham was reviewing his options. The idea of pushing off on his own was very attractive to him; he'd already seen others have independent success outside the team: Cleese with *Fawlty Towers*, Idle with *The Rutles*, even Terry Gilliam with *Jabberwocky*. Amazingly, Keith's death – which should have killed the fragile 'mad movie' project – actually served to kick some life into it. Graham turned his attention again to the 'pirate movie' with an eye to turning it into a vehicle for himself, either as an actor, a director, or a producer – or any combination of the three. (In homage to Keith, Graham and Bernard named the character of 'Mr Moon', the dastardly pirate played by Peter Boyle in the film, after Keith.)

In 1979 Graham and family relocated to Los Angeles for a year. Although the move was largely for tax purposes, it was also designed to explore the lucrative acting opportunities in Hollywood. His recent accolades in *Brian* had made him a hot property and Graham hit Hollywood Boulevard running, attending gala premieres and glittery parties and taking meetings with a lot of people he'd never heard of. 'Graham called me up from Los Angeles and said, "I've met this independent producer, Chris, who is excited by our pirate film idea," ' says McKenna. 'I said, "What pirate film idea?" That's all it was, a pirate film "idea" – we hadn't done any work on it.'

Over the years McKenna had written many projects with Graham for British television including the popular *Doctor in the House* series, *Out of the Trees*, and he was the author of *The Odd Job* script. Because of their established working relationship, McKenna dutifully flew out to the States to discuss the (as yet untitled) *Yellowbeard* project again – but for real this time.

Although Graham had no idea who 'Chris, the independent producer' was, Bernard knew immediately once he heard his name: Chris Mankiewicz, the son of legendary film director Joseph L. Mankiewicz (*All About Eve*, *Cleopatra*), and nephew of Herman Mankiewicz (playwright, member of the Algonquin Round Table and co-author of the screenplay for *Citizen Kane*). Chris Mankiewicz was also a foreign film buff, which pleased Bernard. 'Graham knew nothing about those sort of films,' says McKenna. 'He never had any interest in things like that, but I did. So Chris and I hit it off immediately.'

Bernard and Graham shared a rented house in Brentwood (a suburb of Los Angeles) and it fell upon McKenna to put a lot of their 'pirate film' ideas down on paper as Graham was also busy writing his autobiography (*A Liar's Autobiography*) at the time. 'The studios were really only interested in getting a Python,' says McKenna. '*Life of Brian* was happening, or it was known about anyway, and Chris Mankiewicz said that all we needed for now was a twelve-page story outline.' As Mankiewicz was Hollywood royalty he had no trouble at all in getting a meeting at Warner Brothers where the pitch session went off without a hitch. In fact, they bought the project before Bernard had even finished reading the outline. "We left the meeting, with Chris, and I said, "Wait a minute . . . have we got a deal?" "Yeah." "Oh, shit . . ." you know, it was like "What?" And Graham said, "I suppose you'll have to live in America now." "Oh yeah, I suppose I will . . ."'

Bernard flew back to England, moved out of his flat and to Los Angeles in order to write with Graham, beginning work before any agreements were signed. McKenna describes the writing process as being a somewhat mixed bag as Graham was on the phone to home a lot to his teenage (adopted) son John, who was having some problems at the time. Plus Graham and Bernard were having problems of their own over the direction the story should take. On the plus side, Warner Brothers allowed the two of them to do nothing for several weeks but watch pirate films and do research. 'We watched them all,' says McKenna. '*Captain Blood*, *The Crimson Pirate* . . . It was wonderful.'

It may come as a surprise to anyone who thinks of *Yellowbeard* as simply a comedy, but it's also historically accurate. Graham and McKenna, along with some help from Graham's companion David Sherlock (who is a history buff), spent several weeks researching pirates and their life and times before committing one word to paper. It was similar to the way the films *Monty Python and the Holy Grail* and *Monty Python's Life of Brian* had been developed. This historical perspective lent not only credence and weight to the work, it also supplied natural springboards for humour. For instance, they uncovered the fact that many pirates used to twist cannon fuses in their hair and beards and then light them for frightening effect. This was later incorporated into the film (the only drawback was that Graham found the fuses in his beard very uncomfortable as the smoke kept getting up his nose). Another was the fact that pirates often smuggled women on board ship disguised as men (having women on board ship was considered unlucky), which was used to great effect with the character of 'Mr Prostitute', who acted as Captain Hughes' aide. (In the film, Mr Prostitute was played by Greta Blackburn, and Captain Hughes was played by James Mason.)

The writing process wasn't all smooth sailing, though. According to McKenna, while they were working on the first draft, Graham told him that work would have to stop until he returned from Australia. McKenna had no idea what Graham was talking about.

'When are you going to Australia?' he asked.

'Tomorrow.' Apparently Graham had agreed to appear

in a beer commercial there, which left Bernard alone to work on the script over the Thanksgiving holiday. While it was sneaky behaviour on Graham's part, the reality was that he was in somewhat dire financial straits at the time (which was another reason why he'd come to America – to make money) and while it no doubt inconvenienced Bernard, in Graham's mind he had little option but to try and make a dollar when and where he could.

After the first draft was turned in, and McKenna had returned to England, things really did turn sour. Warner Brothers read the script – and they didn't like it. The project was dead and if it was to be revived at all then it had to be taken back from Warner's. Graham contacted Denis O'Brien, who was manager for Monty Python during this period. Acting on Graham and Bernard's behalf, O'Brien bought the script back from Warner's for $64,000. He then proposed that his company, EuroAtlantic, produce the film in conjunction with HandMade Films, another company helmed by O'Brien and originally formed with the late Beatle George Harrison (who was hardly hands-on) in order to produce *Monty Python's Life of Brian*. The script now belonged to EuroAtlantic/HandMade, and Graham and Sherlock continued to tweak it through 1979 and into mid-1980, both in LA and back in London. Chris Mankiewicz also stayed with the project as an independent producer working with HandMade. But trouble was brewing. 'When HandMade got involved and wouldn't pay me for rewrites, I didn't rewrite,' says McKenna. 'It wasn't that they refused to pay me any money, it's that what they were offering me wasn't very good. So I stopped writing. Graham was getting plenty of money from Python – and other sources.'

McKenna's reluctance to continue on the script for HandMade caused a problem. Apart from Bernard McKenna and John Cleese (the best-known of Graham's writing partners), there were several others with whom he would often collaborate, chief among them being Barry Cryer (a great set-up-and-punchline-man) and Douglas Adams (later the creator of the *Hitchhiker's Guide to the Galaxy*). There was a brief period (in June 1980) when it looked like Cryer might be brought on board to lend a hand. But Barry was suspicious of the way O'Brien had approached him and so rang McKenna, asking if he was aware that he was being courted. Bernard wasn't aware, so Cryer begged out of the project. In October 1980 Graham enlisted Peter Cook to help with rewrites and polishes. 'Graham got Cook attached, as he was a sort of starry name,' says McKenna. 'It was ironic in that I was working on something else with Cook at the time[2] and Graham kept ringing him up to chat.' Chapman and Cook wrote a new draft in about four to six weeks. While this draft has some brilliant comedic moments,[3] Cook had never had much real experience writing screenplays and it was still in need of some tightening and brightening. So, while McKenna was battling it out with HandMade for payment for the work he'd already completed, Graham approached him to help rewrite the script as it was suddenly and urgently required. A tentative deal was stuck with O'Brien and they

2 *Peter Cook and Company.*
3 This second draft is quite different from the filmed version and reads much more Pythonic. For instance, there is a very long sequence in the draft concerning a character named Woolfitt, the leader of a troupe of thespians, who is enticed to join the adventure in order to bring Shakespeare to the island barbarians. While it's extremely funny it had nothing at all to do with Yellowbeard, or the search for his treasure, and so was cut out. 'I think Cook put that in because he wanted to play the role,' says McKenna. Many characters such as Blind Pew, El Segundo, Moon, Gilbert, El Nebuloso and Triola are mere bit parts and, for much of the film, Yellowbeard himself is absent. In this script Dan actually kills Yellowbeard (thus proving himself a true pirate) and makes off with the treasure. In a funny bit of in-joke humour, one of the pirates who comes in for particular abuse is named O'Brien.

worked from 8 November 1980 through 2 January 1981 ('We even worked on New Year's Day – and me a Scotsman, too!' says McKenna).

In January, pre-production suddenly began at Pinewood Studios. Without Graham's knowledge, Denis O'Brien had employed a whole team of production managers, assistants, set designers, location managers, model builders, secretaries and various accountants to work on the film. He also hired Clive Donner to direct. A proposed shooting schedule was drawn up with principal photography set to begin on 21 April 1981. When Graham finally caught up with O'Brien he learned that the schedule had them filming in the UK and Sri Lanka. When Sri Lanka proved to be too expensive it was switched to the UK and the island of Malta. Graham went to Malta at his own expense to scout locations (O'Brien didn't want him to go) and came back saying that Malta wasn't suitable for a tropical isle location, although a rewrite using Maltese locations was done by Graham and David Sherlock.

Things under O'Brien began to accelerate, and once 'production had started at HandMade,' says McKenna, who was still waiting to be paid for his work on the script, 'they realised they were going to have to pay me money. Chris Mankiewicz was over in England, living in John Cleese's house while the film was in pre-production, and I told him the offer I'd been given by HandMade and he told me I should take it as he thought the film financing was going to collapse. So I rang my agent and told her to accept it. She did, and HandMade said, "No, we're thinking about something else."' That HandMade had 'something else' than money in mind as payment for McKenna suggests that, in line with the rumours about the financing, they were stalling. And then, in February 1981, things abruptly halted, and O'Brien cancelled production. Mankiewicz connects the call he had received from HandMade telling him to fire everyone on *Yellowbeard* with the fact that Terry Gilliam had just finished *Time Bandits* for HandMade, and had gone way over budget.

O'Brien didn't inform Graham of events until March. Soon afterward, Graham decided to disengage from O'Brien and drafted a letter stating that he wished to reclaim O'Brien's interest in the *Yellowbeard* property and reimburse him for the money he had paid to Warner's. 'I feel that I would like to deal with the script entirely on my own,' Graham wrote in the letter to O'Brien, 'and have no contractual obligations in this regard and Bernard shares my feelings.'

Despite not having heard back from O'Brien about his letter, Graham moved into more of a producer mode. He put out feelers to find outside investors in New Zealand where the ship, the *Bounty*, was also berthed (they were looking to use the ship in the movie). Months of convoluted talks with EMI Films, Oasis Films (a New Zealand production company) and Filmco (a film financing company in New South Wales) all led nowhere. As if getting *Yellowbeard* moving forward wasn't enough of a headache, Graham was also trying to get another film of his off the ground, *Ditto*. This too was faltering.

In October 1981, Graham contacted Bill Sharmat, a man with extensive experience in financing motion pictures, asking him to get involved in raising financing for *Yellowbeard*. In January 1982, Graham's solicitors finally received word from Denis O'Brien – *Yellowbeard*'s purchase price had escalated from the buy-price of $64,000 (£34,000) to a sell-price of $500,000 (£270,000). (Although there was no hard evidence to support it, there were suspicions that EuroAtlantic/HandMade had caught wind that Graham might want to reclaim the property and had accelerated production in January 1981 in order to raise incurred costs and therefore the sell-price of the production.) It turned out that O'Brien had sent a letter to Graham's management team offering a price of £250,000 – 'open for acceptance' for three weeks only. Graham's solicitors wrote to O'Brien on 11 February 1982 asking that, since the letter had been 'accidentally' sent to the wrong people, the offer be extended for a further three weeks. O'Brien replied saying there could be no extension, but he would consider any serious future offers in the 'light of other opportunities'. (It should perhaps be noted at this point that Denis O'Brien was also business manager for ex-Beatle George Harrison – who accused O'Brien of fraud and mismanagement in a 1995 lawsuit, and who won a $10.9 million judgment against O'Brien the following year. A Los Angeles court rejected O'Brien's appeal in February 1998 and Denis O'Brien has since left the film business.

Meanwhile, Bill Sharmat had lined up $6,000,000 in interim financing via a labyrinth of English, Australian and United American film financing organisations. The labyrinth extended as far as people like Tony Stratton-Smith, who was something of a legend in the pop music/hip community of the 1970s. In addition to running one of the first truly independent record labels (later sold to Richard Branson, becoming the nucleus of Virgin), Smith had also managed Genesis and the Bonzo Dog Band, among others. He was a friend of Graham's and had helped finance *The Odd Job*. Exactly what Smith's involvement was with the *Yellowbeard* project is unclear, but he is listed as receiving a finder's fee.

In Los Angeles, Graham went to see producer John Daly at Hemdale Films. 'I was approached by Graham in Los Angeles,' says Daly. 'I read the script and liked it very much.' Daly sees himself as 'sort of the early promoter of it; the architect of getting it to Orion, getting it set up there.' Daly took the script to producer Carter De Haven, who called Michael Medavoy,[4] co-founder of Orion Pictures (Sharmat had dealt with Orion before, and *Life of Brian* was distributed by them). 'I told Mike the story of the movie and he liked it,' is the way De Haven remembers it. 'He asked if I had anyone else interested and I said he was the first person to see it. He said, "I'll get back to you next week," and I said, "No, I want an answer by Monday morning, Mike. I want you to commit to the movie." I wish I'd been smarter and said I wanted him to commit to the movie with *a big-name director*, but I didn't. Anyway, he said, "Come on!" and I said, "No, it's too good a movie. I can make this deal in four places now." So bang, Monday morning at ten o'clock he called and said, "You've got a deal." ' Between them, and in whatever proportion of responsibility, Daly and De Haven had got *Yellowbeard* back on track.

During all this, negotiations with HandMade on the purchase-price had come to a head, with O'Brien's last offer being $320,000, payable on receipt of financing. 'Once John Daly put up some money and Orion put up some money, the picture got made,' says De Haven. O'Brien was duly paid off, as was Chris Mankiewicz. (Not being party to all the recent financing and rights issues, it must have looked to Mankiewicz as if Graham had gone right ahead and made a deal behind his back with Orion. He calls this 'the great betrayal': 'Orion dumped all of us and said,

4 Michael Medavoy is something of a legend in the film industry. A real-life Horatio Alger story, Medavoy started out working in the mailroom at Universal Pictures, eventually working his way up to become a casting director. He then worked as one of Hollywood's biggest talent agents in the 1970s, managing the careers of Gene Wilder, Marty Feldman, Steven Spielberg, Jane Fonda, Michelangelo Antonioni and Peter Boyle. At that time, Medavoy also was the vice-president in charge of the IFA motion picture department and was responsible for helping to promote such seventies blockbusters as *The Sting* and *Jaws*. In 1978, Medavoy and others created Orion Pictures after becoming frustrated with the policies of United Artists where Medavoy had been serving as the senior vice-president of West Coast productions since 1974. Still a power player, Medavoy currently heads Phoenix Pictures.

"Sue us."' McKenna softens this somewhat, saying he doesn't feel Graham ever knowingly stabbed anybody in the back, simply that he often didn't realise that his actions could be perceived as being disloyal.)

'I'm sure Denis was very relieved that he got his cash back,' says John Daly. With Orion's participation things moved faster and much more smoothly. Medavoy gave the screenplay to Chris Chesser, a young production executive at Orion who worked closely under Medavoy. While still at Filmways, Mankiewicz had brought the screenplay to Chesser. He turned it down: twice. Of the first occasion, 'I liked the idea, but I just didn't think the script was as funny yet as it could be,' says Chesser, but after Filmways was taken over by Orion Pictures, Medavoy asked Chesser to take another look since he was already so familiar with it. In a memo to Medavoy dated 24 March 1982, Chesser says, 'Basically, I like the screenplay very much. However there are three problem areas . . .' He goes on to detail several improvements, including having Yellowbeard and crew sent to debtors' prison and then having Dan (finally proving himself to be a prawn of Yellowbeard's loins) lead an escape.

Story issues aside, the first task for the new team was to find a director who knew comedy and who could handle what was shaping up to be an extravaganza unseen since the days of movies like *It's a Mad, Mad, Mad, Mad, Mad World*. There were several directors on Graham's shortlist, some well-known others less so, including Robert Young (who had already directed Cleese in *Romance With a Double Bass* and would later direct him in *Fierce Creatures* as well as Eric Idle in *Splitting Heirs*), Carl Reiner, Alan Parker, Mickey Dolenz (of Monkees fame) and Harold Ramis. But on Carter De Haven's list there was but one name. 'When I went to talk to Mike Medavoy about the script I said that we've got an extraordinary screenplay here and the opportunity to have a huge cast, so it's really important we get the right director. He

14

asked who I had in mind and, because he's a very good friend of mine and he really knows comedy, I said, "Blake Edwards."[5] I gave it to Blake and he said he'd do it for seven hundred and fifty thousand dollars. I told Mike Blake's price, but they had a much smaller figure in mind. I said we couldn't get anybody of any stature for less.' De Haven certainly hadn't considered Graham Chapman's name. 'When the script was sent to me I asked John Daly if there were any attachments to the script, he said, "No, just that Graham wrote it." But when Graham came out to LA to visit with me he said, "You know, I really want to direct this." That was pretty shocking to me because usually that's something somebody says first, not after a while.' De Haven dutifully suggested Graham to Medavoy, but the suggestion wasn't taken too seriously: 'Medavoy, who was a huge Graham fan, thought it would be too much for him to be the star and the writer and the director. Shortly after Orion came on board Graham was told that we had to go a different way,' says De Haven. 'A lot of members of the cast wanted a seasoned director and he'd never done a movie. He didn't have the approach to things like a director does. He was a marvellous performer and writer though. He was fine with the decision, although I'm sure it was a dream of his, but he never mentioned it again.'

Director Mel Damski[6] came to direct the picture through

5 Director of classics such as *The Pink Panther* series with Peter Sellers and *10*, starring Dudley Moore.
6 Damski's directing credits up to that point consisted mainly of American television programmes like *Lou Grant*, *M*A*S*H* and made-for-TV movies. Damski has since carved out a great career in television, directing episodes of several popular US TV series like *The Tick*, *The Guardian*, *Ally McBeal* and *Charmed*. In fact, there's a rather funny plug for *Yellowbeard* in an episode of *Charmed* where a character (played by Nick Lachey) talks about pirate movies: 'I grew up watching pirate movies with my dad . . . I've seen them all. Even *Yellowbeard*. It was a great spoof.' (Damski says that the writer of that episode put the *Yellowbeard* reference in to tease Damski. The original line was not 'It was a great spoof' but one a bit less complimentary. All in good fun.)

Chris Chesser, who knew Damski through the American Film Institute and knew he was looking for a feature to direct. 'He's a good hands-on director, and liked to mix with the actors as opposed to some directors who like to keep a distance. I knew he could relate to them on that level, and could also handle any potential creative problems that might arise on the set,' says Chesser. Ironically, one of the biggest problems that arose on the set was between Graham and Mel Damski. 'Medavoy didn't want to bring in a big-time director with a big ego, either, who would shut Graham out creatively,' says Damski, 'but it was his vision and I was trying to get into his head. I had a complicated relationship with him.' While Damski was trying to get into Graham's head, Graham was getting under Damski's skin. 'When I was directing him as a character we got along great, he totally respected me in a director-actor relationship, the problem was when I directed everyone else. Marty Feldman was a very inventive actor and comedian and he always came up with some fresh ideas and behaviours to make the scene funnier. Almost in every case Graham said he didn't want Marty to do that, he wanted him to stick to the script. It was more him being a protective writer than anything else.' Actually it sounds more like Graham directing by proxy. It makes sense that Graham would be fine when Damski directed him, because he could control his own performance. Besides, he didn't originally envision himself as being the lead actor in the film anyway, he wanted Burt Lancaster or Kirk Douglas to play Yellowbeard. So by controlling the script he was controlling the performances of the other actors.

There were also problems between the two regarding their approach to schedules. 'Let's say I had an early call with Marty Feldman,' says Damski. 'Well, Graham didn't want to wake up early because he wasn't a morning person and because he wasn't in the scene, so he'd call me at night –

at midnight, and I'd already been asleep for two hours – and say, "Now how are you going to shoot that scene tomorrow with Marty?" That kind of thing. I'd tell him, "Graham, I've been asleep for hours. Please either call me earlier or come by in the morning and watch the rehearsal." But he never changed. Graham always called me late at night to discuss things so I was sleep-deprived the next day.' Graham was infamous, especially during his *Python* days, for having a complete disregard for timetables. He was always turning up late for meetings and for filming. In those days a lot of the reason was due to his drinking and late-night carousing, but since giving up the bottle a new seriousness had come over him towards his life and his career. 'Graham took the movie all very serious. More serious than what it deserved really,' says John Daly. But there was a reason for that: finally free from chains of booze and (with this film) the repression of being thought of as 'a Python', he was out to prove himself. He was now worrying about things that he'd never bothered with before such as script, cast, make-up, direction, and money – in addition to acting. It was a lot for any one person to take on and, some felt, was too much for Graham in particular. 'I believe Graham was well in over his head as a producer,' says Bernard McKenna. 'I don't think he had the aptitude for it.' No doubt he could have handled things better with Damski, but then he had no prior experience to go by and (seemingly) little support. Besides, following the path of least resistance and being passive-aggressive was his nature. Despite the conflicts, there was no real acrimony between Damski and Graham. 'He was a very serious person but with a rapier wit,' says Damski. 'He was very shy, almost painfully shy, but had poor people-skills which made it tough for me to relate to him.'

Graham also stepped on Carter De Haven's toes on a few occasions. 'Graham wasn't easy sometimes, a very quiet guy. I don't think he was as accessible as the others on the picture. It was hard to get him to understand that he was just the writer. I had a run-in with him once or twice. There was one big moment when we were running behind schedule and he wanted to spend some money for a shot that we didn't think we needed. I told him he was wrong, that that's not how you make a picture, we have an obligation to the financiers to keep as close to the budget as we can, and he said, "I'll tell you right now, it's not a good idea to disagree with me." Things were pretty cold between us after that.'

Despite Chesser's initial concerns about the script, once Orion decided to go with it he became the script's biggest advocate – and Michael Medavoy's right-hand man on the set, dealing with logistics and problems as they arose. 'I was viewed by some of the others on the set as "the suit",' says Chesser, 'as the man from the studio.' Martin Hewitt, who played the Dan character, recalls Chesser acting almost as an assistant director on the set. 'He worked really hard,' says Hewitt, 'and even though he was Orion's guy, he hung out and was pretty cool. I saw him more than I did Carter De Haven or John Daly.'

Principal photography was set to begin on 4 October, in England, with eight weeks on location in Mexico to follow. At this point even Bernard McKenna was coaxed back into the fold to do rewrites. 'When they got the money together to make it, both Graham and Cook wanted me back on board,' says McKenna. 'They lured me with money and with the location trip to Mexico where I continued to rewrite and we three did a third version (as opposed to drafts).' Previous to the work in Mexico, the three met on several occasions in a London pub to brainstorm. 'It was quite funny,' says McKenna, 'Peter and I were getting very drunk at Graham's expense, literally, improvising lines and having a drunken laugh. The whole time Graham was sober, looking on disapprovingly, trying to get us back on track. It was quite a turn around from how he had used to be.'

The cast of *Yellowbeard* was an embarrassment of riches, containing as it did a 'dream team' of actors and a virtual *Who's Who* of late twentieth-century comedy: Spike Milligan from the renowned *Goon Show* in a bit part; Peter Cook of *Beyond the Fringe* and 'Cook and [Dudley] Moore' fame; Kenneth Mars, Peter Boyle, Madeline Kahn and Marty Feldman representing the Mel Brooks school (with Feldman sharing double duty, with Cleese and Chapman, as an alumni of the *At Last the 1948 Show* and *Frost Report* programmes); American stoner comics Cheech & Chong; three from the Monty Python team (Chapman, Cleese and Idle); and Nigel Planer from heirs to Python, The Young Ones. There were also legends from the British stage and cinema like James Mason, Michael Hordern, Susannah York and Beryl Reid. Not to mention David Bowie in an uncredited cameo. 'They all admired each other's work,' said Graham at the time. 'That was not something I expected when I was casting. It all worked out very well.'

Over the years nothing has caused as much debate and discussion among fans, critics – and even the participants themselves – as the cast of *Yellowbeard*. They have been both praised and disparaged; targeted as the reason for the film's *joie de vivre* and blamed for its box-office deficiency. Michael Medavoy was primarily the man behind the diverse cast. Drawing on his experience putting together the team for Mel Brooks' hit, *Young Frankenstein*, Medavoy suggested hiring Marty Feldman, Kenneth Mars, Madeline Kahn, Peter Boyle and Cheech & Chong. 'We were doing a film for Orion (*The Corsican Brothers*) at the same time,' says Cheech Marin, 'and Mike Medavoy asked us if we wanted to be in the movie. He said that they were looking for a bunch of comedians and we said, "Okay!" Peter Boyle

I had known from before, I don't remember. I think we'd worked on a project.' Martin Hewitt, for one, wasn't very happy to learn that Cheech & Chong were on their way to the set in Mexico. 'The whole Cheech & Chong thing . . . I don't think they fit in at all,' he says. 'I didn't even know they were going to be in it. It was nice to see the *Young Frankenstein* cast together again but, even then, I really didn't think any of us Americans belonged there.' The international cast (slanted, some complained, more towards American tastes) didn't sit well with producer John Daly either: '*Yellowbeard* was meant to be a rather irreverent film, and somehow it started to go slightly Hollywood. Some of the people that became involved, I mean James Mason – he'd never made a comedy in his life! So it took on a slightly more serious tone. I always thought it would have been wonderful if it had been made in the way that Graham had earned his reputation, by making it in this mad way. But once we got Orion involved, suddenly it started taking on a more Hollywood approach.' According to director Mel Damski, he was hired by Orion in order to even-out the overt British humour. 'I was brought in through Orion because they wanted the movie to be palatable to an American audience,' he says. 'They wanted someone with an American ear.' One would think that Graham might have agreed with Daly and fought to keep the style and humour of the movie more in the 'mad and loony' style that he'd helped make famous, but according to Daly, Graham was very hands-on in the casting as well, and actually appeared to push for the mixture of English and American actors and combination of humorous approaches. 'I think he saw it as his break-out movie,' says Daly. 'He wanted a splashy success.'

It's not uncommon during the development of a film to draw up lists of possible actors – a wish-list – to play certain roles. Sometimes people are chosen because one actor really wants to work with another one, sometimes strictly for their marquee value, and sometimes simply to satisfy the needs of the international market. Preliminary notes during development of the *Yellowbeard* project show that it was a mix of all three, and that the film might have been quite a bit different. Hal Linden (most remembered as the star of the US television series *Barney Miller*) was heavily favoured for the role of Clement (eventually played by Eric Idle). Oliver Reed was pencilled in for the role of Mr Moon (the Peter Boyle role), Diana Dors or Ann-Margaret as Betty Beard (the Madeline Kahn part), Liz Taylor as one of the Queen's servants and Larry Hagman (star of *Dallas* and *I Dream of Jeannie*) as Captain Hughes. The importance of getting a Big American Star (well, big at that time) was a driving force in casting, as that meant a better chance of securing financing. Also considered for roles were old friend Alan Bennett (from *Beyond the Fringe* fame) as the Chaplain, Don Novello (best known as Father Guido Sarducci) as either El Segundo or El Nebuloso, Olivia Newton-John as Triola, Spike Milligan as Blind Pew (played by John Cleese) and, as stated earlier, Graham wanted either Burt Lancaster or Kirk Douglas to play Yellowbeard. (Graham intended to play Captain Hughes or Finn if either one of those took the role.) Kirk Douglas begged off as he was busy doing a film in Canada with Sylvester Stallone (*First Blood*, although he pulled out at the last minute), however there is a letter to Douglas from one of his assistants suggesting that he not do the film as '. . . it's a cameo role and unless there's a lot of money for a little time, and you're dying to visit New Zealand [at the time the location of the shoot], forget it'. Also on the short-list for various roles were Robin Williams (as El Nebuloso), fellow Python Terry Jones (as the Chaplain), Elton John (as the Chaplain), Pia Zadora (as Triola), Ringo Starr (as McDonald), Billy Connolly (as McDonald), Denholm

Elliott and Danny De Vito and Christopher Lloyd (both from the US TV series *Taxi*).

Without delving too deeply into pop psychology, there were several instances in *Yellowbeard* where Graham's subconscious obviously came into play. First, and foremost, Martin Hewitt, who plays Dan, Lord Lambourn's adopted son, bears a more than passing resemblance to Graham's real-life adopted son, John Tomiczek. And, as mentioned earlier, Keith Moon appeared in name (in the character of Moon) as well as persona (Graham modelled Yellowbeard on Keith). Also, Captain Hughes' ship is named the *Edith*, which was the name of Graham's mother.

The role of Dan was originally offered to pop star Adam Ant, who agreed and then backed out. In a handwritten letter to Graham dated 12 August 1982, Ant stated his frustrations at production delays and funding problems. Graham must have sensed the possibility of Ant's leaving as he had already offered the role of Dan to Sting in a letter dated 11 June. 'Sting wanted to play Dan,' says Damski, 'but the producers in their ultimate wisdom thought the film was getting "too British" and didn't want him. Granted he wasn't as big then as he is now, but it's ironic because we ended up casting an American kid who, while good, ended up playing with a perfect British accent. So what did we accomplish?' Interestingly, Martin Hewitt (who is American, and played Dan) thinks the same thing. 'They should not have involved an American studio, just kept it all English,' he says. 'I mean, even me – Sting should have had my part. For crying out loud, I would have hired Sting over me any day.' While Hewitt was hired for his obvious heart-throb appeal (his previous film had been Franco Zeffirelli's *Endless Love* starring opposite Brooke Shields) he worked very hard, probably much harder than many of the other actors, in order to overcome the idea that he was merely there as eye-candy. 'I felt that I really had to carry my weight, I had a lot to prove.'

In the letter to Sting, asking him to consider the Dan role, it's obvious that many of the finance and production details of the movie had been finalised, even if all the casting hadn't been ('Casting has only just begun,' Graham wrote, 'but so far we have myself playing Yellowbeard, Peter Cook as Lord Lambourn, Eric Idle as Commander Clement and John Cleese guesting as Blind Pew'). Graham also says that Harry Nilsson[7] was doing the music.

Harry Nilsson had been a great friend of Graham's for many years, and Graham was godfather to one of Harry's children. Along with Keith Moon and Ringo Starr, Harry and Graham comprised a drinking team of Olympic-sized proportions and had been striking fear and loathing in the hearts of pub owners across Great Britain since the early 1970s. Graham and Harry had been searching for a film project to collaborate on for a very long time. Nilsson had offered a song ('Going Down') for *The Odd Job* but the producers had rejected it, and he'd been aware of *Yellowbeard* since its earliest inception in the mid-seventies. It looked like it was to be the movie where the two of them would, finally, be able to work together.

'Harry Nilsson came down to the location in Mexico with his family and hung out for a few weeks,' says Carter De Haven. 'One night we were talking and he said, "You

7 Harry Nilsson was a singer and songwriter best known for the hit 'Without You'. A pal to the Beatles (especially John and Ringo); singer of 'Everybody's Talkin' ', the theme to the movie *Midnight Cowboy* (1969); singer of the theme to the TV show *The Courtship of Eddie's Father*; and composer of the soundtrack to the animated movie *The Point* (with its hit single 'Me and My Arrow'). Nilsson had great vocal range and a pop sensibility that was at turns lyrical and whimsical. He released records in the late sixties, 1970s and early eighties. He died of an apparent heart attack in 1994. Ironically, Nilsson's apartment in London is where both The Who's Keith Moon and 'Mama' Cass Elliott died.

know, this sort of story really lends itself to music," and I said, "Yeah," not daring to think what he was about to suggest. I said, "We need to have a top-notch composer," and he said, "I can be top-notch. Will you give me a shot at it?" I mean, "Give him a shot?!" – he was an incredible musician. I said, "What do you have in mind?" This was the second day of shooting, and I didn't see Harry again for, like, another ten days – I think he's hiding from me or something. We're passing notes to each other. Anyway, he finally appears one night and says he had something to show me. So he pulls out a napkin and writes down the lyrics to this song ('Men At Sea') and sings it to me there at the bar! He said, "I sure want to be a part of the movie, Carter.'" But, in much the same way that the producers of *The Odd Job* had been scared off by Keith Moon's reputation for being a wild man, it was decided by Mike Medavoy that Harry was too much of a risk; that he wasn't reliable enough to turn in a suitable, completed soundtrack on time. 'Harry was okay with the decision,' says De Haven. 'He was a great guy, very smart.' It's a shame that the producers weren't as smart as Harry as his music has appeared in dozens of movies[8] since 1969 and a Nilsson soundtrack would have, no doubt, earned back a great deal of the money that the film didn't. In fact, Harry *did* record several tunes for the movie and Martin Hewitt is one of the only people ever privileged enough to hear Nilsson's phantom soundtrack for *Yellowbeard*. 'Graham invited me to go with him to Harry Nilsson's house in Los Angeles,' Hewitt says. 'We ended up in his basement listening to all this incredible music. I hadn't really put two-and-two together at the time, that this was HARRY NILSSON, all I knew was that the music was amazing. But then I saw all these posters

8 Nilsson's music has appeared in many hit films including *Midnight Cowboy, Reservoir Dogs, You've Got Mail, GoodFellas, High Fidelity* and *Magnolia*.

and gold records on the wall and really listened to his voice and I suddenly realised who the guy was and that I should be impressed. Believe me, I was *very* impressed.'

Although Nilsson did write at least one song specifically for the movie ('Men At Sea') and planned to use at least another one ('Black Sails') that he had released a few years previously on his Lennon-produced record, *Pussy Cats*, Harry did not end up doing the music for the movie. Sadly, Graham never managed to work, on film, with two of his greatest friends: Keith Moon and Harry Nilsson.

Just as Graham and Bernard McKenna had prepared for the writing by watching dozens of pirate movies Mel Damski, too, threw himself into the genre by endlessly viewing Richard Lester's *The Three Musketeers*, hoping to reproduce its mixture of comedy and adventure. The madness had begun.

By the autumn, most of the pieces were in place. Casting had been firmed up and locations had been chosen, Zihuatanejo Bay (on Mexico's West Coast) was to substitute for the tropics, and the English seaside city of Rye was to fill in for Portsmouth. 'Portsmouth had been too modernised,' says Damski. 'But Rye, with its fourteenth- and fifteenth-century thatched cottages and cobbled streets looked more like Portsmouth than Portsmouth.' While shooting began on the picture in mid-October in Rye, the search for a suitable ship was underway. The *Bounty* (as featured in the 1960 remake of *Mutiny on the Bounty*) was now anchored in St Petersberg, Florida, as a tourist attraction. Carter De Haven negotiated for its use and it was restored to its eighteenth-century glory, before setting sail through the Panama Canal for the shoot in Zihuatanejo.

From Rye, the cast and crew trooped to Hertfordshire for scenes at Lord Lambourn's estate and then to Zihuatanejo. 'Our headquarters was actually in nearby Ixtapa,' said

Graham, 'which was a relief to everybody because nobody could get a call out of Zihuatanejo. By the time you learned how to pronounce it, your three minutes were up.' Filming in Mexico was mainly a money-saving move (the entire budget was $10 million, skimpy even by 1983 standards but paltry by today's) so to keep costs down De Haven decided to make the movie a Mexican co-production. The move from England to Mexico was haphazard and caused several problems; usually a production allows a gap of a week or so when moving to a new location in order to make certain things like equipment and costumes and actors arrive, but because money was tight the gap was only a day or two. Consequentially, filming in Mexico was gruelling for both cast and crew. 'We went immediately from English efficiency to Mexican chaos,' says Damski. 'We had a whole box of eighteenth-century weapons sent from England but they were tied up in customs for eight weeks and so had to use the same two pistols in every scene.' Also, Air France had accidentally shipped a whole series of costumes to Paris. This caused the costume and continuity departments trouble as the improvised outfits had to match exactly the ones shot in England, which were now sitting in a Parisian warehouse. Also, several of the extras simply walked off with their costumes and never returned. Damski credits his background in television for the ability to roll with the punches. 'I'm used to improvising and working quickly,' he says.

Because of costs, the *Bounty* ended up playing all three ships needed for the film. First it was painted bright crimson and edged in gilt to play the gold-filled galleon of El Segundo and El Nebuloso. It was then rubbed down and weathered to portray Captain Hughes' armed merchant-man, then a false French flag was flown above the freshly painted gunnels as it became Commander Clement's French frigate.

It was difficult when battle scenes between the warring ships were needed. 'The battle scene between the *Edith* and the frigate was tricky,' Graham recalled. 'First we aged the ship to be James Mason's and took a few pictures, then we whisked it back to dry dock and tarted it up for Eric's boat. Then it was back to Mason again, this time with cannons firing. Then we panned back to Eric's frigate firing, which had to be redecorated all over again when the cannon-ball hit and splintered the mast.' If anything dire had happened to the *Bounty* then the production would have been finished. 'It wasn't like Columbus,' said Graham. 'Let's say the *Niña* hit a whale or something, well he still had the *Pinta* and the *Santa Maria*. But we'd have been right down the drain.' Luckily, the *Bounty* remained seaworthy and finished its filmatic journey at the Churubusco Studios in Mexico City, with one last side trip to Acapulco where the Portsmouth waterfront was created for a few scenes.

Then there were the bureaucratic nightmares. 'We had a censor in Mexico,' says Damski, 'and it was her job to make sure we didn't do anything to insult Mexico in the movie. We kept trying to explain to her that what we were shooting wasn't supposed to take place in Mexico, that we're just borrowing the scenery, but she still had to watch the dailies every day because if she didn't sign-off on them we couldn't ship the film to LA to be edited.' Couple all of this with the heat (nearly 100 degrees centigrade in the shade and there was hardly ever any of that), the lack of toilets, the strange mix of diverse comedians and serious actors, and you have the makings for mutiny. But, surprisingly, everyone generally got along. 'The set was great fun,' says Damski. 'Eric Idle especially was a real cut-up, always "on" and Peter Cook was the funniest person I'd ever met in my life. When he spoke everyone – and I mean everyone – stopped to listen. Marty was a serious person, almost dour when not in character, and Madeline Kahn was a very funny actor but not in person.'

Cheech and Chong arrived once production had settled in Mexico and immediately fell into the spirit of things. 'It was a big lovefest,' says Tommy Chong. 'Peter Boyle was especially kind, a real sweet guy. We were like old friends, such a buddy.' Still, not everyone was happy, and there are differing opinions on who did and did not fit in. 'Michael Hordern was the only one who was a pain in the ass,' says De Haven. 'The only really weird one was Spike Milligan. I don't think he really liked being in someone else's film so he decided to make me the target by goofing on me,' says Damski. 'James Mason didn't really fit in, and neither did Michael Hordern,' says Martin Hewitt. 'They were from an older generation, they did their work and went to their rooms. The rest of us partied.'

David Bowie, who happened to be vacationing in Mexico, says he had been sunning on the beach one day when he saw an eighteenth-century galleon sail past. He went to investigate and discovered half the Monty Python team, Marty Feldman, James Mason and all of the others on board. 'Bang went the holiday,' he said. He was soon roped into making a cameo (as a shark) in the film and then spent the remainder of his time on the island partying with the actors. One evening he and Graham decided to go into town, so they borrowed a Jeep rented to the production and set out, passing Martin Hewitt who happened to be standing in the parking lot. 'I asked if I could come along,' says Hewitt. 'And David looks at Graham and says "Oh, *sure* you can . . ." I wondered what I was getting into, but hey, how much fun could this be, right? Bowie was driving, and he was pretty drunk. I was too. Graham wasn't drunk at all. He was riding shotgun. I climbed in the back. We didn't get too far into town when suddenly David rear-ends a taxi. We hit it so hard that it disabled the Jeep, shoving the radiator fan right into the engine. Graham hit his knee on the dashboard. I was pretty banged-up. Anyway, this taxi driver gets out and says he's got to call the police. David's so drunk that pulls out a big wad of bills, chunks of hundreds, and starts peeling them off, saying to the driver not to call the police, that he wants to buy the taxi! The taxi driver says "No" and goes into this market to call the police. I mean, we're in serious trouble. Then this guy who was working on the film drove by and he saw us. He said, "Get in!" and we sped off.' Graham had hit his knee so hard on the dashboard that he developed water on the knee and missed a week's filming. 'No one was allowed to go into town after that,' says De Haven.

Often filming took some rather odd turns, such as the night that James Mason asked Bernard McKenna to kiss him. 'I did a small part in the movie, playing the character of Askey,' says McKenna. 'We were filming together very late at night in Acapulco and James asked me if I'd ever seen this film he did where this woman kisses him and then he turns to her and says, "Don't you ever do that again!" – it's a chilling moment in the movie – so he says, "Shall we do that?" and I go, "What?" thinking, "Is James Mason asking me to kiss him?" I said I wasn't sure about that, so he says, "Just think, Bernard, you'll be the only man I've ever kissed in a film." So I thought, "Okay, I'll do it for that reason."' Bernard McKenna stands as the only man James Mason ever kissed in a movie. For Damski, controlling the improvising impulses of the cast was a constant struggle as almost everyone in the movie was a star and he had to be constantly on watch to make sure no one tried to steamroll him. 'I felt like I was conducting an all-star orchestra,' he says, 'and all of these guys were stars, they could all do solos.' Michael Hordern said that Damski did a good job of controlling the egos. 'Mel was very much in command,' Hordern said at the time. 'Very democratic.'

Production went fairly smoothly throughout October and November. The biggest concerns for the producers were filming aboard a constantly rocking ship, and the constant praying for good weather. As Yellowbeard, Graham had a hard time filming one scene which required him to swim a few hundred yards towards the ship. His pirate boots kept filling up with water and he was in serious danger of being dragged under, but the stunt coordinator (who was swimming behind dressed as a pirate) shouted out instructions and Graham managed to reach the boat unscathed. Towards early December the filming was wrapping up. There was a general feeling of satisfaction among the cast and crew at having captured at least a little magic in the bottle, the anticipation of the upcoming Christmas holidays, and the melancholy actors always feel when leaving a movie and having to bid adieu to on-set friends. Early in the morning of 2 December, Carter De Haven was sitting down to breakfast in Mexico City when he received a panicky telephone call. 'I was staying in the same hotel in Mexico as Marty, on the floor below his. I got a call in that morning saying that Marty was ill, that he'd a heart attack or something. I told them to stay calm; call the hotel doctor and the hotel manager but nobody else. I ran up to Marty's room in my bathrobe.'

When De Haven arrived in Feldman's room he found Marty lying on the bed without his shirt, resting. He asked Marty how he was feeling, although De Haven could tell that things weren't right. 'It was quite apparent he wasn't going to make it.' The hotel doctor arrived soon afterwards and began to examine him. 'Marty had said to me the night before that he wasn't feeling good,' says Tommy Chong, 'and I told him he should get acupuncture. I think he did.' Feldman said he had chest pains. An ambulance was called but it didn't arrive for four hours. 'It was a long wait for the ambulance,' says Chong, 'so he had time to phone home, check his messages, tell everybody goodbye . . . The last thing Marty had said to me was, "I feel much better now."

Then he died.' Feldman's death was not only a tragic loss to his family, his friends, and the entertainment industry, it also posed seemingly insurmountable problems for the producers. According to Chris Chesser, the man responsible for handling the logistics of getting Marty's body back to the States, there was an immediate (and unfounded) fear that Marty might have died on drugs. 'We didn't know why he'd had a heart attack, just that he'd had one, so we had to be careful. No autopsy. We had to get him back to LA and to his family.'

Getting Marty's body out of Mexico was a problem. 'The Mexican government is very strict about things like that,' says De Haven. 'But the ambassador to Mexico happened to be an old friend of mine, an actor by the way, and I asked him to help. He said, "Give me an hour." And it was taken care of.' The news of Marty's death hit the cast and crew very hard. 'Marty had flown down to Mexico with me,' says John Daly. 'And I had to come back knowing that he was returning in a coffin.' Peter Boyle was especially distraught. 'Peter and I had a beer together,' says Martin Hewitt, 'and he just poured out his guts to me about Marty, about a lot of things actually. He was really upset.' Chesser says that he had to go to everyone's room individually – many of the cast and crew had known and worked with Marty for years – and break it to them that their friend was dead. 'Can you imagine what that was like?' says Chesser.

'We had about ninety-five per cent of Marty's scenes shot already,' says Damski. 'Ironically, the scene we still had to shoot was his character's death scene. We used a stunt double.' Amazingly, all of the actors managed to pull it together and finish the final few scenes of the movie. 'That's what makes actors actors,' says Hewitt, 'we have the ability to pretend when we have to.' For his part, Graham wasn't aware that Marty had died as he had been on set until late. 'I'd heard he'd been taken to hospital,' he said at the time, 'but that was all. He'd been in perfect spirits the night before and had, I believe, actually been out shopping that morning. It seemed to happen out of the blue.'

The cause of Feldman's death has been put down to many things. Michael Mileham, one of the production people on the film, believes Marty may have died of shellfish poisoning from a dirty knife used to cut coconuts he and Marty had eaten while visiting an island off the coast. Others believe that it was the thin air of Mexico City. 'If you've got heart problems it's not a good place to be,' says Chong. Marty was buried in Forest Lawn Cemetery in Los Angeles, California near his idol, Buster Keaton, in the Garden of Heritage, lot 5420. For Graham, *Yellowbeard* was book-ended by sadness with Keith Moon dying before it got off the ground and Marty dying at the end. 'But I try to look at the positive side,' he said at the time. 'I take pleasure in knowing that Marty was back on form for his last role.' Surprisingly invigorated by the experience of *Yellowbeard*, Graham actually made plans to star in another island adventure, a serious acting role about Robinson Crusoe. 'It will be a serious movie, filmed in Australia,' Graham told the *Melbourne TV Scene*, 'with a cast of two. I'll hopefully start work on it in October, and I'll be able to look at a bit of Australia.' But funding was never solidified, and the movie was never made.

In October 1982, Geoffrey Strachan, publisher of Methuen Books, wrote to Graham expressing interest in publishing the *Yellowbeard* novel which Graham intended to write with David Sherlock, whose historical research and eye had played an important part in the project from the start. Now, with the movie in the can, Graham turned his attention to the writing of the novel. While he and Sherlock used the shooting script as a blueprint for the book, writing in a prose narrative gave them much more room to crowd in details, story and atmosphere that the film simply didn't allow. While in some ways the novel parodies the grandiose story-style of Robert Louis Stevenson's *Treasure Island* (as well as other classic adventure tales by writers like Stevenson), it was not intended to be a spoof of the genre. '*Yellowbeard* has a story that, although ludicrous, hopefully sweeps you along with it,' Graham told the press at the time. 'The characters are slightly larger-than-life but not wholly unbelievable.' Work on the novel got seriously underway after the Christmas holidays, written in the clear strong longhand of David Sherlock. ('Graham didn't have the best handwriting,' Sherlock has said. 'He could write legibly when he had to though, if he knew someone else would be reading it.') Since Strachan/Methuen had published Graham's autobiography previously, and had been responsible for the publication of all the classic Monty Python books, it is a surprise that the novel did not go out under the Methuen imprint (perhaps Graham simply took too long about it). Instead, Sphere Books published it in 1983 to coincide with the release of the movie. It was a deluxe, magazine format with several dozen illustrations from the film. However, like most movie tie-in books, it had a relatively short shelf life (about the length of the film's theatrical run). It was never published in the US. Consequentially the novel (like the film) has been out of print for over twenty years and is a hot collector's item, exchanging hands at several times its original cover price – assuming you can find it.

Yellowbeard was released on 24 June 1983. While it received a fair amount of critical praise ('There are many moment of hilarity here,' wrote the *Los Angeles Times*) and did well in test screenings, for some reason it didn't catch fire at the box-office. 'I remember going down to San Diego for the preview,' says Michael Medavoy of Orion Pictures.

'It went very well. I don't know why the movie didn't do as well as expected when it was released, but it's a funny movie and today it's a sort of big cult film.' There are almost as many theories as to why *Yellowbeard* didn't perform (economically) as there are actors in the movie. Some say it was an uneven combination of British and American humour, others point fingers at the odd mix of comics and stage actors. Still others claim the movie just 'looked flat' and had no visual style. Eric Idle believes *Yellowbeard* would have worked better if it had parodied the look and style of classic pirate films, in much the same way *Life of Brian* had parodied Biblical epics.

In Graham's handwritten notes following the first edit he wrote down many areas that he felt needed addressing (Graham was not allowed in on the edit of the film):

Opening credits too long with too little happening, reminds the audience to expect too much. Promotion should stress adventure/comedy and less emphasis should be laid on the large number of fantastically funny cast members – no film could live up to this sort of promise. On several occasions jokes have been included which are not on the same level of comedy as the rest of the movie; okay to have tried them but the tried (part) is over; e.g. Clement stepping in shit, Mr Crisp speaking outside window (illogical) . . . We must not make jokes too obvious for the audience; e.g. the second viewing of the joke that the sailor is nailed to the deck. The audience must be allowed the privilege of working these things out for themselves.

His notes were not taken onboard, however. Many of the low-brow jokes (like the Clement/shit scene) stayed in, and the movie was heavily promoted as a 'star-studded comic romp'.

While it's not always a good idea to judge the merit of any movie by how much money it made, the question remains: Why didn't *Yellowbeard* do better business? A quick look at the top movies of 1983 shows that it may have simply been out of sync with the times. *Return Of The Jedi*, *Terms Of Endearment*, *Flashdance*, *Trading Places*, *WarGames*, *Octopussy*, *Sudden Impact*, *Mr Mom*, *Staying Alive* and *Risky Business* were the hits of 1983. It was the year of Eddie Murphy, Michael Keaton and Tom Cruise, not a mad swashbuckling pirate extravaganza. Even the British hits of 1983 (*Educating Rita* and *Local Hero*) were gentler and more thought-provoking. If *Yellowbeard* had been produced a year or two earlier, or released a year or two later, it might have been a different story. In fact, it *is* a different story today. The fact that it hasn't been available on video for years, and has never been released on DVD, has mythologised *Yellowbeard*. 'It's got a cult audience for sure,' says Damski, 'and I've had some weird experiences with it since. For instance, I was at a blackjack table in Reno, Nevada a few years ago and somehow found myself sitting next to this guy I knew from high school. He said, "Mel, didn't you direct *Yellowbeard*?" and I go, "Yeah," and then the blackjack dealer starts doing dialogue from the movie! He's going, "Stagger left, stagger right, crawl, crawl . . ."'

ABOUT THE SCREENPLAY

There are at least four (and possibly more) drafts of the *Yellowbeard* screenplay (including one in Spanish, which was most likely for the censor hired to make sure the film didn't portray Mexico in a bad light). While all of them have their pluses and minuses the version which follows was chosen primarily because it bears a close-enough resemblance to the final, filmed, version so as to be familiar to those who have seen the movie and yet still offers something new. This screenplay differs in many key ways from the others: first and foremost the focus here is more on the plot (the quest for Yellowbeard's treasure) so it moves faster, unlike the filmed screenplay which had a tendency to wander and give too much screen time to minor characters like Blind Pew. The emphasis on El Segundo and El Nebuloso is also greatly reduced, and the stories of Clement and Mansell and Gilpin and Lambourn are expanded, all of which serves to round out their characters. Also, Betty Beard has a lot more to do with the story which gives more insight into her motivations. This version begins and ends completely differently than the filmed script, has a surprise twist involving the map and is, without a doubt, the funniest (and most Pythonic) of all the drafts. It is the script that is truest to Graham and Bernard McKenna's original vision, the most unadulterated version, and the one they turned in to Warner Brothers (and the one they rejected). Perhaps this rejection by part of the

Hollywood establishment says more about this screenplay's credentials than anything else could. I believe that after reading this draft you will agree with me that Warner Brothers was wrong.

BIOGRAPHY OF YELLOWBEARD

Taken from Yellowbeard press kit

There has always been a pirate in the Beard family. Blackbeard. Bluebeard. And the one called Redbeard whom history tells us had no beard at all, just a dreadful case of spots. But the worst of all was Yellowbeard.

Yellowbeard didn't enter puberty, he invaded it. Coming of age at thirteen, he drove a cutlass through his giblets then took command of his father's crew and became the scourge of the Spanish Main ('A one-man Bermuda Triangle' – Pirate's Gazette) and his raiding parties were the high spots of the Tortuga social season. Year after year Yellowbeard won the 'Roger', piracy's equivalent of the Oscar.

With five thousand slit throats to his credit, Yellowbeard amassed a fortune in gold and jewels which he buried in a cove (or a cave, he could never remember which). But his glory ended abruptly when he was betrayed by his bosun, Mr Moon, clapped in irons and returned to London on a passing packet boat. There, from a dank and fetid cell, he plotted his revenge.

CAST & CREW OF YELLOWBEARD

Directed by
Mel Damski

Produced by
John Daly   Executive Producer
Carter De Haven   Producer

Writing credits (in alphabetical order)
Graham Chapman
Peter Cook
Bernard McKenna
David Sherlock

Cast (in credits order)
Graham Chapman   Captain Yellowbeard
Peter Boyle   Moon
Cheech Marin   El Segundo
Tommy Chong   El Nebuloso
Peter Cook   Lord Lambourn
Marty Feldman   Gilbert
Martin Hewitt   Dan
Michael Hordern   Dr Gilpin
Eric Idle   Commander Clement
Madeline Kahn   Betty
James Mason   Captain Hughes
John Cleese   Harvey 'Blind' Pew

Kenneth Mars	Mr Crisp and Verdugo
Spike Milligan	Flunkie
Stacy Nelkin	Triola
Nigel Planer	Mansell
Susannah York	Lady Churchill
Beryl Reid	Lady Lambourn
Ferdy Mayne	Mr Beamish
John Francis	Chaplain
Peter Bull	Queen Anne
Bernard Fox	Tarbuck
Ronald Lacey	Man with parrot
Greta Blackburn	Mr Prostitute
Nigel Stock	Admiral
Kenneth Danziger	Mr Martin
Monte Landis	Prison Guard
Richard Wren	Pirate
Gillian Eaton	Rosie
Bernard McKenna	Askey
John Dair	Big John
Carlos Romano	Priest
Álvaro Carcaño	Beggar
Leopoldo Francés	Helmsman
Ava Harela	Flower Girl
Garry O'Neill	Sergeant of the Marines
David Bowie	The Shark (uncredited)
Michael Mileham	The Coxan (uncredited)

Assistant Director
Clive Reed

Original Music
John Morris

Cinematography
Gerry Fisher

42

Film Editing
William Reynolds

Casting
Michael McLean

Production Design
Joseph R. Jennings

Art Direction
Jack Shampan

Set Decoration
Tim Hutchinson
Peter James
Teresa Pecanins

Costume Design
Gilly Hebden
Stephen Miles

Production Management
David Ball
Miguel Lima

Art Department
Arthur Wicks

Sound Department
Jeremy Hoenack
James D. Young

Special Effects
Arthur Beavis
Andy Evans

Stunts
Michael Cassidy
Loren Janes
Walter Robles
Buddy Van Horn
Terry Walsh
Chuck Waters
George P. Wilbur

FILM TRAILERS

These two scripts (to my knowledge, never produced) were intended to promote the film before its release.

Yellowbeard Teaser

1   SHOT OF EDITH AT SEA FLYING PIRATICAL FLAG
    (CAPTION OVER: 'YELLOWBEARD') THEME MUSIC

                                                    CUT TO:

2   *EXT. MAIMED FOX (RYE)*
    The Inn sign creaks in the wind.

                                                    CUT TO:

3   *INT. MAIMED FOX (STOCKERS FARM)*
    Various piratical and very seafaring CUSTOMERS are
    enjoying themselves. A DISTRAUGHT MAN enters.

                    DISTRAUGHT MAN
            Yellowbeard's escaped from prison!

Alarm quickly spreads throughout the bar. The LADY
OWNER, a robust wench, swiftly hides her 'cash box'
under a floorboard. A BEASTLY LOOKING MAN, who
had been doing a trick with a cigar-butt turning it
round so the lighted end is in his mouth, swallows the
cigar. SEVERAL CUSTOMERS run out, creating a

45

minor stampede, OTHERS take off items of jewelry and hide them. ONE CUSTOMER simply 'pales' and passes clean out.

CUT TO:

4   *EXT. VILLAGE STREET (STOCKERS FARM)*
SHOTS of shutters being placed over the windows and PEOPLE running every which way.

ALL
Yellowbeard! He's out! It's Yellowbeard!

CUT TO:

5   *EXT. UNDERTAKER'S (STOCKERS FARM)*
A BUNCH of GUYS laze around a half-built coffin. DISTRAUGHT MAN sticks his head in the doorway:

DISTRAUGHT MAN
Yellowbeard's out!

Some of the MEN spring into action to construct new coffins, flailing away wildly with their hammers. ONE MAN, resigned to his fate, simply runs himself through with a dagger.

CUT TO:

6   *EXT. HOUSE (STOCKERS FARM)*
A MAN pulls up at a gallop and stops his cart in front of his house. His WIFE and THREE DAUGHTERS are sitting outside their home, sewing. The MAN is in a panic and quickly and firmly ushers his protesting DAUGHTERS inside. He rushes back and bundles his WIFE inside.

WIFE
It is an earthquake or something?

46

MAN

Worse . . .

Almost as an afterthought even GRANNY, who is
sitting comatose by the door, is grabbed and pulled
inside. The door is locked. The MAN emerges yet again
and ushers a goat inside the house and GRANNY
outside. The door is finally bolted.

CUT TO:

7   *INT. MAIMED FOX*
The OCCUPANTS have closed shutters, hidden
everything of value and barricaded the door. A few
nails are being hammered around the door. The
CUSTOMERS sit drinking with weapons ready.

BEASTLY MAN

Even he can't get near us now.

There is a tremendous explosion. The door is blown in,
with wood and bricks flying every which way.
EVERYONE cowers, whimpers and screams.
YELLOWBEARD bursts through the splintered
woodwork, the fuses woven through his beard blaze.
He leaps and FREEZES in MID-AIR.

ANNOUNCER

Yellowbeard – the filthiest, nastiest, smelliest
pirate you've ever seen! Vile and scurvy and –
AAAARRRGGGGH!

YELLOWBEARD (VO)

Shut your noise!

ANNOUNCER

(As he dies) Yellowbeard . . . coming soon . . .

47

Yellowbeard Trailer

Portrait gallery of a venerable British Museum . . .
Walls covered with oils of piratical scenes and
portraits. Tour Guide (PETER COOK) and TOURISTS in
foreground. Guide is lecturing.

> PETER COOK
> The golden age of piracy was a time of deeds
> dark and heroic . . . of treasures lost and won
> . . . of plots, perils and passions. And through it
> all rang the dreadful names of the most daring,
> dangerous and hated swashbucklers of them all,
> Bluebeard and Blackbeard.

Camera zooms in on side-by-side portraits of Bluebeard
and Blackbeard. A sword comes slashing through rear
of gallery wall between the two portraits and GRAHAM
CHAPMAN (in full Yellowbeard costume) crashes
through. Graham starts waving the sword and
advancing on the group (and towards camera). He
becomes increasingly more worked up as his speech
continues.

> GRAHAM CHAPMAN/YELLOWBEARD
> Bluebeard? That pint-sized pissant? Blackbeard?
> That nasty little nance? It was a sad day for the
> Jolly Roger when those two twits set sail! How
> many men tasted their steel? How many
> women tasted their lips? I was the boldest
> buccaneer to ever shiver a timber, walk a plank
> or bound over the main! I was the most
> puissant pirate to ever poop a deck . . . I was the
> scariest and the hairiest . . . and soon the world
> will tremble again at the sound of my name . . .

Totally apoplectic, he charges the group (and camera), swings his sword directly at camera which will catch and freeze him in this ferocious posture just as he roars out his name.

> GRAHAM CHAPMAN/YELLOWBEARD
> Yellowbeard!

Freeze on Graham.

> NARRATOR
> For horrendousness, brutality, outrageousness, offensiveness . . . even a stuffed alligator and sheep, be watching for Yellowbeard! Starring Graham Chapman, Eric Idle, Peter Cook, Marty Feldman, John Cleese and the fiercest band of irate pirates to ever blunder towards plunder!

Super title: Yellowbeard.

Super title: Star names.

> NARRATOR
> Coming soon from Filmways Pictures.

EL NEBULOSO'S SONG

This song to El Nebuloso, sung to him by his men before they committed suicide, was cut before the first draft screenplay.

Nebuloso comes to give us peace,
Nevermore shall we betray our friends,
Nevermore shall we upset our ends,
Nebuloso he will show us how to cease.
Nebuloso esse portentous,
(Nebuloso is ominous)
Ferox magis esse guam villosus,
(Fiercer than his fury)
Nebuloso maior triginto annos natus
(Nebuloso is older than thirty)
Nebuloso esse maculosus
(Nebuloso is a North American salamander with red
   feathery external gills).

YELLOWBEARD

BY

GRAHAM CHAPMAN

AND

BERNARD McKENNA

CAPTION: YELLOWBEARD

1   EXT. ESTABLISHING SHOT OF EIGHTEENTH
    CENTURY PRISON

    Three or four PRISONERS are being brought through
    the gates in a caged cart. As they enter, a cart laden
    with two or three wooden coffins is wheeled out. The
    gate closes.

    CAPTION: 'ENGLAND 1712'

    CAPTION: 'HER MAJESTY'S PRISON ST VICTIM'S FOR
    THE EXTREMELY NAUGHTY'

2   EXT. EXERCISE YARD OF ST VICTIM'S

    Prisoners, including YELLOWBEARD, are shuffling
    slowly round in a circle. The new prisoners are
    dismayed to see two prisoners drop to the ground and
    be unceremoniously thrown into waiting coffins which
    are loaded on to a cart.

                                                CUT TO

    YELLOWBEARD AND GILBERT

    YELLOWBEARD is a fierce-looking wiry man with
    missing teeth and scars and weatherbeaten skin. He
    has a straggly, yellowish beard. GILBERT is an oily
    fellow prisoner.

                        YELLOWBEARD
            Pathetic! Taking the easy way out like that.

                            55

GILBERT

How do you mean?

YELLOWBEARD

Dying. They'd only been in 15 years. You won't
catch me dying. They'll have to kill me before I die.

GILBERT

As many a man has tried, Captain Yellowbeard.
And soon you will be at large again.

YELLOWBEARD

With a hand-picked crew of the hardest
bucanneers that ever stained the seven seas
with Spanish blood.

GILBERT

T'was most unjust for locking you up for doing
your duty.

YELLOWBEARD

20 years for killing 5,000 dagoes and walloons.
Betrayed by my right-hand man, that bastard
Moon.

GILBERT

But he never found out where you hid the
treasure, did he, Captain Yellowbeard?

YELLOWBEARD

No, nor will he ever.

GILBERT

(casually)

Where *did* you put it by the way?

YELLOWBEARD
You won't catch me out with those trick
questions.

A GUARD fetches YELLOWBEARD a terrible blow with
a baton. No reaction from YELLOWBEARD.

YELLOWBEARD
What really pisses me off is . . .

An even heavier blow lands on him.

YELLOWBEARD
What is it now?

GUARD
You have a visitor.

YELLOWBEARD
Oh, I expect that will be the Queen with my pardon.

CUT TO

3 INT. SMALL STONE DUNGEON IN WHICH
PRISONERS ARE KEPT SEPARATE FROM THEIR
VISITORS BY A WALL WITH SMALL IRON GRILLES

BETTY (YELLOWBEARD'S WIFE) watched over by A
GUARD, is seated waiting for YELLOWBEARD. Other
PRISONERS and FAMILIES hold conversations with
difficulty. ANOTHER GUARD enters and lays into a
family with a big stick.

Suddenly stops. Realises where he is. Looks at number
on door. Realises his error.

GUARD

(lightly)
    Sorry!

GUARD EXITS, YELLOWBEARD ENTERS

BETTY

Hello, poppet.

YELLOWBEARD

What, you again?

BETTY

Again? I haven't seen you for ten years.

YELLOWBEARD

What is it this time?

BETTY

Well, what with you being let out next week, I thought it was my duty as a wife to bring you up to date on a few things. Remember just before you were arrested we were having a cuddle?

YELLOWBEARD

I was *raping* you, if that's what you mean.

BETTY

Well, sort of half cuddle, half rape. Well, something happened which I have been meaning to tell you about for the past 20 years.

YELLOWBEARD

Get on with it, woman.

BETTY

Well, I haven't told you this before because I
wanted him to be brought up like a gentleman
and not a pirate.

YELLOWBEARD

Who are you on about?

BETTY

The fruit of your loins, poppet.

YELLOWBEARD

Are you mad, woman? I haven't got fruit in my
loins. Lice, yes, and proud of them.

BETTY

It's a biblical phrase, poppet. The fruit of your
loins means that we have spawned a son.

YELLOWBEARD

What?

BETTY

You have just become the father of a 175-
pound, 20 year-old bouncing boy called Dan.

YELLOWBEARD

Ahhh. A son. Takes after me does he?

BETTY

Well, er.

YELLOWBEARD

By the time I was 20 I had killed 500 men.

BETTY

Well, he's not quite so *extrovert* as you, but he's
... er ...

YELLOWBEARD

A thief?

BETTY

No.

YELLOWBEARD

A rapist?

BETTY

No.

YELLOWBEARD

Oh, bloody hell. I give up. What is he then?

BETTY

Well, he's sort of quiet.

YELLOWBEARD

QUIET? You've brought him up to be QUIET? A
Yellowbeard QUIET?

BETTY

Well, it's not all my fault. Remember Lord
Lambourn? You strangled his gardener.

YELLOWBEARD

Oh, that old loonie.

                    BETTY

Yes, he's been ever so good to Dan. He's even
given him a job up at the Hall.

                 YELLOWBEARD

He's got a job? No Yellowbeard ever had a job.
Are you sure it was you I raped before I was
arrested?

                    BETTY

It *was* me, poppet.

                 YELLOWBEARD

What's this job he's got?

                    BETTY

A gardener.

YELLOWBEARD is hit by the guard on the back of his
neck which he doesn't notice.

                 YELLOWBEARD

A Yellowbeard gardening? I'll see about that
when I'm out.

Receives an even heavier blow.

                 YELLOWBEARD

What is it?

                    GUARD

Time's up, sir.

Pulls down iron shutter in front of BETTY. He mocks
YELLOWBEARD.

GUARD

So your son's a gardener eh?

YELLOWBEARD

(threatening)

    Watch it. You could get your shrubbery kicked
    in.

4   CAPTION: 'THE COURT OF HER MAJESTY QUEEN
ANNE'

Ante-Room. Small queue of ambassadors waits to see
the Queen. In it COMMANDER CLEMENT is
resplendent in commodore's uniform.

FLUNKIE announces loudly:

FLUNKIE

    Next, the head of her Britannic Majesty's Secret
    Service. Not to be read out loud.

Pauses. Realizes. At the same time, there's a flurry of
interest in the queue, they look at each other;
COMMANDER CLEMENT is very uncomfortable.

FLUNKIE

    Excuse me.

Goes back into the room. Hurried conversation.
FLUNKIE comes out.

FLUNKIE

    Joking apart ha, ha . . . er . . . next.
    Royal Navy Commander Clement.

COMMANDER walks awkwardly and furiously in while ambassadors write his name down.

5   INT.   'THE COURT'

A SERVANT is shading in pink bits of the world that are British. Battle areas of Europe are marked. Very flattering painting of a youthful Queen Anne. H.M. QUEEN ANNE is seated on the throne, next to her is LADY SARAH CHURCHILL, nearby PRINCE GEORGE is standing at an odd angle.

> FLUNKIE
> Her Majesty's the fat one on the throne. She's not too well this morning. I should kneel upwind of her if I was you. The skinny one's Lady Sarah Churchill, the brains of the outfit, and that . . .

(points to Prince at angle)

> . . . is Prince George of Denmark.

CLEMENT stiffly steps forward and kneels upwind.

> QUEEN
> State your business.

CLEMENT stands.

> CLEMENT
> Your Majesty. We in the Naval Department while being keenly aware of recent spirals in Defence Expenditure . . . humbly submit . . .

> QUEEN
> Are you the Prime Minister?

63

CLEMENT is taken aback. He puts fingers to lips, looks furtively around and whispers.

> CLEMENT
>
> Secret Service.

> QUEEN
>
> Oh, Charades . . . You're a beekeeper.

He is about to say 'no.' SARAH cools it with a nod and polite applause.

> SARAH
>
> That'll do . . . for her.

> CLEMENT
>
> Will it?

> QUEEN
>
> What do you want?

SARAH nods him to explain.

> CLEMENT
>
> The Pirate Yellowbeard is due to be released in two days, and despite twenty years of imprisonment and unpleasantness, he has told us nothing about the treasure he has hidden. However, I have a detailed plan here.
> (he proffers it to Queen)

> SARAH
>
> I doubt if she could manage more than the label on a gin bottle. Just tell us.

CLEMENT

Well, milady . . . once we let him go he'll make
straight for the treasure. I need a fast ship to
follow him.

SARAH

A sensible request, I think, Your Majesty.

QUEEN

A plateful of steamed fish.

SARAH

I sometimes think I'm running this sodding
country on my own. However, my 'usband, the
Duke of Marlborough, needs that gold for his
glorious slaughter of the French who are a load
of bum-biting foreigners. From what I've heard,
there's enough to buy the whole of Bavaria, and
some nice pink bits for me map.

CLEMENT

I didn't expect such bluntitude, Mrs
Marlborough. Will Her Majesty agree to this?

He hands over document for signature.

SARAH

In her state, of course she will.

She wakes the Queen up slightly.

SARAH

The beekeeper would like this signed.

QUEEN

Oh!

                        SARAH
        Request for a new hive for the Royal Navy.

                        QUEEN
(signs it)
        Certainly.

                        CLEMENT
        Oh, thank you, Ma'am.

                        SARAH
        It was your flashing blue eyes that done it. I'm
        only in this for the perks.

She fondles his bottom as he bows.

                        SARAH
        What's in this for you?

                        CLEMENT
        Pardon? Oh, er . . . Since you mention it . . . my
        wife always hankered after me being . . . Sir
        someone or other.

                        SARAH
        If you get that loot pronto, you'll be a Duke, like
        my husband what goes away a lot.

CLEMENT stoically accepts another fondle.

                        CLEMENT
        Duke, eh . . .

6   EXT. 'MAIMED FOX', PIRATICAL PUB

                                              CUT TO

7   INT. THE BAR OF THE 'MAIMED FOX'

BETTY is serving BLIND PEW.

                    BETTY
(as she finishes pouring)
          There you are, Mr Pew.

                    PEW
          I said a double.

                    BETTY
          It is a double.

                    PEW
          Come off it, Mrs Beard. I can hear a double
          when I hear one.

She continues pouring.

                    PEW
          When! Are you trying to get me drunk or
          something?

He taps his way over to a table where a drunken man,
HODGE, is seated.

DAN ENTERS, reading 'NAVIGATION TODAY'.

                    BETTY
          Ah, there you are, Dan. You got a moment?

                    DAN
          I'm reading something.

He sits in a quiet corner of the bar.

                              BETTY

          Read! Read! There's more important things in
          life than reading, son. Keep an ear on the bar
          would you, Mr Pew?

She goes over to DAN in corner.

                              BETTY

          If there's one thing I've learnt in life, it's that
          learning things never taught me anything.

She tears the book out of his hand.

                              DAN

          All right, Mother.

                              BETTY

          Books are the worst. Last time I read a book I
          was raped, so let that be a lesson to you.

                              DAN

          What do you want?

                              BETTY

          Well, Dan, it's about your father.

                              DAN

          What about him?

                              BETTY

          Well, when I said he was – er – dead, I was
          trying to cushion the blow.

                              DAN

          What blow?

                              68

                    BETTY
Well, he's alive. He's kept himself to himself
since the – um – since the – er – the
misunderstanding.

                    DAN
What misunderstanding?

                    BETTY
Well, he and the Crown didn't see eye to eye on
the way he ran off with their business. He
wouldn't brook interference with the principles
of free enterprise.

                    DAN
He was a pirate?

                    BETTY
Sort of.

                    DAN
A pirate like Yellowbeard?

                    BETTY
Very like Yellowbeard. In fact he is Yellowbeard.

DAN is stunned.

                    BETTY
At last, your Daddy's coming home.

                                        CUT TO

8   DELETED

9   EXT.   ST VICTIM'S PRISON. COACH DRAWS UP TO
     THE GATE

                        COACH DRIVER
(shouts out)
          Commander Clement and Lieutenant Mansell,
          for their appointment with Governor Barclay.

Coach is waved through.

10   INT.   GOVERNOR BARCLAY'S OFFICE

CLEMENT is in full and angry flow.

                        CLEMENT
          Governor Barclay, after 20 years of unmitigated
          torture you still haven't the slightest idea where
          Yellowbeard has hidden his treasure?

                        BARCLAY
          Well, he did say one thing about it.

                        CLEMENT
          Yes.

                        BARCLAY
          He said, 'Where I hid it ain't been found yet.'

                        MANSELL
(who is a bit of an idiot, not saying the whole of an
idiot)
          Ah, that could mean he's hidden it somewhere
          which hasn't been discovered yet, which makes
          things easier.

CLEMENT

How?

MANSELL

I mean, um, least we know everywhere it *isn't*.
It's where it *is* that we don't know.

CLEMENT

We've known that for years.

MANSELL

You mean where it is?

CLEMENT

No, where it isn't.

BARCLAY

(confused)

Where isn't it?

CLEMENT

(impatient)

Look, he's due to be released tomorrow. We'd
better think of something fast.

Door opens and DR GILPIN enters.

BARCLAY

Ah. Commander Clement, this is Dr Gilpin.
Found any medical reasons for us to detain
Captain Yellowbeard?

GILPIN

I've had a look at him. Wouldn't have thought it
possible for anyone to survive more than a
month in this place.

BARCLAY

Ah. Thank you.

GILPIN

He's fit enough to be released.

MANSELL

I've found his plea of mitigation: 'I regard the slaying of 50,000 Spaniards as justifiable homicide and ask for 10,000 future offences against the French to be taken into consideration' - sounds reasonable enough to me.

BARCLAY

I'll be sorry to see him go. He scares the shit out of the other prisoners.

CLEMENT

We have to know the whereabouts of his treasure.

GILPIN

Surely, the best way to find that is to release him, as agreed by Her Majesty's Government, and then follow him.

CLEMENT

No, what I am suggesting is that Yellowbeard be allowed to escape, but not know that we have allowed him to escape. Mansell, I want you to arrange the facilities.

MANSELL

Yes, sir. What sort of facilities?

CLEMENT

Use your head, Mansell. I mean, when you are
in prison, what are you surrounded by?

MANSELL

Prisoners, sir.

CLEMENT

No, walls.

MANSELL

Got you, sir. So L. A. D. D. E. R.?

CLEMENT

Precisely, but don't make it too obvious.

MANSELL   exits.

BARCLAY

All right, send him in.

YELLOWBEARD   enters.

BARCLAY

Ah, Mr Yellowbeard.

YELLOWBEARD

Captain Yellowbeard to you, you scum.

BARCLAY

Quite, sorry, Captain Yellowbeard. Um – twenty
years ago today, Captain Yellowbeard, you were
sentenced to jail.

73

YELLOWBEARD
Yes, and now I am due to be released.

BARCLAY
Yes, or rather no. Now twenty years ago,
Captain Yellowbeard, no man was expected to
live twenty years in the filthy, horrendous
conditions that existed then and indeed, still
exist today. So, when the judge sentenced you,
he had no idea that you would *survive*. In light
of these factors, Her Majesty the Queen has
graciously agreed to extend your sentence a
further forty years. Case dismissed.

YELLOWBEARD is dragged screaming and roaring
from the room.

11   EXT.   DAY

MANSELL is completing the task of disguising himself
as a bush outside the high prison wall. Above him, we
see the top of a ladder peeping over the wall.

CUT TO

12   INT.   PRISON YARD

YELLOWBEARD returning from the Governor's office
encounters GILBERT. Prominently in the background
we see the ladder placed against the wall. A cart load
of coffins is being driven towards the gate.

GILBERT
Went well did it?

                    YELLOWBEARD
No.

                    GILBERT
Um – so you – er – won't be leaving us then?

                    YELLOWBEARD
They broke their solemn word.

                    GILBERT
That's governments for you, isn't it? I expect
they wanted to know about the treasure.

                    YELLOWBEARD
Yes, and that's something they'll never know.

                    GILBERT
Well, until you tell them about the treasure, the
only way you're going to leave here is feet first.

As GILBERT continues musing YELLOWBEARD rushes
away, picks up an empty coffin, runs with enormous
speed behind the cart which is about to exit and in
one move throws the coffin on to the cart and himself
into it. The gate clangs shut behind him.

                    GILBERT
Must be an awful strain being the only man in
the world knowing where this treasure is. Why
don't you share the burden with a friend?

He looks round, realises YELLOWBEARD is gone. He
sees the ladder and assumes that this has been his
escape route.

                        75

GILBERT rushes to the ladder.

CUT TO

13   EXT.   OF THE WALL

MANSELL, now totally disguised as bush, awaits
YELLOWBEARD.

GILBERT drops heavily on to him. There is a brief
struggle before GILBERT runs away. MANSELL
follows.

MANSELL
That disguise doesn't fool me, Yellowbeard.

CUT TO

14   INT.   BAR, 'MAIMED FOX'

YELLOWBEARD bursts through the door, rushes past
blind man and HODGE, the drunk man, straight up the
stairs.

CUT TO

15   INT.   BETTY'S BEDROOM

YELLOWBEARD rushes in, locks the door and puts a
chair against it. As he turns to BETTY we see that she
is undressing rapidly.

BETTY
I do wish it didn't have to be such a rush every
time.

76

                              YELLOWBEARD

    What?

Realising she is expecting sex.

                              YELLOWBEARD
                   I haven't got time for that now.

He takes out two daggers and goes to a part of the wall
in which he starts to hack a hole. BETTY is displeased.

                                BETTY
                   It's been 20 years since we had a little cuddle,
                   and what do you do? Come in here and give me a
                   kiss? No, you rush in and hack a hole in the wall.

Plaster and brickwork fall out easily. YELLOWBEARD
stops hacking.

                              YELLOWBEARD
                   Where's the map?

                                BETTY

    What map?

                              YELLOWBEARD
                   (advancing on her with the daggers)
                         If you say you don't know where it is, I'll nail
                         your tits to the table.

                                BETTY
                   Oh, I – er – know where it is. It's – it's burnt.

                              YELLOWBEARD
                   (advancing on her)
                         You burnt my map?

BETTY

But only after I'd copied it.

YELLOWBEARD is relieved but still menacing.

YELLOWBEARD

Where's the copy?

BETTY

Well, when little Dan came along . . .

YELLOWBEARD

Who's Dan?

BETTY

My, and probably your, son. When he was two
minutes old I tattoed it on his head.

YELLOWBEARD

Does he know about this?

BETTY

Oh, no, no. Nor does anybody else. I thought of
that, that's why I kept him in a cupboard for
three years. That may be why he's a bit odd
with all these books and stuff.

YELLOWBEARD

Where is he now?

BETTY

Lambourn Hall.

YELLOWBEARD

I'll go up there and cut his head off.

YELLOWBEARD starts undressing which arouses false
expectations in BETTY's mind.

> BETTY
> Oh, how nice. You've still got time for a cuddle
> before you kill your son.

YELLOWBEARD wrenches open cupboard which
contains a large array of frocks and dresses.

> YELLOWBEARD
> Where's my pirating outfit?

Finds it. Starts to put on his flamboyant pirate
outfit.

> YELLOWBEARD
> Where did you get all these frocks?

> BETTY
> Well, Lord Lambourn - you know the one I said
> has been ever so kind to Dan - well, he's been
> ever so kind to me.

YELLOWBEARD comes across a suit of male clothing.

> YELLOWBEARD
> What's this?

> BETTY
> Oh, that's Lord Lambourn's as well. He's such a
> kind man, he thinks of everyone. He left those
> here in case you escaped and needed a change
> of clothing.

YELLOWBEARD

I'm sure I killed the last one I raped. It can't
have been you.

BETTY

The afterplay was a bit on the rough side, but
not fatal.

YELLOWBEARD

What does this Dan, or whatever you call him,
look like?

BETTY

Well, a little bit like Lord Lambourn.

She pauses as she realises her error.

BETTY

But a bit more like *you* than that. Much more
like you in fact.

YELLOWBEARD climbs out of the window.

CUT TO

16   EXT.   'MAIMED FOX'

GILBERT in search of YELLOWBEARD arrives outside
'Maimed Fox'. He is followed at an almost discreet
distance by MANSELL. GILBERT passes before the
main door of the inn and to seek a more clandestine
entrance goes round to the rear of the inn.
YELLOWBEARD lands on him heavily from above and
dashes off towards Lambourn Hall without pausing or
noticing the body. MANSELL's face cautiously appears

80

round the corner of the building and registers
puzzlement at the recumbent figure of GILBERT
whom he still takes for YELLOWBEARD. Suspecting
the lying on the ground to be some sort of ruse,
MANSELL takes up a watching position. Cautiously he
peeps round a couple of times.

16A   DISSOLVE/FADE UP

It is night time. We see the figure of CLEMENT
working round the outside of the inn. He sees
GILBERT's body. Examines it. Sees MANSELL soundly
asleep at a watching angle. Resignedly CLEMENT
walks up and taps him on the shoulder.

CLEMENT
Where's Yellowbeard?

MANSELL
(rapidly wakening, points at Gilbert and whispers)
He's up to something, been like that for hours.

CLEMENT
Up to what?

MANSELL
Not moving.

CLEMENT
Two points, Mansell.

MANSELL
Thank you, sir.

CLEMENT ignores this.

                    CLEMENT
     I wish to *make* two points. *One:* he's not doing
     anything because he's unconscious.

                    MANSELL
Uhu.

                    CLEMENT
     Two: it's *not* Yellowbeard.

                                        CUT TO

17   INT.   'MAIMED FOX'

     Smoke-filled, booze-laden atmosphere. Lots of seafarers
     include man with one wooden leg, man with two
     wooden legs and a variety of one-eyed, one-armed,
     scarred, drunken, piratical types.

     A customer roars with laughter. His false eye pops out
     and lands in his drink. Without reacting he fishes it out,
     wipes it on his grubby trousers and pops it back in.

     CLEMENT and MANSELL burst in.

                    CLEMENT
     Royal Navy here.

     General moans.

                    CLEMENT
     Where's Yellowbeard?

                    BEAST
     He's gone.

CLEMENT

(to assembled crowd)
    Well, if he's gone you must have seen him.

Chorus of 'NO'.

All shake their heads.

CLEMENT
    Not one of you saw Yellowbeard?

General shouts of 'NO'.

The BLIND MAN raises his white stick.

CLEMENT
    What did you see? Oh, I'm sorry.

PEW
I saw nothing, but I heard something. I heard a
man of about fifty-five years of age in a prison
uniform and I heard a strange violent look in
his eye and a long, yellow, grizzled beard.

CLEMENT
What else did you hear?

PEW
An' I 'eard him climb up the stairs and I 'eard
'im open the door to his wife's bedroom and
then I heard him shout something very loud
indeed, but I didn't catch that.

CLEMENT
Come on, Mansell.

CLEMENT and MANSELL dash up the stairs.

83

18   INT.   BETTY'S BEDROOM

BETTY is tidying up. YELLOWBEARD's prison costume is still littered all over the floor.

CLEMENT and MANSELL burst in and are immediately aware of the 'stink' from the clothes.

> CLEMENT
>
> Where's Yellowbeard?

> BETTY
>
> He's in prison isn't he?

> CLEMENT
>
> Your husband escaped this morning and we know that he came straight to you.

> BETTY
>
> (thinking hard)
>
> Oh, come to think of it, someone did come in here a while back, but I don't think it was my husband.

> MANSELL
>
> These are his clothes.

> BETTY
>
> (clearing up the pile of clothes)
>
> Oh, wait a minute, someone did pop in and rape me. These must be his clothes.

> CLEMENT
>
> That was Yellowbeard.

BETTY

Prison has reformed him. He never bothered to
take his clothes off in the old days.

CLEMENT

Where did he go?

BETTY

I've no idea.

CLEMENT

Bring the clothes, Mansell, we'll need a scent for
the dogs.

Start to leave.

BETTY

But – um – if it *was* my hubby who raped me, I
imagine he's dashed off to rape somebody else.
He was never satisfied with just the one.

CLEMENT and MANSELL rush out clutching the
clothing.

CUT TO

19   INT.   BAR, 'MAIMED FOX'

HODGE drunkenly approaches PEW.

HODGE

You didn't tell everything you heard to those
two gentlemen what just left, did you,
shipmate?

                              PEW
        Yes I did.

                              HODGE
        I didn't hear you mention much about treasure.

                              PEW
        What treasure?

                              HODGE
        Yellowbeard's. What any pirate worth 'is salt
        would give 'is eye teeth to get 'old of.

                              PEW
        You're drunk again, Hodge. Your mind's
        wandering.

                              HODGE
        And my 'ands will be wandering towards your
        throat, Pew, unless you tell me what you 'eard.

                              PEW
        So you can pass the information on to Captain
        Moon. Huh, over my dead body.
        (withdraws sword from his white stick)

                              HODGE
        (already blind drunk and seeing double takes a large
        swig of drink)
                If those are your conditions.

        HODGE takes a lunge at PEW. His cutlass pierces
        straight through the woodwork of an open door next
        to PEW. He struggles but fails to free it but snatches a
        sword. The inn falls silent.

BETTY appears and in a routine way collects cash box from behind bar and disappears upstairs with two pistols. She closes the door with imbedded sword and tut tuts.

CUT TO

20   EXT. 'MAIMED FOX'

The terrific noise of the fight inside can be heard in background. GILBERT still on the ground is beginning to revive when a hook through his coat collar suddenly pulls him in one move to an upright position. The hook replaces the left hand of MR MOON, a formidable, huge, muscular man with scarred face who is unexpectedly gently spoken with well-hidden menace.

> MOON
> You mean to say you've lost Yellowbeard already.

GILBERT is surprised to see him.

> GILBERT
> Oh Mr Moon, sir, I tried to follow him, but I was being followed, if you follow me.

> MOON
> Who was following you?

> GILBERT
> Some stupid naval prat.

87

                              MOON

          Well, we've got to follow Yellowbeard and make
          sure no-one else is following him, or I'll never
          get the treasure. Do you follow me?

A scream from the inn causes MOON to react.

                              MOON

          What's going on in there? That sounds like my
          man Hodge.

The noise in the inn stops abruptly. MOON and
GILBERT exchange looks and head for the inn.

21   INT.   'MAIMED FOX'

The room is now a total wreck. All the spectators are
unconscious or dead. PEW finishes attacking some
upholstery. He cackles satisfactorily, sheaths his sword
into white swordstick and finds a wall with his stick
and taps his way along feeling for a door. The door
with HODGE impaled on his own sword through it is
flung open by MOON and GILBERT. PEW, the innocent,
harmless, blind man, taps his way out and as he
passes MOON:

                              PEW

          Afternoon. Sounded as though there's been a bit
          of a fight.

EXITS.   MOON and GILBERT, wide-eyed, take in the
room. PEW closes door revealing HODGE behind
MOON.

                                              CUT TO

22   EXT.   LAMBOURN HALL (which has seen better days)

Preparations for a society garden party. DAN is
wheeling a wheelbarrow-load of manure towards the
kitchen gardens which are at the rear of the house.
Bunting is in the trees and a banner reading 'Welcome
to Her Majesty' is draped above the porch.

                    LADY LAMBOURN
(to Flunkeys)
          I want the garden spic and span. We must 'ave
          an h'air of courtly dignity h'about the 'all.

                         DAN
          Don't you mean 'Hall', your ladyship?

                    LADY LAMBOURN
          I do not. The letter 'H' is not being aspirated
          this season by 'er Majesty 'oo 'ates it. Dan, stop
          that man pissing on the 'edge. It's imported.

LADY LAMBOURN goes off with FLUNKEYS to
supervise decor.

LORD ARMATRADING AND LORD LAMBOURN have
been observing this from a safe distance.

                    LORD ARMATRADING
          So, Lambourn, the Queen really is coming this
          afternoon?

                    LAMBOURN
          Of course not. The woman is mad. God knows
          what I ever saw in her.

LORD ARMATRADING

Well, she is very rich.

In the distance behind them, we see YELLOWBEARD burst through some bushes into the garden. He looks around for DAN, sees LADY LAMBOURN in all her finery. Decides after twenty years in prison he is a little randy. He rushes over to her and hauls her away into some bushes. We hear LADY LAMBOURN's screams of delight and fear, and clothes being ripped.

LAMBOURN

You know, John, that chap who just dashed up and seized hold of the wife, sure I've seen him somewhere before.

LORD ARMATRADING

He seems to have taken a bit of a shine to Lady L.

LADY LAMBOURN, extricating herself from the bushes, very much on her dignity, adjusting her dishevelled dress. All eyes on her. LAMBOURN sniffs a strong whiff of YELLOWBEARD.

LADY LAMBOURN

Should you be a wonderin' 'oo that was, it were an emissary from 'er Majesty, apologisin' and saying that she is on 'er way, but in the meantime, she suggests that we all 'ave a few sips of brandy.

23   DELETED

CUT TO

24   EXT.   REAR OF LAMBOURN HALL – KITCHEN
      GARDEN

DAN is reading a nautical tome.

YELLOWBEARD is munching from a whole leg of lamb
and a flagon of wine.

YELLOWBEARD draws his cutlass.

                    YELLOWBEARD
      Is your name Dan?

                         DAN
      Yes.

                    YELLOWBEARD
      I need your head, my lad.

                         DAN
      You're my father.

                    YELLOWBEARD
      So your mother says, but that's no reason to
      believe it. Never trust a woman or a
      government.

                         DAN
      Pleased to meet you.

                    YELLOWBEARD
      I haven't got time for idle chit-chat, I need your
      head.

DAN

That makes a change. Mother seems to
disapprove of me using it at all.

YELLOWBEARD

You're not going to use it, you're going to lose it,
lad ... *I'm* going to use it. Right, put your neck
on that stool, it'll be cleaner that way.

DAN

You want to cut my head off? What for?

YELLOWBEARD

I don't want to lug your body half way round
the world do I? Your 'ead's got a map on it that
I need.

YELLOWBEARD brings cutlass down, narrowly missing
DAN's scalp. DAN springs out of the way and manages
to keep his distance successfully as YELLOWBEARD
chases him round the garden lopping tops off plants
and trees.

DAN

You don't need to kill me for it. Why don't you
copy it?

YELLOWBEARD

What, and have two maps. Bugger off.
(has him by the hair)

DAN

If you cut my head off, it will start to putrefy.

YELLOWBEARD

What?

DAN

Putrefy, go rotten.

YELLOWBEARD

Yes, it would pong a lot. Heads do. But I can live
with that.

Having cornered him, he raises his sword.

DAN

Stop! I could help you, Dad. Everyone will be
following you – the naval authorities, rival
pirates. If they catch you, they'll have the map.

YELLOWBEARD

Bugger them. I'll eat it first. Won't be the first
head I've eaten.

DAN

Then you'll have lost it for ever. Wouldn't it be
better to leave it where it's safe?

YELLOWBEARD

And take you along? You're not pirate material
– you wouldn't fit in.

LAMBOURN enters. Picks up plant-pot, produces bottle
and swigs. Looks at the lopped-off plants.

LAMBOURN

Hello, Dan. Been doing some gardening?
(to YELLOWBEARD)
I know you. You're not an emissary. You're that
pirate chappie.

YELLOWBEARD

All right, Dan. If you're my son, prove it.
(hands DAN a dagger)
Kill this stupid old bugger.

LAMBOURN

Oh, hold your horses.

DAN

I can't kill him. He brought me up – just like a
father.

YELLOWBEARD

Oh, you mean he's beaten you and kicked you
and smashed you in the teeth?

DAN

No, he's been kind and gentle.

YELLOWBEARD

What kind of father is that? Kill 'im.

DAN

No.

YELLOWBEARD throws him to the ground and has his
cutlass to his throat in one move.

YELLOWBEARD

I'll do it.

DAN

(playing for time)
Don't, don't, he could be useful.

94

LAMBOURN

Could I? Oh, yes, yes, I could. Why not? I could
er ... I could ...
What could I do?

From outside we hear the sound of orders being
shouted and hounds baying.

DAN

They've followed you here.

YELLOWBEARD

I'll kill 'em all.

DAN

Quick, hide in here.

He motions him to a wheelbarrow of manure.
YELLOWBEARD climbs in with relish.

DAN

We'll go to Dr Gilpin's.

YELLOWBEARD

And then kill everybody.

DAN

Whatever you like, Dad.

Hounds are getting nearer. DAN wheels the barrow out.

25   EXT.   LAMBOURN HALL. MAIN GARDENS

LADY LAMBOURN, having regained her composure, is
talking to LORD ARMATRADING.

> LADY LAMBOURN
> I would like your advice on a matter of
> etiquette. Does one curtsey while saying ''ello',
> or does one go down while speaking?

A pack of hounds, followed at a distance by a panting
MANSELL, burst through the hedge following
YELLOWBEARD's scent. They make straight for LADY
LAMBOURN and swarm all over her.

> MANSELL
> The game's up, Yellowbeard. That frock doesn't
> fool me.

He tries to drag her away from the hounds by pulling
her feet first across the lawn.

> LADY LAMBOURN
> Excuse me, Lord Armatradin', while
> I just 'ave a word with this gentleman . . .

26 INT. GILPIN'S HOUSE

It's more like a laboratory than a home. Jars
containing herbs, shelves and benches full of chemist's
equipment, retorts, crucibles, etc.

GILPIN is examining DAN's head. YELLOWBEARD is
the other side of the room helping himself to drinks.
The others are aware of YELLOWBEARD's stench.
LAMBOURN opens a window.

> DAN
> I'd like to go with my father to get the treasure.
> I've got the map of the island.

YELLOWBEARD
But it doesn't tell you which island, does it?

LAMBOURN
(to DAN)
It'll be dangerous.

YELLOWBEARD
Oh, it'll be dangerous. Do the boy good to get a bit
of senseless violence into his life, and he'll get a
share of the loot if he comes along with me.

LAMBOURN
Oh no, Dan. I can't allow you to go off with this
creature. He needs watching.

YELLOWBEARD
(menacing)
So what are you going to do about it?

LAMBOURN
I'll come with you.

GILPIN
What?
(pleading)
Look, you'd be criminals and never able to
return to England . . . But, if the government
gets the treasure, they'll only waste it on
warmongering in Europe.

DAN
Then you'll come with us too, Doctor. Think of
all the new plants and medicines you could
discover.

GILPIN muses.

GILPIN

Mmm. Well, if we were really going on a
botanical expedition in search of medicinal
herbs and . . . er . . . this person . . . happened to
find his treasure then . . . er . . . that's fine by
me.

LAMBOURN

A botanical expedition it is then.

YELLOWBEARD

A botwhatical?

DAN

A voyage of scientific discovery.

YELLOWBEARD

Eh?

DAN

Seeking out hitherto unknown plants and herbs.

YELLOWBEARD

And killing them?

DAN

Whatever you like, Father.

27   EXT.   DR GILPIN'S HOUSE

PEW is tap-tapping his way past GILPIN'S DOOR. He
hears something of interest and takes up a begging
position to cover up his eavesdropping.

CUT TO

98

YELLOWBEARD is partially dressed in different clothes
and is being shaved by GILPIN. DAN is gathering up
YELLOWBEARD's manure-covered outfit and holding it
at arm's length.

> GILPIN
> Better take these out and burn them.

> YELLOWBEARD
> You'd better not unless you fancy seeing your
> giblets nailed to the ceiling. I want them.

> LAMBOURN
> (unconvincing)
> Sentimental value, eh?

> YELLOWBEARD
> What's *that*?

> GILPIN
> Try and clean them up for him and put them in
> the bottom of his bag. We don't want him to be
> recognised.

DAN puts them in a washbowl.

> DAN
> How is this botanical expedition going to reach
> its destination?

> LAMBOURN
> Indeed and what is the destination?

99

                    YELLOWBEARD
(reluctantly)
          Mmm ... well ... first we'll steal a ship in
          Portsmouth, and head for Jamaica.

                    LAMBOURN
          I think we'll try something a little less
          conspicuous. I'll pay for our passage.

                    YELLOWBEARD
          I've never paid for anything in my life.

GILPIN finishes shaving him.

                    GILPIN
          There you are.

YELLOWBEARD catches sight of himself in the mirror.

                    YELLOWBEARD
          That looks nothing like me.

                    DAN
          That's the whole point, Dad.

There is a loud knock on the door.

                    LAMBOURN
          Good God, they're here. Let's hide.

                    YELLOWBEARD
          Kill!

                    DAN
          There's no need to.

GILPIN

You'd better have a name. How about Professor
Anthrax?

All assume a casual air as GILPIN opens the door to
reveal BETTY.

BETTY is turned to PEW outside.

BETTY

Bugger off, you evil git.
(she changes when she sees Gilpin)
    Oh, afternoon, Doctor. Just sayin tata to Mr
    Pew.
(as she enters)
    Oh, hello, Lord Lamb ... oh ... Dan? ... and ...

She looks at uneasy YELLOWBEARD.

GILPIN

This is Professor Anthrax.

BETTY

It's Yellowbeard.

YELLOWBEARD

I'm in disguise, you stupid tart.

BETTY

Well, no-one told me. Anyway, there's been a bit
of a fight up at the inn.

GILPIN

Oh dear. Not many injured I hope.

BETTY

Oh no . . . all dead, so there's no need for you to
rush. Just thought I'd let you know.
(to DAN)

You've met your father then.

DAN

Yes . . . er . . . got some exciting news.

BETTY

You're all goin' after the treasure.

Chorus of denials.

LAMBOURN

An expedition . . .

GILPIN

Botanical . . .

YELLOWBEARD

Killin' plants.

BETTY

Well, I'm entitled to my share – what with all the
lying and cheating and tattooing I've done over
the years.

DAN

Don't worry, Mother, you'll get your share.

BETTY

I don't ask for much. I'd just like to make a few
of my little dreams come true. You know I've
always wanted to buy Denmark and be richer
than the Queen.

                                    DAN

            If you do your job, Mother, that'll all come true.

                                   BETTY

        What job?

                                    DAN

        Cover our tracks. Make sure we are not
        followed.

                                   BETTY

        Oh, I'm used to that. If any of those bloody
        militia come by, I'll spin 'em a yarn.

                                  GILPIN

        Tell them we died of the plague.

                               YELLOWBEARD

        Death's a pretty good alibi.

                                 LAMBOURN

        Oh yes. Do tell my wife that I'm dead.

                                   BETTY

        Oh, yes, don't worry, lambchop – I've got loads of
        bodies up there. Now piss off out of it before the
        marines get here.

                                                          CUT TO

29   INT. ROOM

     Where LADY LAMBOURN, much bruised and
     dishevelled, is having her manacles and chains taken
     off by an embarrassed MANSELL.

                                103

CLEMENT

I do apologise, Lady Lambourn, but mistakes
can happen in the best run navies. Now this
man who assaulted you. Did he have a long
yellow beard?

LADY LAMBOURN

He might have done, but I've told you it was all
over in a flash.

CLEMENT

After the incident, did he happen to mention his
- er - likely movements?

LADY LAMBOURN

There was no mention of likely movements at
all. I had enough likely movements to last me
a lifetime thank you very much, Captain
Clement.

MANSELL

Just a thought, sir.

CLEMENT

What is it?

MANSELL
(out of the side of his mouth to his superior)
Well, putting myself in Yellowbeard's shoes, the
first thing I'd do after raping her ladyship would
be to have a stiff drink.

CLEMENT
(briefly eyeing Lady Lambourn)
You could be right, for once, Mansell. Let's try

the inn. It seems to be the centre of life round
here.

CUT TO

30   EXT.   'MAIMED FOX'

MOON and GILBERT are behind a hedge watching the
dead customers being piled in a heap. PEW is going
through pockets.

> MOON
> That's that blind bastard that killed Hodge.
> Knows too much for his own good.

> GILBERT
> I'll slit his throat.

> MOON
> No ... no ... somethin' more in the way of an
> accident.

BETTY approaches PEW.

> BETTY
> Stop that, you thief.

She shoves him out of way and starts to go through
the pockets, helping herself to possessions. CLEMENT
and MANSELL appear.

> CLEMENT
> Oi!

                    BETTY
        I'm only takin' what's my due . . . to cover
        legitimate expenses. Should see the mess they
        made.

                    CLEMENT
        What happened?

BETTY is aware of their importance.

                    BETTY
            Plague.

CLEMENT and MANSELL step back.

                    CLEMENT
(incredulous)
            Plague?

                    BETTY
        All sudden like. Lucky I was out.

                    MANSELL
        That man's got a sword in him.

                    BETTY
            He fell on it.

                    CLEMENT
(suspicious)
            Has Yellowbeard been round here?

                    BETTY
        He's dead too, and Lord Lambourn and Dr Gilpin
        . . . oh, and my son Dan. All gone . . . ooooh.

                    106

She attempts a convincing wail.

> MANSELL
> Oh hell. If they're all dead, sir, what'll you tell
> the Queen? I mean we're supposed to follow
> him to the treas . . .

CLEMENT gives him a shin-shattering kick and sees
PEW who has been listening.

> CLEMENT
> (shouting)
> Halt, in the name of the law.

> PEW
> All right, I'm not deaf.

> CLEMENT
> Good. Have you heard anything about
> Yellowbeard?

> PEW
> Well, I might have heard something . . .

CLEMENT takes out a bag of coins and jingles them.

> PEW
> . . . A heavier jingle might get me ears in tune
> again.

CLEMENT pulls out another bag and jingles that.

> PEW
> It's extraordinary, no doctor can do anything
> for me, but I find the old gypsy remedy of two

bags of coins in the pocket does wonders for my earsight.

CLEMENT places the bags in his pocket.

                    PEW
Ah, that's better. You were asking about . . . ?

                    CLEMENT
Yellowbeard.

                    PEW
Ah, him. He's not dead and neither are the others.

MOON and GILBERT react from behind the hedge.

                    PEW
I did hear something about a town - they were 'eaded for Portsmouth, that's what I 'eard.

MOON dispatches GILBERT with a nod.

                    MANSELL
Is that all?

                    PEW
It's more than anyone else knows in these parts.

                    CLEMENT
Right. You find them in Portsmouth, Mansell, and I'll meet you there with the frigate as soon as I can.

They exit in different directions. THE BLIND MAN taps his way with a stick along a wall at side of the inn. At the end of the wall a bit of the wall continues with him. We see that this is a large rock being carried by MR MOON. This bit of wall is moved in a semi-circular fashion towards an outhouse at rear of the inn into which PEW taps himself. The outhouse then explodes.

CUT TO

31   EXT.   BUSTLING STREETS OF PORTSMOUTH

Lots of exceptionally poor beggars, dandies, sailors, tarts.

With GILBERT lurking in the background, LAMBOURN, GILPIN, DAN and YELLOWBEARD arrive at door with brass plate on it saying:

CLOVIS WHITFIELD
MERCANTILE AGENT

In the window is another sign:

'WHY PAY MORE?'
CHEAP OFF-PEAK PASSAGES
TO: 50 gns.
Barbados
Port Au Prince
Jamaica
Mustique
Tobago

DAN
This is the place, look, Jamaica.

109

All shush him. He points to sign.

THE EDITH. A THREE-MASTED
SQUARE RIGGER LEAVING
TOMORROW.

> LAMBOURN
> Mmm. Let's try here, they're all the same these
> places.
> (showing the way)
> Professor Anthrax.

They go up the steps. YELLOWBEARD, who is bringing
up the rear, has his coat tugged by a very pretty, blue-
eyed, fair-haired, eight-year-old GIRL, dressed very
poorly. She's very sweet and orphanic.

> GIRL
> (pointing)
> Mister, someone's following you.

YELLOWBEARD sees GILBERT dashing off.
YELLOWBEARD chases after him. The GIRL
approaches DAN.

> GIRL
> Oi, mister, give us three farthings for a lump of shit.

> DAN
> I beg your pardon?

> GIRL
> I said give us three farthings for a lump of shit.

> DAN
> Certainly not.

The little GIRL hurls a lump of shit in his face.

> GILPIN
> (philosophically)
> Society's to blame.

They enter. LAMBOURN is about to leave, turns to GIRL.

> LAMBOURN
> (sympathetic)
> Here's three farthings for you, lass.

She takes it, smiles sweetly – and LAMBOURN
violently kicks her down stairs and wanders into
house.

CUT TO

32   INT.   DRAWING ROOM OF HOUSE

Room is richly overfurnished. Dominating the room is
CLOVIS WHITFIELD, a fop who is as overdressed as the
room. He wears an enormous vast peruke. He stands
in front of the mirror with a brown spaniel which he
is trying out in the crook of his arm. A sycophantic
SALESMAN is hovering attendantly. On the floor is a
sack of dogs. WHITFIELD pulls a face. He is selecting
dogs for his muff.

> CLOVIS WHITFIELD
> Mmm . . . not sure.

> SALESMAN
> Oh, that really suits, sir. I think you'll find this
> one just the thing for chilly evenings.

111

CLOVIS WHITFIELD

Mmm . . .

(not sure)

It's a bit too brown . . . more of an afternoon
dog. Have you got something that'll set the coat
off a little better?

SALESMAN

I see. Sir would like a more formal-looking
beast.

CLOVIS WHITFIELD

I think so, don't you?

(hands it back)

Something a bit less 'ectic.

SALESMAN

Ah . . .

A speaking tube whistles. CLOVIS WHITFIELD answers.

CLOVIS WHITFIELD

'Ello?

VOICE

Some gentlemen to see you about a passage to,
er . . .

(does a covering-up cough)

CLOVIS WHITFIELD

Send 'em up.

He returns the sack of dogs and peers in at the
moving, yapping bundle.

112

CLOVIS WHITFIELD
Something in a darker brown possibly?

SALESMAN
You've seen the whole collection, sir.

CLOVIS WHITFIELD
Oh! Well, let me have the grey one then, it does
go well with the peruke.

He adjusts his wig as SALESMAN produces grey one
from sack. WHITFIELD holds it up next to wig.

SALESMAN
Oh, very nice, sir, and extremely less 'ectic.

SALESMAN packs up the rest of dogs.

SALESMAN
Good day, sir.

He goes with his lumpy sack. WHITFIELD poses with
his new dog. As the SALESMAN goes, so our group
enter.

WHITFIELD turns and greets them.

CLOVIS WHITFIELD
Ah . . . you must be the gentlemen who wanted
the passage to . . .
(coughs meaningfully)

LAMBOURN
Quite. One of your 'why pay more' passages.

WHITFIELD motions silence. Goes to door, quickly opens it to look for prospective listener.

He shoves hanky down speaking tube, puts whistle cork back in.

                    CLOVIS WHITFIELD
          I'm afraid we're fresh out of those. You could
          opt for one of our 'Why pay less?' passages
          which works out a bit treblish.

                    DAN
          One hundred and fifty guineas? For the four.

                    CLOVIS WHITFIELD
          Each. There are four of you?

                    GILPIN
          (shocked)
          Where is Professor Anthrax?

                    DAN
          There are four.

                    LAMBOURN
          Should have bloody good cabins for that.
          (he gets money out)

                    CLOVIS WHITFIELD
          Finest.

                    GILPIN
          What ship do we go to?

> CLOVIS WHITFIELD
> Ah . . . you don't. You'll be met this evening at ten o'clock at the 'Stoned Crow'.

CUT TO

33   INT.   PORTSMOUTH BROTHEL

Central 'reception area' from off which are the curtained doorways of booths. A fat, tarty MADAME supervises. A few horrible SLAGS sit around in boredom. Everything is a bit tatty. A pathetic gesture has been made in the direction of erotica. Out of one booth comes the tall, imposing figure of CAPTAIN HUGHES, followed by a ravishing-looking BLONDE, with retroussé nose and pert tits.

> HUGHES
> Oh Miss Purvis . . . thank you for the eels, they were absolutely delicious. Worth every penny.

He hands over a bag of coins with which she is well pleased.

> PURVIS
> Oh, thank you, Captain.

We see MOON's face peer out from behind a curtain to look at HUGHES.

CUT TO

34   INT.   MOON'S BOOTH

He is lying flat on his back on a couch. His unstrapped hook stands upon a bedside table. DORIS, a tart,

115

wearing lace-up bodice and frilly petticoat, is seated
astride him facing away from him. He is finishing off
the rum from a bottle with smashed-off neck and
puffing a curious-looking pipe.

>   MOON
>   Who's that?

>   DORIS
>   Sounded like Captain Hughes.

>   MOON
>   Which is his ship then?

>   DORIS
>   The Edith.

                                            CUT TO

35   INT. 'RECEPTION AREA'

GILBERT hastily enters. The girls grin seductively. He
ignores them.

>   GILBERT
>   Mr Moon?

Their smiles disappear and one points to his booth.

36   INT. BOOTH

GILBERT enters. MOON is seated on couch strapping
on his hook. DORIS is carrying a tray of
'embrocations'.

                         MOON
     Thank you, Doris.

                         DORIS
     But we . . .

                         MOON
     Thank you, Doris.

DORIS goes.

                        GILBERT
(whispering)
     They've booked a passage on a ship called . . .
(fumbles out a piece of paper)

                         MOON
     The Edith.

                        GILBERT
     That's right, Captain by the name of . . .

                         MOON
     Hughes.

GILBERT is in awe of MOON's ability and checks the
other side of the paper.

                         MOON
(whispers)
     So Yellowbeard's going to be aboard the Edith.

We see YELLOWBEARD listening in an adjoining
cubicle.

                    MOON
    I reckon Captain Hughes needs a new Bosun.

                    GILBERT
Eh?

                    MOON
And a bosun's mate.

                    GILBERT
Aha . . .

                    MOON
Doris.

She appears. He tosses her a coin.

                    MOON
    Thank you for the eels.

They leave. YELLOWBEARD emerges and chuckles.

                    DORIS
    Are you anything to do with Yellowbeard?

                    YELLOWBEARD
    No, I'm Professor Anthrax, a bonatical expetide.

He hurries off leaving DORIS confused.

37/39   DELETED

  40   EXT.   QUAY AT PORTSMOUTH

        YELLOWBEARD strides up ramp searching for the
        others, as they pass beneath the ramp looking for him.

                      118

They stop outside a nautical accessory shop evidenced by a large anchor, coils of rope, lanterns, charts, telescopes, knives, etc.

DAN has just completed a sizeable purchase. He has three hats under his arm and several books and charts. He is wearing a new cocked hat. LAMBOURN staggers up to him followed by GILPIN from another direction as clock strikes the hour.

> LAMBOURN
> I've . . . been in every tavern this side of town and there's no sign of 'Professor Anthrax'.

> GILPIN
> I've looked in all the knocking shops.

> LAMBOURN
> The what?

> DAN
> Brothels.

> GILPIN
> The 'Eel Houses'.

LAMBOURN is a bit embarrassed.

> GILPIN
> The 'Professor' is bound to find you, Dan, before we sail – so I think we should stick together.

They start to walk off.

LAMBOURN
Perhaps I should take a quick look in a couple
of brothel knocking places before . . . er . . .

CUT TO

41   ANOTHER PART OF THE QUAYSIDE

A small marquee has been erected among the vendors.
It bears a sign: 'SIGN ON FOR THE ROYAL NAVY'.

CAPTAIN HUGHES stands impressively before it. He
addresses the public.

HUGHES
Any fit young man keen to shoulder
responsibility and serve their country while
enjoying the finest comradeship?

HUGHES becomes conscious that A SPOTTY YOUTH is
the only one paying attention.

HUGHES
(pause)
Free board and lodging?
(pause)
More tail than you ever dreamed possible?

Still no response from the SPOTTY YOUTH (ALAN).

HUGHES
Train for a good career at our expense?

ALAN smilingly starts to enter tent.

HUGHES

That's right, laddie. Step inside and leaf through
the brochures.

42   INTERIOR OF TENT

A HUGE BOSUN strikes ALAN a terrible blow from
behind. He falls to the ground and TWO SAILORS
quickly bundle him up and drag him under the back of
the tent.

There is a ripping sound as MOON's sharpened hook
tears its way neatly through the canvas walling of the
rear of the tent. MOON appears through rip unseen by
BOSUN, places the point of his hook on the BOSUN's
throat. The BOSUN freezes.

MOON

Here, Bosun, I heard you were thinking of er . . .
becoming an ordinary seaman again.

CUT TO

43   EXT.   OUTSIDE TENT

MOON appears in BOSUN'S UNIFORM and salutes
HUGHES.

HUGHES

Well done, Bosun.

MOON

Where to next, sir?

121

> HUGHES

I think a tour of the local pubs.

> MOON

Aye, aye, sir.

> HUGHES

(to the man next to him)
Didn't notice that hook when he signed on.

> GILBERT

He's right-handed, sir.

HUGHES accepts explanation.

44 EXT. 'STONED CROW'

Lots of hubbub from loutish CUSTOMERS as they sit on benches at tables talking and drinking. GILBERT comes over and looks around. He sees DAN, GILPIN and LAMBOURN sitting long-faced and fed-up, their trunks nearby. GILBERT watches from a discreet distance.

> DAN

He's run out on us, he's the worst father anyone ever had.

> LAMBOURN

He's the nastiest person I ever met.

> GILPIN

Quite clearly demented.

Pause while they all mumble agreement.

122

                                        DAN
                        But he wasn't dull.

LAMBOURN and GILPIN agree.

                                    LAMBOURN
                        Gave me the best day of my life.

                                        DAN
(sighs)
                        We've lost him. We've got the map but, without
                        him, we might as well go back home. So that's
                        that.

GILBERT hurriedly exits.

From down the quayside, MOON arrives with GILBERT
and some naval psychopaths.

                                        VOICES
                        Press-gang!

Shot of our group with LAMBOURN indicating to DAN
that press-gang should be fun to watch.

                                        MOON
                        What? No . . . no . . . we're just out for an
                        evening of heavy sarcasm.

Some people accept this. Some look puzzled.

                                        MOON
                        I'm sure some of you gentlemen would like to
                        volunteer for an adventure holiday upon a
                        modern, rat-free, leakproof ship. We'll give you

                                      123

ample opportunity to kill foreigners, perverts, blacks and hottentots. All those wishing to volunteer should lie down on the floor with their eyes shut.

MOON proceeds to bash a few customers about the head, as do his press-gang.

GILBERT gives the nod to MOON as to who our group are.

> MOON

(over-polite)
> Would you be bound for . . .
(coughs meaningfully)

> LAMBOURN
> No, as a matter of . . .

MOON knocks 'em out. Bodies picked up by men.

> MOON

(to tarts)
> Thank you very much, ladies . . . be back in half an hour.

As they're carried out MOON glances at trunks. He gestures to GILBERT to bring them. As he exits, we see that YELLOWBEARD has observed all this from behind a stall.

CUT TO

124

45   EXT.   PORTSMOUTH QUAYSIDE. MORNING

Quayside in PORTSMOUTH – An armed merchantman, the EDITH, is being made ready for her departure. The quayside is bursting with activity. The tall, imposing figure of CAPTAIN HUGHES is standing by an ill-attended signing-on table. The occasional, rather stupid-looking volunteer signs on by making his mark. He is given a shilling by HUGHES and climbs the gangplank. As soon as he's aboard, he passes red-clad MARINES who close ranks behind him indicating that there's no leaving the ship now.

Supplies are being loaded up another plank. We see a cartload of press-gangees, still dazed, some still drunk and all in chains. MOON is supervising their being loaded like cargo. Among them, we see our three unconscious heroes.

On the quayside are many opportunist vendors including liquor vending stall, pipe and tobacco and snuff stall, a stall selling medicaments for maritime ailments and other quack remedies, musical instruments including squeeze boxes, tin whistles, fiddles, and we see a SAILOR happily buying some bagpipes. A parrot vending stall is doing good trade.

Sign saying: E. B. BRADSHAW – PURVEYOR OF CRUTCHES, WOODEN LEGS AND HOOKS TO THE GENTRY.

Another sign: ADULT BOOKS AND TAPESTRIES.

SALESMAN
Can't go wrong with Chaucer, page three of the Miller's Tale.

125

Wraps up book in brown paper and hands it over.

> SALESMAN
> If you fancy something a bit stronger there's
> some wood carvings round the back.

A half open-topped crate of pigs stands on a landing
net about to be hoisted aboard. YELLOWBEARD, seeing
this, chooses his moment and stealthily climbs in with
the pigs. A few moments later the crate is hoisted
aboard. Also being carried on to the ship are various
potted plants and the odd pig and goat. HUGHES gives
them a cursory glance and nod of approval as they're
taken aboard. An OFFICER is boarding and being
followed by a CABIN BOY who is lugging the officer's
chest. The CABIN BOY has an ample pair of breasts
and conceals her face with the officer's sea chest. The
officer's name is CRISP.

> HUGHES
> Mr Crisp.

> CRISP
> Sir.

> HUGHES
> What is that?

> CRISP
> My box, sir.

> HUGHES
> No, no, carrying your box.

CRISP

(feigning innocence)

Oh . . . er . . . cabin boy, Smith, sir.

HUGHES

Smith's got tits.

CRISP

Er . . . well, he's been a bit ill . . . er.

HUGHES

Get her off.

CRISP

Yes, sir.

CRISP sadly takes his box from SMITH. They gaze fondly at each other as SMITH reluctantly leaves. CRISP turns and boards.

HUGHES next spots three sailors carrying a large, stuffed crocodile on their shoulders.

HUGHES

Just a minute. What is that?

GILBERT

Crocodile, sir.

HUGHES

What's it for?

GILBERT

Each sailor is, by tradition, allowed a pet, sir.

127

                    HUGHES
        One pet per sailor. Parrots preferred.

                    GILBERT
        Ah, well . . . we like . . . clubbed together, see . . .

                    HUGHES
        That's bigger than three parrots.

                    GILBERT
        Not if they're in cages.

                    HUGHES
        Open it up.

                    GILBERT
        Open it, sir?

                    HUGHES
        Yes, it's got buttons down the side.

The sailors reluctantly lower the crocodile and undo
the buttons. DORIS climbs out. HUGHES shows his
contempt with a look.

                    GILBERT
        Good try, Doris.

As DORIS shuffles down gangplank, the three sailors
sadly board. DORIS passes a sailor waiting to board. He
carries a big, woolly sheep. DORIS taps it on the head.

                    DORIS
            I shouldn't bother, love. They're fairly strict on
            this one.

The sheep bleats as it's carried on board.

CAPTAIN HUGHES is supervising the loading of press-gangees. CLOVIS WHITFIELD has joined him and points out LAMBOURN, DAN and GILPIN.

> CLOVIS WHITFIELD
> That one and that one, and the fat one there.
> Officer material. Well educated.

CAPTAIN HUGHES hands over the money. DAN groggily sees this. DAN, although manacled, attempts to get to CLOVIS WHITFIELD.

> DAN
> You thief and liar.

> CLOVIS WHITFIELD

(indignant)
> You wanted a passage to Jamaica – you've got one!

DAN is thwacked on head by MOON.

> CLOVIS WHITFIELD
> Carrying much cargo?

> HUGHES
> A few cosmetic luxuries and farming
> equipment.

> CLOVIS WHITFIELD
> *Farming* equipment?

> HUGHES
> Mainly manacles and chains.

CLOVIS WHITFIELD

Ah, yes . . . Always a pleasure to do business
with you.

The ship is ready to sail.

Lots of the regular crew and officers are lined up on
deck, including MOON.

MOON

All hands present and correct, sir.

HUGHES

Thank you, Bosun. Officers and men of the
Edith. The ancient superstition that a woman
on board brings bad luck is nowadays a proven,
scientific fact.

AN OFFICER appears on deck with a struggling, naked
woman under one arm. As though jettisoning a piece
of rubbish, he flings her into the harbour. HUGHES is
smugly satisfied.

HUGHES

(with great solemnity)

And now that you're all on deck, I should like to
make sure that this rule is being obeyed. I
appreciate that this is going to be a bit
embarrassing for us all, but it won't be if you all
close your eyes. Bosun Moon.

MOON

Sir!

                              HUGHES
                   Give the orders . . .
          (he whispers to him)

                               MOON
          (his eyes widen)
                   You sure about that, sir?

                              HUGHES
                   Oh, yes.

          MOON takes a deep breath.

                               MOON
                   Right, men. Close your eyes and take your . . .
                   willies out.

          There is a general murmur of surprise and protest.
          MOON's eyes are shut as he fumbles with his trousers.

                               MOON
                   Come on, it's an order. Have you got them out?

          A chorus of unhappy 'Yesses'. HUGHES walks through
          the ranks, inspecting them. He stops in front of
          ASKEY, taps him with a stick.

                              HUGHES
                   You, man. See the ship's surgeon. Mr Crisp.
                   Make ready for sail. Hoist the petard.

                               CRISP
                   Aye, aye.

          Nautical music and fanfares.

                                                    CUT TO

                              131

46 DELETED

47 EXT.   THE EDITH IN FULL SAIL IN OPEN SEA.
    DAY

                                        FADE INTO

48 THE BILGES OF THE EDITH

The very lowest level. Hardly any lighting, the
planking is awash. The beams from the deck above are
only a few feet above them. The movement and noise
of the sea is great. The occasional rat swims past. The
press-gangees are all in chairs and barely keeping
their heads above bilge-water.

LAMBOURN is using GILPIN as a pillow and staring at
rows of forlorn, manacled men who all realise their
predicament. They stare blankly back. LAMBOURN
looks at his manacles, shifts uneasily in water. A rat is
perched on his head.

                    LAMBOURN
          You know, I've just been thinking. If this cabin
          cost us three hundred guineas a head, thank
          God we didn't fall for one of the cheaper ones.

A particularly gloomy-looking man speaks out. He
speaks with a Scandinavian accent.

                    FINN
          It's all right for you English with your well-
          known laughing in adversity type behaviour. We
          Finns prefer to face the stark reality of the
          wretchedness of life. Why turn it into

                        132

happiness? What we have here is high quality
misery. Accept it for what it is.

Suddenly hatch opens and MOON appears and unlocks
chains so that all are free to move but their hands and
feet are still manacled.

                    MOON
          Gentlemen. I'm afraid I shall have to interrupt
          your morning bath. Now, on your knees and
          crawl up here on the double.
(orders)
               Left, right, left, right . . .

49   INT.   GUN DECK – STAIRWAY

All press-gangees shuffle along and ascend stairs on
knees.

                    BURGESS
          When you've successfully survived your
          training as able-bodied seamen, you'll be
          permitted to crouch freely in this deck.

He moves up to main deck. Our group hangs back on
the gun deck. In background men are stowing
hammocks and mopping floors. Slops are thrown out
of gunports through which occasional waves crash in.
The odd loose cannonball rolls about. MACDONALD
and ANOTHER MAN frantically work ship's pump.

                    LAMBOURN
(to men on pump)
               What did you do to deserve this?

133

MACDONALD
We were the first to store our hammocks.

GILPIN
Is that wrong?

MACDONALD
(indignant)
No! Pumping is an honour. All the rest got sent
up the rigging.

There is a scream and a dull thud on deck above them.

MACDONALD
Was Mike in the rigging? Sounded like Mike.

OTHER MAN
Yeah, it did.

DAN
Listen, things aren't as bad as they seem. All
right, we've been press-ganged, but that means
nobody knows where we are.

LAMBOURN
Including ourselves.

DAN
We do, this ship *is* going to Jamaica, and we've
got the map even though we've lost Yellowbeard.

We see MOON listening through the hatch above.

ALL
Ohh!

                    LAMBOURN
        I shall go directly to the Captain and tell him
        who I am and demand a cabin.

                    GILPIN
        We're safer if no one knows who we are. All we
        have to do is keep out of trouble until Jamaica.

MOON yells down the hatch.

                    MOON
        Right! I shall be keeping a very close eye on
        you three. Up here on the double.

They hurriedly clank their way up the main deck.

49A   EXT.   THE EDITH SAILING ON THE HIGH SEAS

                                        DISSOLVE TO

50   EXT.   MAIN DECK ANOTHER DAY

        As the gangees come out of hatch on to deck, they're
        unshackled and herded into a line by marines. The
        rest of the ship's company is assembled. The ship is
        in full sail. There is no land in sight. The CHAPLAIN
        is finishing a prayer over a recent burial at sea.
        Standing near him are two sailors with a plank and a
        flag. A third is mopping up a nearby bloody mess on
        deck.

                    MOON
        (shouts)
            All hands present on deck, Mr Crisp, sir.

All crew assemble on main deck. MR CRISP is on quarter deck.

>   CRISP
>   Thank you, Bosun.

CRISP walks to rear of quarter deck and salutes CAPTAIN HUGHES and stands beside him with two other officers, one of whom happens to be an absolutely ravishing blonde in pink-beribboned dress with huge tits and pouting lips, retroussé nose and an obviously drawn moustache, MR PROSTITUTE. CAPTAIN HUGHES strides briskly to front of quarter deck. The officers stand behind him. The gangees react to the woman. The Bosun's mate pipes 'attention for the Captain'. ALL enlisted men and officers rapidly stand to attention. The gangees follow suit. He addresses ship's company.

>   HUGHES
>   My name is Captain Hughes. These are my
>   officers. This is Lieutenant Martin who is
>   responsible for discipline; and Lieutenant Crisp
>   who is responsible for discipline and this is Mr
>   Prostitute who is responsible for . . .

There is a snigger from O'DRISCOLL.

>   Nail that man's foot to the deck.

He quickly continues his sentence.

>   . . . discipline.

BURGESS has taken hold of O'DRISCOLL. We hear the sound of nailing and screaming.

HUGHES

Now in fairness to you all, I'm honour-bound to
ask the question, 'Is there anyone here who does
not wish to be a member of Her Majesty's navy?'

ASKEY steps smartly forward.

ASKEY

Me, sir.

HUGHES pulls a pistol and shoots him dead.

HUGHES

Chaplain!

The CHAPLAIN rushes forward while two sailors place
ASKEY on a plank permanently jutting out from the
side of ship. A flag is hastily put over him. CHAPLAIN
conducts his prayer with great haste.

CHAPLAIN

(fast)

O Lord, we hereby commit the body of our dear
departed

(the body is dumped)

into the sea. Amen.

HUGHES re-addresses the ship's company.

HUGHES

Anyone else want out?

No-one replies.

HUGHES

Right, at first, some of you may find the
discipline on this ship slightly on the harsh side

of strict. It is our duty to seek out and destroy
Her Majesty's enemies, the foul and most
foreign French, and indeed anyone whose vile
hearts are set upon selfishly grabbing whole
continents which rightfully should only be
governed by those fit to govern.

(pause)

The English. It has recently been proven by that
eminent English scientist Sir Christopher
Newton that it is one of the fundamental laws of
nature that all bodies given freedom of choice
must eventually come to rest in the state of
being English. While the entire world is sooner
or later bound to be of this opinion, in the
meantime it is our most urgent task to push
things on a little. Carry on, Mr Crisp.

                      CRISP

Aye, aye, sir.

                      HUGHES

(turning)

Mr Prostitute, Mr Martin, luncheon duty.

They descend to main deck and enter Captain's cabin.
CRISP remains on quarter deck.

                      BURGESS

(who carries a knotted rope.
To DAN and LAMBOURN)

You two sanding and scouring.

BURGESS goes to others. Orders them to hurry up.
Whacks a passing sailor.

138

LAMBOURN

What do we do?

DAN

Er . . . stand and scour. Better do it I suppose.

They shade eyes and scour the horizon.

LAMBOURN

What are we scouring for?

DAN

Don't know but do it hard or we might get ahhgh . . .

Both are whacked by BURGESS.

BURGESS

I told you to sand and scour.

Indicating buckets of sand and scouring stones and
another man who is furiously scrubbing for his life,
having cleaned a considerable portion of the deck.

LAMBOURN

We evidently misheard what you . . . ahhgh.

Gets bashed behind the knees with BURGESS's knotted
rope. LAMBOURN falls to his knees near stones and
sand which he hurriedly begins to use. DAN joins him.

BURGESS

If you haven't finished by the time I get back
you'll get more of this.

Whacks deck with rope. They scrub furiously.

139

50A EXT. DECK

LIONEL BARRYMORE heads for the Captain's cabin
carrying a tray with a whole, roast, garnished chicken
covered by a napkin. On his way, he passes the pig
pen. A hand swiftly darts out and quickly removes the
chicken from under the napkin. Oblivious, LIONEL
BARRYMORE continues on his way.

CUT TO

50B INT. PIG PEN

YELLOWBEARD ravenously devouring chicken
surrounded by envious pigs.

CUT TO

50C INT. CAPTAIN'S CABIN

LIONEL BARRYMORE enters carrying tray. HUGHES,
MARTIN and MR PROSTITUTE are sitting at the table
and look up expectantly.

HUGHES
Thank you, Barrymore.

BARRYMORE
Sir.

He leaves. HUGHES removes napkin with a flourish to
reveal garnish only.

CUT TO

140

50D   EXT.   DECK

DAN is completing a section of the deck which
includes O'DRISCOLL nailed to it. He accommodatingly
raises the un-nailed foot for DAN to scrub under it.
Someone else further along is receiving a beating for
poor scrubbing. LAMBOURN has made little progress
and is in danger. DAN quickly swaps with him and
scrubs furiously. He is spotted by BURGESS as having
done very little compared with LAMBOURN and has
one of his hands ground into deck. DAN cries out in
pain.

                    BURGESS
        Oh, you liked that eh? Now the other hand.

MOON appears.

                    MOON
            Burgess, stop that.

BURGESS stops and scurries away.

                    DAN
            Thank you.

CRISP, matter of factly, selecting the most vicious set
of cat o' nine tails from a box and hanging over rail in
readiness.

                    CRISP
        (shouts from bridge)
            You going soft, Bosun?

141

                    MOON

        Oh no, sir. Burgess wasn't putting his weight   .
        into it.

                    CRISP

        Jolly good.

                    MOON
    (out of corner of his mouth)
        Scream.

                    DAN

        What?

                    MOON

        Scream!

    We see MOON place his foot over DAN's hand so that
    the weight rests totally on the heel. He twists from
    side to side, DAN begins to scream and enjoy his
    portrayal of agony. CRISP nods to MOON approvingly.

                                        CUT TO

51   INT. CAPTAIN'S CABIN

    HUGHES, MARTIN and MR PROSTITUTE sit with
    empty plates in front of them. HUGHES has a face like
    thunder.

                MR PROSTITUTE
        I always prefer a light luncheon.

    MARTIN is examining his empty plate which has the
    ENGLISH COAT OF ARMS on it. He considers it.

                    142

MARTIN

... Very strange, isn't it ... that the English flag
should have lions on it? I mean, there aren't
any lions in England are there?

HUGHES

In the normal course of events their numbers
swing from none at all to few. I think, Mr
Martin, you're missing the whole point of the
Royal Standard. Would you have our nation
employ as its proud emblem the sheep? the
spaniel? the pussycat? Or perhaps our furry
little friend, the fieldmouse?
(to MARTIN's face)
Squeak, squeak!

MARTIN AND PROSTITUTE exchange nervous looks.

HUGHES

The point of three lions being the English
emblem is to display a degree of ferocity
symbolic of their national fortitude.

He roars ferociously into MR PROSTITUTE's face. She
and MR MARTIN look awkwardly at each other and
wish they weren't there.

During this, LIONEL BARRYMORE returns and
removes the untouched tray.

HUGHES

Mr Martin, I'm taking Mr Prostitute on a tour of
the ship, him being new to it or should I have
said he being new to it?

                    MARTIN
        Don't think it matters these days, sir.

HUGHES and MR PROSTITUTE leave for the deck.

52/53   DELETED

54   MAIN DECK

CAPTAIN HUGHES and MR PROSTITUTE stroll on to
main deck.

CRISP salutes him and HUGHES.

                    HUGHES
(to Gilbert)
        That man over there yawned. Give him
        swimming lessons.

GILBERT grabs the man and throws him overboard
and resumes duty.

HUGHES and MR PROSTITUTE pass the FINN and
another man who are stripped to the waist and are
tied either side of the stairway leading to the quarter
deck. They are being lashed with a rope's end by MR
BURGESS. Man screams out as he is lashed.

                    FINN
        Oh you English, you always complain. Where I
        come from we are stripped nude and beaten
        with logs and thrown into the snow for fun.

LAMBOURN desperately looking around approaches
BURGESS.

LAMBOURN

Excuse me, which way to the bathroom?

BURGESS

(points along deck)
Anywhere along there, just stick whatever bit
wants emptying over the side and shout 'Sorry'.

LAMBOURN

Thanks, I'll wait.

CAPTAIN HUGHES is finishing describing the rigging
on the main mast to MR PROSTITUTE.

LIONEL BARRYMORE carries the tray of garnish along
the deck. It is looked at longingly by crew members and
is taken to the pig pen at forward end near the fo'cstle.
LIONEL throws the garnish to the pigs and goes. After a
pause, the garnish comes flying out again.

CUT TO

54A   EXT.   MAIN DECK AFT

HUGHES

Now over here we have Mr MacDonald who is
our expert in hand-to-hand fighting.

GILPIN is in unarmed combat class. MACDONALD
gives LAMBOURN a sword and dagger.

MACDONALD

Right, you're comin' at me w' a sword an'
dagger.

145

LAMBOURN
Sorry, what's that?

GILPIN
(acting as translator)
You're coming at him with a sword and dagger.

LAMBOURN throws up attacking position with sword
and dagger and advances on him.

MACDONALD
So. What do I do? Stamp on his foot . . .

He does so. LAMBOURN doubles up with pain.

MACDONALD
. . . then hit him round the face wi' your wee
wet sockie . . .

Wallops LAMBOURN across face with sock which
leaves large red stain across his face.

MACDONALD
. . . while he thinks he's bleedin' to death, you
kick him in the balls.

LAMBOURN examines his face and he's kicked in the
balls. He falls in a heap.

MACDONALD
Right, a moothfu' a headies. D'y ken what that is?

GILPIN
A moothful of headies . . . I don't quite know
what . . . that is . . .

146

MACDONALD hits GILPIN on the bridge of nose with forehead.

                    GILPIN
          Arrgh!

                    MACDONALD
          He kens noo.

                    GILPIN
     (pained)
          He knows now.

Having observed this, HUGHES and MR PROSTITUTE move on.

                    HUGHES
          Come, Mr Prostitute, it is time to discuss those
          matters of great nautical gravity.

He goes.

                    MR PROSTITUTE
     (to herself)
          That's twice this morning.

A beam in middle of deck. BURGESS orders DAN to walk across beam.

                    BURGESS
          You. Walk across it.

DAN does so.

                    BURGESS
          Easy, isn't it?
     (turns to all)
          Can you all do that?

All agree. He then points to one fifty feet up.

                    BURGESS
          Good, now that's exactly the same. Walk that one.

They start to climb the ropes. MOON looks on
anxiously and is about to make his move when the
ship's bell rings.

                    MOON
          We'll carry on from here after lunch.

MOON relaxes.

55   GUN   DECK

A SAILOR comes out from behind some crates marked
'FARMING EQUIPMENT'. He is carrying a wooden
female TAILOR'S DUMMY. He passes it up to another
SAILOR on the gun deck and goes about his business.

All are seated round a table. Bruised and battered.
GILPIN with a bleeding nose and two black eyes.
LAMBOURN is covered with cow's blood and walks
with a pronounced stoop. Gruel is being dished out.
GILPIN looks around surreptitiously and lights up a
pipe. He is spotted by BURGESS who pulls the pipe out
of his mouth and puts it back in with lighted end
inside and is punched in face. GILPIN reacts to
burning throat.

                    148

                        BURGESS
          Smoking is only permitted on the upper deck.

LAMBOURN is just about to eat his gruel.

                        BURGESS
          I wouldn't eat that if I were you.

LAMBOURN tastes it.

                        LAMBOURN
          No, it's not awfully nice.

                        BURGESS
          In fact, I wouldn't eat anything if you're going
          to climb up that rigging in one minute flat this
          afternoon.

                        LAMBOURN
          Eh?

                        BURGESS
          Because for every second you're over the
          minute, I'll have the surgeon cut off a pound of
          that.

Pokes him in the tummy.

GILPIN mumbles unintelligibly but urgently.

                        LAMBOURN
          What?

GILPIN takes a swig of water.

                           149

                         GILPIN

        Argh!
(gasps?)
                  I . . . think we should . . . tell . . . them . . . who
                  we are . . .

                         LAMBOURN
        Quite agree . . . otherwise . . . we'll all be dead
        before we get to Jamaica.

                         DAN
        Five men dead already . . . all before breakfast.

                         LAMBOURN
        And now lunch will have taken its toll.

                         DAN
        We must *do* something.

                         GILPIN
        You mean mutiny?

Nearby MACDONALD is listening from behind a pillar.

                         DAN
        No, not mutiny.

                         LAMBOURN
        No - no - not mutiny. That would be - that
        would be - that would be - um - that would be -
        um - that would be - mutiny, wouldn't it?

                         DAN
        I think once the Captain realises who we are
        we'll get an easier passage.

                         150

                    GILPIN

Failing that we could offer him a cut of
Yellowbeard's treasure.

                     DAN

If word of that gets about we'll all have
swimming lessons. Right! I'm going to try to
talk to the man rationally.

                    GILPIN

No, no, lad. You're too young, Dan.

                   LAMBOURN

Yes, it should be me.

                    GILPIN

No, you're having enough difficulty
remembering your own name, let alone
appealing to anybody's reason.

                   LAMBOURN

I am the boy's guardian and the senior member
of our group.

                    GILPIN

And I am a doctor. Tell you what – strike a
compromise – can't say fairer than that – why
don't we both have a . . .

He looks round and sees that DAN has gone.

                                        CUT TO

56   EXT.   MAIN DECK

DAN continues on his way past sailors who are
scrubbing blood off decks. He then nods politely to
O'DRISCOLL, who is nailed to the deck, and is looking
very bored and tapping his unnailed foot. He passes
the CHAPLAIN who is just finishing another last rites
ceremony. Under the flag are just a few lumps.

                    CHAPLAIN
          . . . and commit these remaining bits of our dear
          departed friend to the deep.

DAN also passes FINN tied in reef knot.

                    FINN
          I've learnt it now . . . reef knot . . . it's left over
          right and then right over left.

DAN arrives at the entrance to cabin area. A SAILOR
OF THE WATCH challenges him.

                    SAILOR OF THE WATCH
          Halt.

                    DAN
          Permission to see the Captain.

                    SAILOR OF THE WATCH
          (sarcastically)
          Oh! The Captain?

                    DAN
          Yes, I have a request to make on behalf of some
          paying passengers.

                    SAILOR OF THE WATCH
        Have you now? You'll have to ask Mr Burgess first.

                           DAN
              Oh! He won't mind me asking?

                    SAILOR OF THE WATCH
              Oh *no* – he'll love that. Pass.

He steps aside. The CHAPLAIN, who is passing and
hears this, turns to his assistants.

                        CHAPLAIN
              Er . . . we'd better wait a moment.

They do so. MOON also observes from nearby. DAN
knocks.

57   INT.   BURGESS' CABIN

BURGESS is just placing a couple of lobsters and rats
in a sack on the floor which obviously contains a man
who is giggling and 'ouching' from inside.

                        BURGESS
        Yes?

                           DAN
              Do you know that you have three paying
              passengers on board, who are being treated as
              abominably as the rest of the crew?

                        BURGESS

(mock shock – knocks out man in sack with marlin
spike)
        Really?

                          153

                    DAN

          I want to speak to the Captain to stop this
          senseless cruelty.

                    BURGESS

          You mean like this?

He gives DAN a tremendous shove.

                    DAN

(on floor)

          I can see there's only one thing you'll
          understand . . .

(he gets up)

                    BURGESS

(smiles)

          Oh, yes? And what pray . . .

DAN quickly grabs a large wooden slop bucket from
floor and smashes him in face with it. BURGESS is
unaffected.

                    BURGESS

          . . . might that be?

DAN is hit a blow by BURGESS and keels over.

BURGESS wipes his knuckles.

                    BURGESS

          Right . . . let's finish it.

He walks towards him. Suddenly he is wrenched into
an upright position by a furious YELLOWBEARD.

                    154

Before he can react he is punched fully in the face. He
flies across cabin and . . .

CUT TO

58   INT.   CAPTAIN'S CABIN

HUGHES is sitting up in bed, demurely. MR
PROSTITUTE sits scantily clad puffing on a cigar.
Knock-knock at door. MACDONALD enters.

                    MACDONALD
          Oh, I'm sorry, sir.

                    HUGHES
     What for?

                    MACDONALD
     Er . . . interrupting you.

                    HUGHES
     Oh, I was only smoking a cigar.

                    MACDONALD
     Oh yes, sir. I came to tell you that the son of
     Yellowbeard is on this ship!

                    HUGHES
     What th . . . ?

There is a scream and a crash as a figure flies past
window.

                    MACDONALD
     That was Mr Burgess.

58A   INT.   BURGESS' CABIN

DAN recovers consciousness and looks round the now
empty cabin. He sees the hole and staggers out.

59   EXT.   MAIN DECK

DAN comes out and THE SAILOR OF THE WATCH
nods to him as DAN heads for below decks. It
gradually dawns on him that DAN is unscathed.

59A   INT.   BURGESS' CABIN

SAILOR OF THE WATCH looks into BURGESS' CABIN
and sees hole in window.

59B   EXT.   SEA

He looks over rail into the sea where we see BURGESS'
hat. SAILOR OF THE WATCH blows a whistle.

59C   EXT.   ANOTHER PART OF MAIN DECK

A SAILOR is drumming. SAILORS are in strategic
positions. Some are issued arms. HUGHES strides on
deck and cocks his pistols. Swivel guns are in position.
Suddenly on to deck DAN, LAMBOURN, GILPIN are
dragged, bound and gagged, before HUGHES. The
ship's company is assembled.

MOON stands by. HUGHES looks on cruelly.

                    HUGHES
          Officers and men of the Edith.
          These three people posing as pressees are

156

stowaways. The perspicacity of Mr MacDonald has led to the discovery of a conspiracy against the Crown.

All gasp.

> HUGHES
> There is no doubt in my mind that the one in the middle is the son of the evil *Yellowbeard*.

Lots of loud gasps. 'Ooh's and aah's' from the crew. MR MOON reacts, knowingly.

> HUGHES
> And now his son has dispatched dear Burgess to the deep. His purpose clearly being to take over the ship. We must deliver these traitors to the authorities. Set course for Plymouth. Mr Moon, you know what to do.

HUGHES stands smugly. MOON nods to his henchmen GILBERT and MINION. They grab HUGHES by the ankles and lift him vertically at such a speed that he sails into the air like a rocket and describes a perfect arc and then plummets head first into the sea.

A big cheer goes up. MOON steps forward and hushes the men with a gesture. Several sailors have quickly disarmed the armed sailors and officers.

> MOON
> Oh, dear. The Captain would appear to have gone for a swimming lesson.

There are choruses of 'ohh' and 'shame'. MOON gestures to men to untie DAN and company.

MOON

Right, me hearties. So who do you want for your new Captain?

Chorus of 'Me', 'the one in the middle', 'Mr Prostitute', (he gets hit) – 'Him' (man pointing to DAN). 'Yes him'!

MOON and GILBERT and MINION triumphantly descend to DAN.

MOON

It's unanimous then. The ship's yours, Captain. (pause)
To take where you will.

DAN is taken aback as are LAMBOURN and GILPIN.

DAN

Me? Oh . . .

MOON and GILBERT lift him up on their shoulders and carry the bewildered DAN through the crowd. Men are cheering and shouting, hanging from rigging. 'The Jolly Roger' is hoisted. Barrel of rum comes out. Sailors dance. Lots of applause. LAMBOURN and GILPIN bewilderdly follow MOON, DAN and HENCHMEN to Captain's cabin. They lower him at cabin door.

MOON

Hope you didn't mind me throwin' Captain Hughes overboard, sir.

158

                    DAN

No, er . . . not at all.

                    MOON

I was only following your lead . . . Well . . . You
killing Mr Burgess was an example to us all . . .

                    DAN

I only hit him with a bucket and then
everything went blank.

                    MOON

It's like that. Killing.

60   THE CAPTAIN'S CABIN

Interior of cabin is dominated by painting of HUGHES
which GILPIN takes down and throws out window.
There are naval charts, nautical instruments, also
portrait of Queen Anne.

LAMBOURN opens the booze cabinet and pours three
drinks. GILPIN and DAN go through trunks. DAN has
tried on Captain's best hat.

                    LAMBOURN

(sitting down)
          This is a bit more like it. Well, here's to our
          heroic Captain Dan.

                    DAN

Must have hit Burgess harder than I thought.

                    LAMBOURN

Just like your father.

                    159

                    DAN

        Huh, some father. If only he had told us which
        island . . .

                    GILPIN

        Er . . . Do you realise that we're *all* pirates now?

                    LAMBOURN

        Mmm? Oh yes . . . I suppose we are . . . quite fun
        isn't it?

Swigs from bottle.

                    GILPIN

        But I think we'll need to keep a very close eye
        on that Bosun Moon.

Knock on door as it quickly opens to reveal MOON and
GILBERT. They all try to look nonchalant.

Throughout the ensuing scene MOON and GILBERT
try to sneak glimpses of any kind of clue to the map.
They look at any maps on desk, leaf through books,
etc.

                    MOON

        Oh, er . . . when you've got a moment, sir, could
        you pop up to supervise the execution of the
        officers on the quarter deck?

                    DAN

        Certainly.
    (realises)
        The what?

                    160

MOON

The quarter deck.

DAN

(aghast)

Execution?

MOON

We're only helping you to complete your
mutiny.

DAN

My mutiny? Look, no more killing on this ship.

MOON

With respect, sir . . . the presence of officers
aboard could be prejudicial to your authority.

GILPIN

Yes, they could be trouble. Why not set them
adrift. They'll be all right – I mean they're sailors.

DAN

Good idea. They can't give us away. They don't
know where we're going. See to . . . er . . . a
longboat, Mr Moon.

The room bears evidence of GILBERT's search.
Ornaments upside down, half-open drawers. A slashed
cushion. Painting of Queen Anne slightly askew, and
one corner peeled back.

MOON

Aye, aye, sir. Er . . . where *are* we going, out of
interest?

161

LAMBOURN and GILPIN start to speak at the same time.

> LAMBOURN   GILPIN
> Ah, well, we're not absolutely . . . Um, we're
> not, um . . .

> DAN

(with authority)
> I'll let you know when it's time.

> MOON
> Well, as soon as possible, let me know. The lads
> like to know where they're going – otherwise
> they – er – well, they get restless.

> DAN
> . . . Mr Moon . . . er . . . there's a man nailed to
> the deck. Release him at once.

> MOON
> Aye, aye, Captain.

DAN rather likes his title and is also embarrassed by it.

> GILPIN
> Did you find what you are looking for, Mr
> Gilbert?

GILBERT, who has been shaking a book hoping for the map to drop out, quickly pretends to have been reading.

61   EXT.   LONGBOAT BESIDE EDITH. EVENING

A longboat with food and water supplies is already in
the sea at the side of the Edith. MR CRISP, MR MARTIN
sit with oars. MR PROSTITUTE sits at the tiller.

62   EXT.   MAIN DECK OF EDITH. CREW ARE LINED UP
TO WATCH

Quarter deck. DAN, GILPIN and LAMBOURN are now
dressed as officers, gentlemen pirates. That is, they've
borrowed articles of uniform from HUGHES and his
officers' wardrobe and look altogether grander.

> LAMBOURN
> Couldn't Mr Prostitute stay . . . I'm sure we
> wouldn't have any trouble from him.

> GILPIN
> (referring to crew ogling her)
> Oh yes we would.

> MOON
> The longboat is ready to put away, sir.

> DAN
>
> Right.

The three descend to main deck.

> MOON
> I thought, sir, that perhaps it might be a kindly
> gesture on your part to donate this fine guiding
> lamp to the gentlemen and they won't think so
> badly of you, sir.

163

DAN nods approval and the lamp is lowered to
longboat.

> DAN
>
> There you are, Mr Crisp. No hard feelings.

CRISP takes lamp.

> CRISP
>
> I'll take note of your consideration.

The longboat puts out from the Edith.

> DAN
>
> (loudly)
>
> Er, now, Bosun. Set course for Madagascar.

> MOON
>
> Eh?

> DAN
>
> Yes.
>
> (he winks conspiratorially)

> MOON
>
> Oh yes. You heard what the Captain said. So, it's
> Madagascar!

63   LONGBOAT.   NIGHT

We hear creaking and sloshing of boat. We can barely
make out the boat which is hardly visible.

> CRISP'S VOICE
>
> Pass that big lamp, Mr . . . er . . . Prostitute.

PROSTITUTE'S VOICE
Aye, aye, sir.

CRISP'S VOICE
Got a flint at the ready, Mr Martin?

MARTIN'S VOICE
Yes, sir.

We hear the flint being struck followed by an
enormous explosion.

CUT TO

64   THE BRIDGE OF CLEMENT'S FRIGATE – NIGHT

CLEMENT
What the Hell's that?

MANSELL
The explosion, sir?

CLEMENT
What do you think?
(shouts)
Three points South, Mr Beamish.

MANSELL
I thought you meant this.
(holds up soggy portrait)
Just fished it up, sir.

CLEMENT
It's Captain Hughes, of the Edith.

MANSELL

Doesn't look much like Captain Hughes.

CLEMENT

It says so here.
(pointing at brass plate)

MANSELL

Oh I know that, sir, but it doesn't look much like him.

CLEMENT

Shut up, Mansell. We're on the right course, full sail as she goes.

CUT TO

65 THE EDITH AT NIGHT

The HELMSMAN is checking the lie of the wheel and lashing it into position. He lights up a pipe. There are lots of ship's creaky noises as we pan along main deck past sailors huddled asleep under tarpaulins to the pig enclosure, the lid of which creaks open.
YELLOWBEARD nimbly jumps out and scampers silently back along deck.

The deck is deserted except for a SAILOR carrying the wooden woman which he passes down the hatch to the orlop deck.

The HELMSMAN's room is lit from within. As he steers ship YELLOWBEARD goes to the gunport nearest the HELMSMAN, opens it and lowers a nearby bucket into the sea.

166

Cheech & Chong as the dastardly Spanish spoilsports determined to have Yellowbeard's treasure for their own. Yellowbeard was one of the last movies that Cheech & Chong would film together as a team.

Eric Idle enjoys a quiet moment with Mrs Beard (Madeline Khan). Khan, along with Peter Boyle and Marty Feldman, were from 'the Mel Brooks school' of comedy. *Yellowbeard* featured a virtual who's who of modern-day comic talent.

The Python meets the Goon. Idle and Spike Milligan pose for the cameras.
Milligan (and *The Goon Show*) was a great early influence on Idle's writing.
Milligan also did a cameo in Monty Python's *Life of Brian*.

Graham as Yellowbeard, a role based in large part
on the character of his best friend, Keith Moon.

Graham on set in his role as film producer; a job that
few of his friends felt he was capable of handling.

Graham and writer Bernard McKenna discuss a few ideas. *Yellowbeard* grew
out of Graham and Bernard's attempt to develop a film project for Keith Moon.

Graham takes a critical look at how things are progressing. Graham's desire to direct the movie was quashed early on, and his decisions as one of its producers were usually second-guessed by others.

He may be blind but he's 'got 'acute earring.' John Cleese as Blind Pew, doing his best impression of Jethro Tull's Ian Anderson.

The face that sunk a thousand ships. Marty Feldman captured days before
his death. Marty began his career as a comedy writer and later shot to fame
as a performer in *At Last the 1984 Show* (with Cleese and Chapman).
By the time of his death he was a fully fledged movie star.

'Bang went the holiday!' David Bowie turns in a funny cameo as a shark.

Graham was against the marketing of the film as a
Pythonesque romp, but that didn't stop the film studio.

Sir Michael Horden and
Peter Cook go looking
for Dan. Horden was an
exceptionally talented
actor able to play everything
from broad comedy,
*A Funny Thing Happened
on the Way to the Forum*,
Brechtian satire,
How I Won the War, to
Shakespeare, *The Tempest*.

The late, great Peter Cook. Cook was a great influence on Cleese and Chapman's early writing, and a fellow member of The Cambridge University Footlights Club. Cook and Chapman were reunited on screen some six years later in *Jake's Journey*, a proposed television series for CBS-TV. Although a pilot episode was filmed, the series was not picked-up. It was Graham's last real film performance.

The *Lady Edith*, so named after Graham's mother. This ship pulled triple duty as the *Edith*, Clement's boat as well as the Spanish galleon.

Blind Pew (John Cleese) and Gilbert (Marty Feldman) conspire at the Maimed Fox.
Cleese and Feldman first worked together on *The Frost Report* in 1966.

Yellowbeard puts the
'rat' back in pirate.

66   INT.   HELMSMAN'S ROOM

He is maintaining the course, taking occasional
glances at compass and puffing on his pipe. The
hourglass is full, he turns it and shouts:

                    HELMSMAN
        All's well.

We hear the creaking of ship. Sound of sails and the
wind. A spray of water catches the HELMSMAN in
the face. He wipes his face, checks that his pipe is
still lit, checks compass and continues to steer. He
now receives what amounts to a cupful of spray in
the face. He pulls out rag and dries his face. He sips
a steaming mug of chocolate and continues his watch
and steering. Suddenly a bucketful of spray catches
him full on. Angrily he lashes the wheel steady with
a loop of rope and strides outside to see who or what
is the cause. Sees nobody but notices the open
gunport. Goes over to close it. We now see
YELLOWBEARD standing on opposite ship's rail and
as the HELMSMAN leans to secure the gunport door
YELLOWBEARD swings in on a rope across the deck
and, with both feet, boots the HELMSMAN through
the gunport. As the HELMSMAN falls towards the sea
he screams. YELLOWBEARD converts this by
finishing it with a similar sounding.

                    HELMSMAN
        Aaaaa . . . !

                    YELLOWBEARD
        . . . 'lls we . . . e . . . e . . . ll

167

He scurries into the HELMSMAN's room, unlashes the wheel and turns it vigorously. Then checks the compass and lashes the wheel in its new position and · scurries off.

67   EXT.   QUARTERDECK. EARLY A.M.

GILPIN is standing on port side at the rail. Lining up the sun using the most up-to-date sextant. DAN is with him taking notes for the ship's log.

68   MAIN DECK

Just below them on main deck are MOON and GILBERT similarly engaged but MOON using a less modern navigational cross staff. MOON and GILBERT exchange looks. GILPIN addresses him from quarter deck.

>   GILPIN
>   We went ten degrees South off course overnight.
>   Did you notice that, Mr Moon?

>   MOON
>   Indeed I did, sir.
>   (to Gilbert aside)
>   Our captain didn't bump the helmsman off did
>   he?

>   GILBERT
>   No, didn't leave his cabin.

They knowingly look up towards quarter deck.

                         GILPIN
(aside to DAN)
        Did – you order a change of direction?

                          DAN
        No.

                         GILPIN
        Well, I think *someone*
(nodding in Moon's direction)
        knows where the island is.

                          MOON
(aside to GILBERT)
        See, they're leading us to it.
(loud to DAN)
        Shall I maintain this course, Captain?

                          DAN
        Well, it's a pretty good course isn't it, Mr Moon?

                          MOON
        Aye, aye, sir.

Both groups are pleased with themselves.

                                           CUT TO

69   MONTAGE SHOTS OF THE EDITH sailing safely on her
      way in a variety of maritime conditions, indicating
      passage of time.

70   INT.   CAPTAIN'S CABIN

CLOSE-UP of MAP showing their course and the ten degree difference causing them to miss Jamaica. DAN, LAMBOURN and GILPIN sitting round having a drink. Map on table. They've been following their new course.

                      LAMBOURN
      I hope it's not *that* island.

                      DAN
  Why?

                      LAMBOURN
      It's got a huge green beast on it.

                      GILPIN
      I suppose you think there's a group of huge, fat, nude boys blowing a fleet of ships up the English Channel.
(taps map showing this)

                      DAN
      I feel uneasy just following a course set by Mr Moon.

                                    CUT TO

71   CLEMENT'S FRIGATE

Cleaving its way through the tropical ocean.

                                    CUT TO

72 QUARTER DECK OF CLEMENT'S FRIGATE

MANSELL is scouring the seas around. There is
nothing in sight.

CUT TO

73 CLEMENT'S FRIGATE AT SEA

CUT TO

74 CAPTAIN'S CABIN

CLEMENT has BETTY seated at his desk. They are
engaged in building up an identikit picture of islands.
He cuts out a piece of map and places it on top of a
map in front of BETTY.

BETTY
No, it still doesn't look right.

CLEMENT
(exasperated)
I don't think you're being as helpful as you
promised when we agreed to bring you along.

BETTY
I'm doing my best.
(pause)
Tell you what it was like. It was like our Freda's
Uncle's nose.

CLEMENT
Was it? . . . er . . . this any good?

171

CLEMENT proffers another piece.

> BETTY
>
> Oh, yes . . .

MANSELL enters.

> BETTY
>
> That's better, but it was wider than that, and
> more knobbly at the end.

> MANSELL
>
> Oh, sorry, sir.

MANSELL turns his back and stays so.

> CLEMENT
>
> Mansell, come here.

> MANSELL
>
> Sorry, sir, I thought you were . . .

> CLEMENT
>
> You thought what?

> MANSELL
>
> Nothing, sir.

> CLEMENT
>
> Turn round, Mansell. What did you mean?

> MANSELL
>
> I thought . . . Oh, er . . . nothing.

Nothing in sight, absolutely nothing at all,

nothing, sir. Talk about clear horizons. This is it.
We've been weeks without sighting anything, let
alone the Edith.

CLEMENT
Shut up! Oh, I'm sorry, Mansell. I know I'm a bit
tough on you sometimes, but then men often
are on the very people they - um—

MANSELL
What, sir?

CLEMENT
Well, men are often hard on the people they - um—

MANSELL
Hard on, sir?

CLEMENT
Nothing, Mansell. Forget what I said.

MANSELL
Oh, what was it, sir?

CLEMENT
About what you thought.

MANSELL
Oh, yes. About what I thought and the hard-on
bit . . .

CLEMENT
Oh, never mind, Mansell. You can think what
you like when we've caught that bastard
Yellowbeard.

173

Sail Ahoy!

CLEMENT and MANSELL dash for door.

CUT TO

75   CLEMENT'S FRIGATE – QUARTER DECK

MANSELL arrives first and scours the horizon ahead
of them. He is followed by CLEMENT.

MANSELL

There you are, sir. Nothing again.
Nothing whatsoever.

CLEMENT, without telescope, has spotted something
behind them. He raises his telescope to look at it, then
taps MANSELL on shoulder from behind.

CLEMENT

Behind you, Mansell.

MANSELL

(without turning)
Ah, so you are, sir.

CLEMENT

A *ship* is behind you.

MANSELL spins round, hitting CLEMENT full on the
back of his head, knocking him sprawling. (MANSELL
is unaware of this.)

174

                    MANSELL
        Good Lord, sir. It's the Edith.

He turns back, and is surprised not to see CLEMENT.
He raises his telescope and spins round to look at the
Edith again, and once more catches CLEMENT who
has just risen to his feet. CLEMENT angrily grabs the
telescope and peers at the Edith.

                    CLEMENT
        It's the Edith, all right.

                    MANSELL
        Er . . . if we're supposed to be following it, sir,
        and it's behind us . . . er . . . how can we be?

CLEMENT finally loses his cool and gives MANSELL a
mighty shove. MANSELL falls to the deck bewildered.
CLEMENT springs into action.

                    CLEMENT
        Strike the colours, Mr Keating. Hoist the French
        flag and hard about!

                    KEATING
        Aye, aye, sir.

                    CLEMENT
        They mustn't know we're after them, Mansell. If
        we can convince them that we're French, they'll
        avoid us and perhaps then we can return to
        following them discreetly.
(takes his hat and coat off)
        I'll stay out of sight below. Don't get too close.
(as he goes)
        And remember we are a *French* ship.

                    175

MANSELL

Yes, sir ... Oui, sir ... oui, Monsieur ... *Oui*,
mon Capitaine.

CUT TO

76 QUARTER DECK OF THE EDITH

DAN, LAMBOURN and GILPIN and MOON are looking
through telescopes.

DAN

What sort of ship is it?

MOON

Some kind of frigate.

DAN

We wouldn't have come across it if we had kept
our course.

MOON

No, no, we wouldn't.

They eye each other suspiciously.

DAN

It's not flying a flag.

GILPIN

Perhaps we'd better take ours down. They've got
twice as many guns. We don't want to look too
aggressive.

MOON

Wait a minute. There is a flag. They're French
and they're rounding on us.

LAMBOURN

Why don't we fly a French flag?

GILPIN

They might want to talk. Does anyone speak
French?

ALL

No, no. Not at all.

LAMBOURN

We could try a Spanish flag.

MOON

Anyone speak any foreign language?

LAMBOURN

Well, Gilpin speaks Latin.

There is the sound of an explosion as the frigate fires
on them. They dive for cover. There is a terrible thud,
and splinters of wood fly as a cannonball smashes the
larboard stairway and imbeds itself in the wall of the
ship.

CUT TO

77   MAIN DECK OF CLEMENT'S FRIGATE

CLEMENT rushes out of the Captain's cabin and along
deck to MANSELL who is standing proudly next to a

177

smoking cannon, which is being re-prepared for firing.
MANSELL is posturing exaggeratedly and shouting
through a loud hailer at bewildered gunners.

> MANSELL
>
> Canard à l'orange . . . mon amour.

> CLEMENT
>
> What the hell are you doing with the bloody
> cannon?

> MANSELL
>
> (proudly)
>> Aha. They won't believe that we're really a
>> French frigate unless we fire on them.
>
> (shouts through hailer)
>> A bientôt concombres d'habitude . . .

> CLEMENT
>
> Shut up, Mansell.
>
> (to men)
>> Cease fire.

CUT TO

78   MAIN DECK – THE EDITH

> MOON
>
> Our only hope is to fire as much as we can, and
> keep them at their distance. Especially if we aim
> for the mainmast and rigging.

Cannons are hauled forward, elevated and aimed.

                          DAN
        (from the quarter deck, down to MOON)
                Stand by to fire, aiming at the mainmast and
                rigging.

                                            CUT TO

79 CLEMENT'S FRIGATE - MAIN DECK

                          CLEMENT
                So, let's just sail quietly past.

                          MANSELL
        Aye, aye . . .

Before he can finish, there are explosions from the Edith,
followed by cannonballs smashing into the deck and
woodwork around them. As the smoke clears, CLEMENT
drags himself out from beneath a fallen sail. In
background, INJURED SAILORS are aided and carried off.

                          CLEMENT
                Are you all right, Mansell?

MANSELL emerges from debris, cheerily unscathed.

                          MANSELL
        Yes, thank you, sir.

CLEMENT grunts disappointedly.

                          CLEMENT
                What do the fools think they're doing? We
                outgun them, we've got more men and we're
                faster.

                          179

                                    MANSELL
                    I think it's that French flag of yours, sir.

CLEMENT sighs, then shouts at GUNNERS:

                                    CLEMENT
                    Well, to avoid suspicion, we'd better appear to
                    retaliate by firing at them a bit, and missing
                    them a lot.

                                    MANSELL
                    That's a much better idea, sir.

Another salvo of cannonballs hit the woodwork.

                                    CLEMENT
                    More sail, Mr Keating. Let's get out of here!
                    Now, FIRE!

                                                              CUT TO

80   THE EDITH - MAIN DECK

     Everyone dives for cover as the frigate fires. The
     cannonballs fall short into the sea, or else whistle over
     their heads and generally miss in all directions.

                                                              CUT TO

81   THE EDITH - GUN DECK

     Lots of smoke and noisy activity as the guns are fired
     and reloaded. Through the smoke we see
     YELLOWBEARD swiftly moving along the deck towards
     two guns which are ready to fire. He motions the crew

                                    180

to hold fire, while with impressive strength, he alters the firing angle of one piece and checks the trajectory of the other. In the smoke and confusion, the GUNNERS accept his presence without question. From above comes the order to fire. They do so.

82   CLEMENT'S FRIGATE

Close-up of frigate as cannonballs thud into it. We see two simultaneously bursting through the woodwork.

CUT TO

83   CLEMENT'S FRIGATE – GUN DECK

Water gushing in through breached hull. SAILORS escaping aloft.

CUT TO

84   THE EDITH – GUN DECK

THE GUNNERS turn to congratulate their advisor, but he's gone.

CUT TO

85   THE EDITH – MAIN DECK

A BIG CHEER goes up from men and firing resumes with gusto.

CUT TO

181

86 CLEMENT'S FRIGATE - MAIN DECK

The ship is now sinking. There is considerable
wreckage and confusion as CLEMENT picks his way
through the debris, taking a confused BETTY by the
hand.

CLEMENT
Lower the longboats larboard! Abandon ship!

They join MANSELL, who gazes towards the Edith.

MANSELL
Gunnery like that makes you proud to be
English, doesn't it, sir?

CUT TO

87 THE EDITH - MAIN DECK

All are assembled on deck to watch the frigate
disappear beneath the waves. CLEMENT and CREW are
in longboats.

MOON's hook rests heavily on DAN's shoulder. DAN is
very wary of it. MOON grins.

MOON
Well done, lad.

DAN smiles uneasily.

LAMBOURN
Well done, *Captain*!

MOON
Oh, yes . . . no disrespect intended, your
Lordship.

Removes hook.

CUT TO

88   THE EDITH AT SEA

89   THE EDITH - GUN DECK

MEN in hammocks asleep. Some on floor chatting,
drinking, pleased with battle result. Behind a tarpaulin
across deck, GILPIN is tending dressings for injured
sailors, which places him in good position to eavesdrop
the following . . .

SAILOR 1
That Captain Dan, eh? He done in Burgess,
what we was scared to, takes over the ship and
now sinks a naval frigate. Whoever heard of
that? Somethin' odd about him. Son of
Yellowbeard, isn't he? You could scarcely call
him human.

SAILOR 2
Somethin' odd about the whole eeling ship.

SAILOR 1
Yeah, there was that helmsman what eeling well
disappeared, that same night Spriggit were
havin' a smoke on the fo'c'stle when there were
this unearthly smell.

183

SAILOR 3

(an old salt)

And the wooden woman, we've only got the top
half left, that's inhuman.

SAILOR 1

And the talking pig.

SAILOR 2

Talkin' pig?

SAILOR 1

Yeah . . . other mornin' I was throwin' the pigs
some of the Captain's slops, and I could've
sworn the pig said 'Not fish again'.

SAILOR 3

There be tales of fearful monsters in these parts.

SAILOR 2

What? Just their tails?

SAILOR 3

Don't you be ruining the atmosphere, young
John.

SAILOR 2

Oh, sorry.

SAILOR 3

They do tell of 'uge spiders with shiny fins, what
bite deep into the top of your head at night and
suck out all your bones, leaving you feeling seedy.

CUT TO

DAN and LAMBOURN are having a drink - DAN from
a glass, LAMBOURN from the bottle.

LAMBOURN

Damned good idea of yours, me boy, to hit them
beneath the waterline.

DAN

Was it? But I didn't do . . .

LAMBOURN

Nonsense . . .

He drains bottle as GILPIN appears.

GILPIN

Gentlemen, from what I've just heard down on
the gun deck - sooner or later, Moon is trying
to turn the men against us.

LAMBOURN

I don't think you need worry about the men.
They respect you, Dan, fear you as though there
was something of your father about you.

DAN

(pleased)

Really?

GILPIN

Yes. They're a gullible bunch. While I was down
there, some old lunatic started talking about
ghosts coming through the deck with unearthly

185

smells and huge monsters with sharp feet. Never
heard such a load of superstitious rubbish.

90A   EXT.   SEA

As they smile at this, a HUGE SEA SERPENT can be
seen through the window behind them passing the
ship, unobserved by the THREE.

90B   INT.   CABIN

                    LAMBOURN
        I was just thinking . . .

                    GILPIN
    Yes?

                    LAMBOURN
        Can brandy make you see things?

                    GILPIN
        If you drink enough of it.

                    LAMBOURN
        Ah, that's what it was then.

                    DAN
        That's what what was?

                    LAMBOURN
        That island I thought was over there.

He points out of side window.

DAN and GILPIN look.

186

                              DAN
          It *is* an island.

90C   EXT. ISLAND

          Through window, we see an EXQUISITE TROPICAL
          ISLAND. They rush on to deck.

                                                  CUT TO

91   THE EDITH - MAIN DECK

          As they erupt on to deck, DAN shouts.

                              DAN
                    Land ho . . . o . . . o . . . !

          There is great excitement as THE CREW rush to get a
          better view of the island.

92   THE EDITH - ANCHORED JUST OFFSHORE OF THE
      LUSH TROPICAL ISLAND

93   THE EDITH - QUARTER DECK

          It is a beautiful sunny day. DAN addresses the CREW,
          A SHORE PARTY prepares to leave.

                              DAN
                    Now, men, a group of us are going to put ashore
                    here for provisions . . .

          MOON and MEN exchange dubious looks.

                              187

                    MOON

            Provisions? Oh, yes . . . of course, sir.

        MOON nods to some of the SHORE PARTY, who quickly
        conceal shovels as they climb into the longboat.

94   THE EDITH - QUARTER DECK

        DAN, LAMBOURN and GILPIN prepare to go ashore.

                    LAMBOURN

            Could be a mirage, you know. I think I saw one
            once. Looks rather like what I saw - if I saw it.

                    DAN

        (aside)

            Is it anything like the map on my head?

                    GILPIN

            I'm sure it tallies. This is the island - Moon's
            men have shovels.

94A   EXT.   THE EDITH'S HULL - TOWARDS THE STERN

        YELLOWBEARD climbs over the ship's rail and with great
        agility makes a speedy and silent descent into the sea.

                                        FADE UP ON

95   THE SHORE - THE LONGBOAT IS REACHED

        All kneel in prayer. The CHAPLAIN is in the midst of a
        Thanksgiving speech. In the far distance we make out
        the shape of YELLOWBEARD disappearing into the
        jungle.

                        188

CHAPLAIN

And, Oh Lord, we give thanks for deliverance
from thy bounteous but vicious sea to this land
of wondrous beauty in which we fervently trust
there are no dreadful serpents, none of thy
tropical fevers nor any of thy great nasty
creeping bitey creatures which thou in thy
wisdom may have caused to lurk in the at first
sight harmless foliage.   Amen.

The CHAPLAIN raises his head and immediately claps
his hand to neck and collapses. GILPIN, seeing this,
rushes over to examine him.

GILPIN

(removing hat)
        He's quite dead I'm afraid.

DAN

How?

GILPIN

Insect bite. He was in a very feeble state. For
the last few weeks he's done nothing but drink
wine and eat wafers.

LAMBOURN

I always suspected God had a bit of a cruel
streak in him.

DAN

We could all do with some good food and clean
water. Ready a hunting party, Mr Moon.

MOON

Aye, aye, sir. Why don't you go ahead and forage
and me and a few of the lads will stay behind
and guard the boat.

DAN

Very good, Mr Moon.

MOON

The lads are clearing space below decks ready
for anything you might find.

(winks)

DAN

Come on, men.

They set off.

SAILOR 2

(to MOON)

They're going to get the treasure. Shouldn't we
go with them?

MOON

No. We'll just have every gun on that ship ready
for them when they return, *Bosun* Gilbert.

GILBERT

Aye, aye, *Captain* Moon.

FADE

96   FADE UP ON DAN and his party, having arrived at a
      spring, water bubbling through rocks in the
      undergrowth.

                              DAN
        Dr Gilpin tells me we've got quite a way to go.
        We'd better be well prepared for the journey.
(to LAMBOURN)
        Lord Lambourn, you stay here and supervise
        the loading of water. I'll take these men and see
        if we can't bag a wild boar or something. There
        must be some animal life around here, eh,
        Doctor? Where's Dr Gilpin?
(looking around)

                            LAMBOURN
        Oh, he wandered off somewhere – the man's
        quite beside himself with all these weird plants
        around. I'll keep an eye open for him from up
        here.

Climbs up on top of rocks and sits. Starts to work on a
hip flask. The men beneath him, having quenched
their thirst, begin to fill water barrels. GILPIN arrives.

GILPIN walks out of the undergrowth working with a
pestle in a mortar. He carries a bag over his shoulder
brimming with herbs, leaves and roots. He dips a quill
into the mixture in the mortar which he begins to
prick into his arm.

                             GILPIN
        I think I may have found the stuff which the
        Indians use to . . .

He collapses paralysed.

                            LAMBOURN
        Indians used to what?

As he turns towards GILPIN, he sees him on the
ground and rushes to him. After a few seconds GILPIN
carries on speaking from the ground.

> GILPIN
> . . . knock beasts out with.

97   JUNGLE

DAN's party, foraging stealthily. There's a rustling in
the bushes. He motions silence.

> DAN
> (whispering)
> Could be wild boar.

They creep towards their hoped-for prey. Suddenly
there's a blood-curdling scream and from out of the
trees and bushes surrounding them appears an
attacking horde of Spanish clergy, led by a cardinal, EL
SEGUNDO. They are armed with cross-shaped clubs,
sword-like crosses, bicycle chain-like rosaries and
weighted thuribles which they swing wildly and lethally.
It is a massacre. Victims are strangled with rosaries
and stabbed with crucifixes and when dispatched are
received into the bosom of the Lord in a multitude of
Spanish 'Extreme Unctions'. Amongst the survivors is
DAN, who is bundled off by EL SEGUNDO.

98   HILLOCK ON TOP OF ROCKS NEAR WATERHOLE

LAMBOURN has telescope.

> LAMBOURN
> They've taken Dan.

GILPIN

Who?

DOCTOR scrambles up to join LAMBOURN.

LAMBOURN

Priests of some kind. Look!

98A   In the distance we see DAN being carried off.

98B   LAMBOURN

Shall we get reinforcements or, or . . . try and catch
them now?

GILPIN

Wait a minute – what's that?

98C   In the distance we see YELLOWBEARD rolling around
on the ground, standing up, lurching from side to side
– intent on some inexplicable business. He is attacked
from behind by a tail-end of two or three straggling
priests. The first priest attempts to fell him with a blow
from behind. It is of insufficient severity and
YELLOWBEARD is incensed. He slices two of them up
a treat, kicks the last one in the face, picks him up and
angrily hurls him a great distance so that he flies
almost horizontally, his head crashing into a tree.

98D   GILPIN

There's our reinforcement.

LAMBOURN

What?
(grabs telescope)

193

Good Lord . . . how did *he* get here? Seems to
have taken a dislike to the priests.

> GILPIN
> We'd better get after them while we can.

> LAMBOURN
> Come on, men, we must save our Captain.

They barely stir.

> GILPIN
> (pointedly)
> And the treasure . . .

They spring into action!

99   EXT. HUGE MONOLITHIC ROCKY OUTCROP IN THE
JUNGLE

In which is built EL NEBULOSO's rocky fortress. The
entrance to this intrapetric complex consists of
imposingly fortified steps leading into the rock.
Around the base of the entrance is a courtyard filled
with a 'market place' of huts and tents. These are in
turn surrounded by a wooden stockade with its own
entrance through which DAN's captors appear like a
hunting party with DAN trussed on a pole between
two priests. They pass through gates of stockade past
market stalls and up steps winding through stone
parapets up to the entrance leading to the interior of
the rock fortress.

CUT TO

100   THRONE ROOM IN HIS INTRAPETRIC PALACE

THE HEADQUARTERS OF EL NEBULOSO, self-appointed Redeemer and Emperor of the island. A lavish room in his palace. He is dressed in scarlet and gold. He sits on a very ornate throne, fanned by near-naked ladies with pert breasts. Standing apart from these ladies is TRIOLA.

VERDUGO enters, bowing low.

TRIOLA is dressed in a sensuous mini variation of a nun's habit complete with leather thigh boots, and is incongruously innocent of all which surrounds her.

                    EL NEBULOSO
        Excellent!

He stands and follows VERDUGO towards a nearby torture chamber.

101   A LARGE 'U' SHAPED POOL OF BUBBLING ACID SURROUNDS A PLATFORM ON THREE SIDES. THE FOURTH SIDE IS THE VERTICAL WALL OF THE CAVE. On the platform is a fiendishly intricate torture-chair device. To reach this they have to walk over a plank which bridges the acid pool.

                    EL NEBULOSO
        (as they walk, Triola follows)
                Explain to me, Señor Verdugo, the intricacies of
                this most Holy Instrument of confession.
        (to TRIOLA)
                Triola, I don't think you should see this, my
                daughter.

195

                    TRIOLA
But it's only another torture machine.

                  EL NEBULOSO
I want it to be a surprise for you. Later, my sweet.

                    TRIOLA
Oh, all right, Daddy.

She pouts and reluctantly goes.

                  EL NEBULOSO
(to VERDUGO)
        Now – your new confessional.

                    VERDUGO
Ah, but first you will see, Your Severity, the
instrument is surrounded by this pool of acid
which will destroy anything thrown into it,
except gold and precious stones. But flesh and
bone and iron.
(dips iron rod in which sizzles and dissolves)

They walk across the gangway.

                  EL NEBULOSO
And it doesn't dissolve gold you say?

                    VERDUGO
Even if they've swallowed their valuables there'll
be no need for any more of those messy
searches we used to have.

                  EL NEBULOSO
Unless we want one.

196

VERDUGO

Of course, Your Outrageousness.

EL NEBULOSO

And this is the new confessional.

VERDUGO

(proudly, climbing into the chair to demonstrate)
It works this way, Your Brutality. The prisoner
is totally restrained by means of this iron
banding.

EL NEBULOSO

Excellent! Excellent!

VERDUGO

But there is more to it than that, Oh Blizzard of
the Wrong. By means of the ratchets and
screws, we can place any part of him in any
position we want, for as long as we want, and do
anything to it. You can break every bone in his
hand one at a time.

EL NEBULOSO

And feet?

VERDUGO

And feet!

EL NEBULOSO

And back?

VERDUGO

And back!

                    EL NEBULOSO
        And slowly crush them *and* break them?

                    VERDUGO
        Oh yes – it is very effective, Your
        Horrendousness.

                    EL NEBULOSO
        People will be even more frightened of me when
        they hear I have this.

                    VERDUGO
        Oh yes, definitely, Your Blind Stupidity.

                    EL NEBULOSO
        Even you – Señor Verdugo?

                    VERDUGO
        Well, not me, obviously. I mean, I made it . . .

                    EL NEBULOSO
        Let's see if it works.

VERDUGO hesitates.   EL NEBULOSO motions to
GUARD who begins to adjust ratchets.

                    EL NEBULOSO
        If it does not, I shall have to despatch you with
        Heavenly Force.

From the throne room we hear a shout of

                    EL SEGUNDO (OOS)
        El Neboloso!

                        198

EL NEBULOSO
Excuse me a moment.

As he leaves, we hear a terrified scream from
VERDUGO.

CUT TO

102   THE THRONE ROOM

EL SEGUNDO and his men arrive like a returning
hunting party with DAN firmly trussed and hanging
from a pole carried by two priests. A wooden wedge in
his mouth prevents speech.

EL SEGUNDO
Greetings, Your Vehemence, mission
accomplished. Eight heathen souls by the Grace
of God and Heavenly Force have attained
eternal serenity.

EL NEBULOSO
Only eight. Any money?

EL SEGUNDO
On the paltry side, Your Brutality.

EL NEBULOSO
So . . . your mission was as so much fart gas.

BLOWS RASPBERRY IN HIS FACE.

EL SEGUNDO
Oh no, Your Offensiveness. The ship they came
from is after Yellowbeard's treasure.

                    EL NEBULOSO
(in awe)
          Ah, the treasure of Yellowbeard!!

                    EL SEGUNDO
          Yes, and this is one of his officers, Your
          Molestation.

                    EL NEBULOSO
          We must find out all that he knows. I've got just
          the thing.

EL NEBULOSO returns to the torture room. EL
SEGUNDO follows.

103   TORTURE ROOM

EL NEBULOSO proudly shows his machine.

                    EL NEBULOSO
          There's no time for your old-fashioned
          psychological rubbish. Agony is what is needed,
          and this can be *real* agony.

He motions to a GUARD in the torture chamber who
turns a ratchet and takes wedge out of VERDUGO's
mouth. VERDUGO screams out.

                    VERDUGO
          I can confirm that!

VERDUGO is released and dragged out of the machine
in a state of collapse.

DAN is put into the machine. EL NEBULOSO motions
wooden wedge to be removed.

                    200

                              DAN
        You may torture me, but it will avail you
        nothing.

                                              CUT BACK TO

104   HILLOCK

        DOCTOR, LAMBOURN, YELLOWBEARD and men on a
        hillock in clearing with a view of EL NEBULOSO's
        stronghold/palace. Sunset. YELLOWBEARD is being
        restrained.

                           LAMBOURN
        Dan has been captured and is being held
        prisoner by those Spaniards.

                          YELLOWBEARD
        Yes, the place always was overrun with mad
        dagoes. I'll kill the lot of 'em. I'll kill all of you. I'll
        kill anyone that comes between me and my
        treasure.

                            GILPIN
        If they torture him, they could find the treasure.
        He must be rescued. We'll attack at first light.

                          YELLOWBEARD
        All right. You and your poncey plans – but I'll
        kill anyone that gets in the way of me killin'
        anyone.

                                                  CUT TO

                              201

EL SEGUNDO looks through telescope towards distant jungle. EL NEBULOSO watches from parapet and is attended by officer priests and monks.

> EL SEGUNDO
> Excuse me, Your Monstrosity. That prisoner of ours must be very important. There's quite a little army assembling down there.

> EL NEBULOSO
> Could he be their leader?

> EL SEGUNDO
> No. There's a man of very high rank giving orders.

> EL NEBULOSO
> He must know where the treasure is – he's the one we must capture.

> EL SEGUNDO
> That'll be difficult, Oh Berserk One. He'd be last in the attack and first to escape . . . that's leaders for you.

> EL NEBULOSO
> What did you say?

> EL SEGUNDO
> (realises)
> Oh . . . except for you, Oh Great Mindless Slaughterer.

EL NEBULOSO lets out a great roar.

EL SEGUNDO dives to the floor in fear.

> EL NEBULOSO
> That's the answer. We shall lure their leader to
> the front by allowing their assault to succeed.
> (he paces around excitedly)
>> We will pretend to resist . . . and feign injury
>> and death when they attack.
> (he notices El Segundo on floor)
>> What are you doing creeping around on the floor?

> EL SEGUNDO

Was I?

He quickly stands.

> EL NEBULOSO
> We all saw you, you silly man.

(returns to subject)
>> Once the invaders have reached the throne
>> room my men shall rise up and dispatch them
>> all with maximum Heavenly Force.

> EL SEGUNDO
> Magnificent strategy, Your Arrogance.

> EL NEBULOSO
> It must look realistic. Anyone caught overacting
> I shall personally frighten to death.

106   TORTURE ROOM

TRIOLA enters the torture chamber and approaches
DAN who's strapped in the machine.

203

TRIOLA

Is it too cold for you?

DAN

I'm all right.

TRIOLA

You must tell my father where the treasure is or you will surely die.

DAN

I'll tell him nothing.

TRIOLA

But he only wants it for the grace and glory of God.

DAN

What kind of God is it that kills and tortures men?

TRIOLA

My father's only purpose is to enable heathen souls to enter Heaven more rapidly than they would of their own accord. Please tell him, it hurts me to see you hurt.

DAN

It hurts me to see you be hurt by me being hurt.

TRIOLA

I think I love you.

                              DAN

        You are right, you do, and I love you, and when
        I am rescued, I want you to come with me.

                            TRIOLA

        To come with you would mean leaving here. Are
        you taking the treasure?

                              DAN

        That's right. Triola, you realise your father may
        be killed?

                            TRIOLA

        Oh Daddy won't mind, he's a bit odd about
        things like that. I must pack my things.

        She blows him a kiss and skips off happily.

107 · NEAR EL NEBULOSO'S PALACE

Our main attacking party is assembled on slopes
approaching stockade. Some soldier priests going in and
out are approached by a blind, lame beggar. They take
the contents of his bowl and then on second thoughts
the bowl as well. They hurl the beggar down and move
off towards EL NEBULOSO's palace. The assembled
attackers move quickly and cautiously through the
undergrowth until they're near the main entrance. They
are spotted by EL SEGUNDO from inside stockade, who
motions some of his guards to appear less efficient.

YELLOWBEARD staggers uncaringly through
LAMBOURN's men carrying a keg of gunpowder with
a lighted fuse. With a mighty shove he rolls this at the
main gate.

                              205

> LAMBOURN
>
> When I give the word 'attack' . . .

The barrel arrives and explodes at the gate.

> LAMBOURN
>
> Attack!

His men have already done so. The explosion causes a series of spectacular 'deaths' in dives and falls, one or two of which are too distant from the explosion for credibility. EL SEGUNDO steps forward and gives one of the men a kick to indicate the explosion was too far away.

108   RAMPARTS OF PALACE

On the ramparts EL SEGUNDO catches a keen young priest who with full drama is staggering backwards with a sword under his arm. EL SEGUNDO removes sword and replaces it in the scabbard of the protesting priest.

> EL SEGUNDO
>
> That won't fool anybody.

He is just in time to spot another soldier proudly strolling around with an axe through his helmet greeting another with a spear through his middle. The helmeted one removes his helmet to show his admiring friend. EL SEGUNDO orders them to return to their posts and as he turns he sees a group smoking pipes and cigars and playing dice. They all have rather shoddy attempts at arrows through their heads. He strides towards them and berates them.

More stunt priests fall from balconies and off
ramparts and through awnings for no reason at all.

Our attackers are surprised at the devastation their
aimless firing has achieved and advance.
YELLOWBEARD charges the main building and is
challenged by some guards who put up a perfunctory
struggle. He advances through a door into the main
building. EL SEGUNDO walks up to this group who are
really dead and dying and congratulates them on their
show.

> EL SEGUNDO
> Very good, men – excellent!

One man is groaning with blood pouring from the
corner of his mouth. He tries to speak to no avail.

> EL SEGUNDO
> Don't overdo it, Gonzales.

He walks off to look at the next group. LAMBOURN,
encouraged by YELLOWBEARD's advance, fires a shot
in the air to rally his men.

> LAMBOURN
> This way, men!

A soldier priest rather belatedly and with a great cry
lands at his feet. Much encouraged by this he
unsheathes his sword and waves his party up the
steps towards the entrance. GILPIN pauses a moment
to look at the man who was apparently felled by
LAMBOURN. He lifts the man's eyelids then stands
and thinks, looking at other apparent casualties. They

are left behind as LAMBOURN, quite overcome with bravery, launches his direct assault.

109   ENTRANCE TO PALACE

EL NEBULOSO's main entrance.

An apparently fierce sword fight takes place with five attackers against LAMBOURN. LAMBOURN emerges from mêlée with all five officers' swords entwined on his as in a cossack routine. The five feign fear and flee.

A fast-approaching party of ten soldier priests 'rush' LAMBOURN. He cowers in a heap on the floor. They do an exaggerated stunt-trip over him, landing on a row of conveniently placed barrels; on these they hurtle out of the building, down a slope and crash through a row of market stalls, causing canopies to collapse and more stunt soldiers to fall from parapets and balconies for no reason at all.

GILPIN is seen approaching the 'dead'.

110   INSIDE PALACE

The over-confident LAMBOURN is swashbuckling his way towards the throne room. He attacks one of two guards at the door. The other guard lets out a scream and keels over.

LAMBOURN looks round. The other swiftly clamps his arm over his sword so that when he looks back it appears he's run him through. He then places his boot on soldier's chest and takes sword out with great ferocity. He hurls himself at the door of the throne

208

room which bursts open, 'killing' two guards on the other side.

YELLOWBEARD, having just really killed three men, leaving one wounded man to rush off complaining to EL SEGUNDO, is impressed by LAMBOURN's performance and runs to join him.

110A   INSIDE THRONE ROOM LAMBOURN grabs a torch and holding it at arm's length and recoiling from heat himself he waves it at some priests who fall back

110B   clutching their clothes alight and dive from parapets into horse troughs below where, having extinguished their flames, they drape themselves in improbable postures of death.

CUT TO

111   CLEMENT'S LONGBOAT

CLEMENT, MANSELL and BETTY approaching island shore.

CLEMENT
(peering through telescope)
The Edith's at anchor, with no-one aboard as far as I can see and some kind of battle is underway at what looks like a fortress on a mountain over there.

MANSELL
I expect they'll be fighting over the treasure, sir, won't they? They usually do, sir, don't they . . . sir?

                    CLEMENT
Do they, Mansell?

                    BETTY
About the, er, treasure, Commander Clement. I
was wondering if you'd given any more thought
to that suggestion of mine about you deservin' a
split of the takings.

                    CLEMENT
Mrs Beard, I'm an Officer of the Crown.

                    BETTY
Well, it was only a thought, but with that kind of
loot you'd be able to buy a crown of your own.

                    CLEMENT
No, Mrs Beard.

                    BETTY
You'd look nice in a crown.

                    MANSELL
Yes, you would, sir.

                    CLEMENT
Shut up, Mansell! Head straight for that fort.

112 THRONE ROOM

     Through the open doors to the torture chamber
     LAMBOURN sees DAN in the chair. Beside him is EL
     NEBULOSO.

                    210

                    LAMBOURN
        Release that man!

                    EL NEBULOSO
        Or what?

Advances across the plank into throne room.

                    LAMBOURN
        Or I'll kill you.

                    EL NEBULOSO
        You kill me?

                    LAMBOURN
        Er yes, yes just like I killed all your other men.

LAMBOURN is joined by GILPIN.

                    EL NEBULOSO
        You killed nobody, you English white mice. It
        was all part of one of my more fiendish plans.
        Guards! Stand up!

The two guards 'slain' by LAMBOURN at the door
stand up, grinning.

                    LAMBOURN
        Oh! Ah! I see.
        (he clearly does not)

                    GILPIN
        We still outnumber you.

> EL NEBULOSO
>
> I think not.

113   INT.   ANTE-ROOM

He strides triumphantly to the main door of the
chamber with 'bodies' littered behind him, raises his
arms Lazarus-like.

> EL NEBULOSO
>
> Stand up, men!

They don't.

> GILPIN
>
> I administered a dose of this to them all just as
> a precaution.

Pointing at mortar with his quill with which he jabs
one of the guards who makes to attack him. He is
immediately paralysed.

EL NEBULOSO, suddenly realising he's on his own,
considers making a dash for it away from the room.

> EL NEBULOSO
>
> Very well then, you fools – you've left me no
> choice. I shall have to . . . give in completely.
> Sorry, sorry everyone, I'll, er, just go and set
> your friend free, shall I then?

LAMBOURN and GILPIN are amazed at this and turn
to exchange views. As they do so EL NEBULOSO runs
into the torture chamber. They follow.

EL NEBULOSO is standing on the plank over the acid pool.

> ### EL NEBULOSO
> I'm much too fiendish for the likes of you white-faced persons. You will not find your treasure without your Captain who is in my power.

YELLOWBEARD appears at back of cave through an air vent. The others seeing this rapidly become more interested in EL NEBULOSO's drivel.

> ### GILPIN
> What sort of power?

EL NEBULOSO is taken aback.

> ### EL NEBULOSO
> What?

> ### LAMBOURN
> (aiding)
> What sort of power do you have?

> ### EL NEBULOSO
> My divine right to command over life and death.

> ### GILPIN
> Oh, I thought you meant power . . . you know . . . the rate of doing work . . . mechanical energy . . . that sort of thing.

> ### LAMBOURN
> Yes *I* thought he meant that.

213

Mumbles of agreement from others. YELLOWBEARD lowers himself down on a rope from the vent out of sight of the orating EL NEBULOSO. He hurls the grappling hook at DAN's chair. It catches first time neatly and silently.

> ### EL NEBULOSO
> I meant . . . as ruler my supremacy is absolute on this island.

He makes to turn to DAN.

> ### LAMBOURN
> I thought this was an atoll.

YELLOWBEARD ties his end of the rope to a lamp bracket on the side wall and begins to tightrope walk his way across the acid pool.

> ### GILPIN
> No, an atoll is coral, enclosing a central lagoon. I thought this was an isthmus.

Others agree or disagree.

> ### EL NEBULOSO
> Silence and obey or I will kill your Captain.

YELLOWBEARD arrives on the other side.

> ### EL NEBULOSO
> I have despatched many souls to Heaven and God *is* on my side.

YELLOWBEARD creeps up behind him and taps him on shoulder.

EL NEBULOSO turns round and goes rigid with fear.

> EL NEBULOSO
> Yellow . . . beard!

He screams in horror and reels backwards into the pool, disintegrating in the bubbles.

GILPIN and LAMBOURN rush over to release DAN. He's astonished to see YELLOWBEARD.

> DAN
> Father! We thought perhaps you were dead.

> YELLOWBEARD
> Us Yellowbeards are never more dangerous than when we're dead.

GILPIN and LAMBOURN free DAN.

> YELLOWBEARD
> How are you gettin' on piratin'?

> DAN
> Er . . . well . . .

> YELLOWBEARD
> How many men 'ave you killed so far?

> DAN
> Er . . . one . . . I think.

215

YELLOWBEARD

You think? You'll never kill anyone if you go
around thinkin'.

TRIOLA arrives at the far side of plank joining the
others. Behind her are two scantily clad handmaidens
with her luggage.

DAN

Ah Triola, I'd like you to meet my father.

With YELLOWBEARD's aid, he has disentangled himself
from chair.

YELLOWBEARD

(eyeing her lasciviously)
Been out rapin', lad. Nice work.

DAN

No I haven't raped her.

YELLOWBEARD

No, you wouldn't have, you poncey little git . . .

They cross over the plank.

YELLOWBEARD

. . . you're not the prawn of my loins. Your
mother's a bloody liar – that's what I liked about
her. She couldn't be your mother – no woman
ever slept with me and lived.

TRIOLA

What happened to my father?

YELLOWBEARD

(proudly)

    I killed him.

DAN

    He's gone to Heaven . . .

TRIOLA

    Oh that's nice . . . he's sent all his friends there.

YELLOWBEARD

    She's yours then, is she, Dan?
    Let me 'ave a bit of a prod at 'er first.

DAN

    Father!

There is a cry from the distance. It is MR O'DRISCOLL limping hurriedly towards them, his previously nailed foot, bandaged.

O'DRISCOLL

    Captain Dan! Captain Dan, sir! It's Mr Moon.

YELLOWBEARD

(bellowing)

    Who?

O'DRISCOLL

    It's Mr Moon, he reckons you've got the
    treasure and he's going to attack, before the
    other boats arrive.

DAN

    What boats?

O'DRISCOLL

I dunno, sir, but he said he saw some. He thought they were coming to help you, and he was going to kill all of you before they got here . . .

YELLOWBEARD

Moon! That shithead Moon! It's time I got rid of him!

YELLOWBEARD starts flailing about wildly with his cutlass.

DAN

Dad! Dad! Stop that! We'll all fight Mr Moon.

LAMBOURN

Oh good, another battle! Well done, son! Captain! Dan!

DAN

It won't be so easy this time.

GILPIN

No, they won't all pretend to be dead for us!

YELLOWBEARD

Who's pretending to be dead?!!

GILPIN

Well, some of, er, these Spaniards were only pretending.

YELLOWBEARD

Well, er, I'll go and hack a few of their legs off to be on the safe side.

218

DAN

Very well, Dad.

YELLOWBEARD rushes out. From off we hear his
blood-curdling whoops of delight.

DAN

Right. You men search round anywhere and
bring anything that looks valuable back to this
room. We'll let them find the treasure.

CUT TO

115   ISLAND SHORE

LONGBOATS full of MARINES, landing on shore.
CLEMENT, MANSELL, BETTY et al, disembark and
prepare to march inland.

CUT TO

116   THE FRONT OF THE STOCKADE SURROUNDING EL
NEBULOSO'S

MOON and his men are assembled and armed to the
teeth.

MOON

Right, lads. We shouldn't have much trouble
moppin' up this little lot. Very considerate of
'em to dig up the treasure for us. Come on then,
let's get what we came for.

117   INT.   OF STOCKADE

They charge through into the stockade. Once inside, they stop and look around, bewildered at the number of corpses.

> GILBERT
> What the bloody hell do you make of this? I don't like it, Captain.

> MOON
> (kicking a corpse)
>> Just a few dead men, Gilbert. There'll be more by the time we've finished. We're close to that gold, I can smell the death in the air. Right, you lot! Grab that log. Let's smash that door down and have a look inside.

Twelve or so of MOON's men pick up a log from the debris and charge the door of the stronghold with it. It crumbles easily in front of them.

118   INT.   PALACE

They charge through. Inside, MOON looks around. Sees a closed door at the top of some stairs.

> MOON
> Up there, men.

Men with logs charge off to attack the next door. Uttering an unearthly scream and wielding a cutlass, the figure of YELLOWBEARD hurtles in on a rope and lands in front of MOON.

> YELLOWBEARD
>
> Moon, you bastard what betrayed me.
> We'll see who's greatest pirate of them all, you
> slimy government collaborator. I'm going to
> make you eat both your own buttocks.

> MOON
>
> (aghast)
> Yellowbeard!

MOON in the nick of time pushes a pirate in front of
him who falls on YELLOWBEARD's sword. He then
quickly disappears up the stairs. YELLOWBEARD is
joined by DAN who fights amongst the pirates back to
back with YELLOWBEARD. Their flailing arms look like
a death-dealing Indian God.

The DOCTOR, LAMBOURN content themselves by
picking off men on the periphery of the mêlée with
long sharp pointed sticks dipped in poison. TRIOLA
helping by holding a bucket filled with poison.

CUT TO

119   THE THRONE ROOM

As the men with the log crash through its doors
spilling into the room followed by MOON. MOON looks
around the room, sees a light shining through the
locked door guarding the torture chamber. Runs up to
it and there by the light of a single torch in the room
sees a pile of glittering gold and silver ornaments,
bejewelled crosses, chalices, etc. totally covering the
chair.

>   MOON
>   Here we are, lads.

The men charge the door with the log. The door gives
way easily.

120   TORTURE ROOM

The log wedges itself over the pool as they disappear
into it screaming.

>   CUT BACK TO

121   THE ROOM DOWNSTAIRS

DAN and YELLOWBEARD stand victorious surrounded
by MOON's dead pirates. DAN shakes LAMBOURN's
hand in a congratulatory way.

>   DAN
>   (looking around)
>   Where's Moon?

>   TRIOLA
>   (pointing)
>   He went up there.

>   DAN
>   Where's my father?

He looks around, but YELLOWBEARD is nowhere to be
seen. Rushes off upstairs followed by TRIOLA and less
nimbly by the exhausted LAMBOURN.

>   CUT TO

MOON is crossing the log and has just reached EL
NEBULOSO's baubles. DAN arrives the other side of
the log. An extremely dangerous and vicious cutlass
fight ensues on the log over the pool. Whenever DAN
looks in danger, TRIOLA does her best to distract MR
MOON by assuming provocative poses. MOON is not to
be distracted, however. DAN finally disarms him and
has him at his mercy at sword point. TRIOLA, angry
that she has been ignored, throws the bucket at him.
This knocks him from his perch and he plummets to
his death.

> LAMBOURN
> Oh I say, good shot!

TRIOLA embraces DAN.

> DAN
> Later, Triola. I must find my father . . .

> LAMBOURN
> He went that way.

CUT TO

123   EXT.   JUNGLE CLEARING

DAN watches from the edge of the clearing.
YELLOWBEARD is crawling, staggering, holding his
back as if shot and mumbling to himself and
occasionally falling to the ground and staggering on
again. DAN runs up to join him.

DAN

Are you all right, Father?

YELLOWBEARD is in the midst of his self-directions.

YELLOWBEARD

Oh, bugger me. I've forgotten where I was. You
stupid little sod.

DAN

Well, what were you doing?

YELLOWBEARD

Shut up. Now did I just stay stagger, or was it
crawl?

DAN

I don't know.

YELLOWBEARD

It was crawl. But was it crawl to the right, crawl
to the left or crawl, crawl and then right and
then a stagger or was it – oh bugger, you've
sodded the whole thing up like the stupid little
twerp that you are. I was recreating what
happened twenty years ago man and boy.

DAN

Oh, I see. Why didn't you wait?

YELLOWBEARD

Because I wanted to betray you.

DAN

But why?

YELLOWBEARD

I had to. Betrayal is all part of pirating. If you
don't know that you're not even close to being a
pirate. Prawn of my loins, my foot.

DAN

What?

YELLOWBEARD

You're either born a pirate or not. It's in the
blood, Dan, and it's not in your blood, or you'd
have betrayed me long ago.

DAN

All right, I may not be a pirate but at least I've
got a brain in my head so why don't we just
follow the instructions.

YELLOWBEARD

Right.

With a single swipe of his cutlass he shaves the top of
DAN's hair clean off. He looks at newly revealed scalp.

YELLOWBEARD

There's nothing here.

DAN

Are you sure? No map?

YELLOWBEARD

Perhaps it's deeper down. I'll show you . . .

He is about to take another swipe. DAN protectively
puts his hands on head.

                          DAN

          No!

                      YELLOWBEARD
          You double-crossing swivel-eyed prawn. At least
          you betrayed me. That's something.

                          DAN
          I didn't.

GILPIN and LAMBOURN sheepishly appear.

                        GILPIN
          Er ... we did I'm afraid, didn't we?

                       LAMBOURN
          What? Oh double-crossed him ... yes ... we did
          ... a lot.

                      YELLOWBEARD
          Where's me map?

                       LAMBOURN
          Ah ... yes ... now ... where was it?

                        GILPIN
          In your pocket.

                       LAMBOURN
          Oh yes ...
          (produces map)
                    We thought no-one would think of looking for it
                    there.

                          226

YELLOWBEARD grabs the map (he is allowed to).
Stares at it and paces out the ground then stops and
furiously starts to dig with his bare hands.

DAN points to his shaven head.

>LAMBOURN
>Your mother only said that to make sure you
>got your share of the treasure.

>YELLOWBEARD
>Come on, lad, give us a hand.

DAN does so with gusto.

>YELLOWBEARD
>The way you was fighting back there, there may
>be some pirate blood in you after all.

>DAN
>I tricked Moon and his men into falling in the
>acid.

>YELLOWBEARD
>With *your* head on *my* shoulders we could
>wreck civilisation.

124   JUNGLE

CLEMENT, MANSELL and BETTY followed by a long
line of MARINES.

>BETTY
>Well, Commander Clement, I had high hopes
>that you would see things differently.

227

CLEMENT

Just lead me to Yellowbeard, that's all I want.

BETTY

Well, let me see - as I recall it, it should be in
this direction . . .

She leads off.

BETTY

I still think you'd look nice in a crown.

CUT BACK TO

125   THE CLEARING

LAMBOURN and GILPIN and TRIOLA and
O'DRISCOLL have been helping YELLOWBEARD and
DAN dig up the four large chests now unearthed.
DAN is being allowed the privilege of prising open
the largest one. He uses his dagger for this. The
chest opens and reveals vast quantities of gold and
silver ingots, ornaments and jewels. The whole
group wildly embrace each other and cavort around
dancing with joy. YELLOWBEARD frenziedly hugs
DAN then suddenly staggers back with a startled
look pointing to DAN's dagger now imbedded in his
stomach.

DAN

But . . . I didn't . . . oh no!

YELLOWBEARD's startled look transforms into a
delighted smile as he falls to the ground oozing blood.

YELLOWBEARD

You *are* a Yellowbeard!

DAN

Eh?

YELLOWBEARD

Killin' your father as I killed my father before
me . . .

DAN

Oh Dad . . . the blood!

DAN cradles him in his arms.

YELLOWBEARD

BLOOD! That's what I like to hear. You *are* my son.

He dies happily.

This bewildered tableau is interrupted by the arrival of
CLEMENT and MANSELL and MARINES with guns at
the ready.

CLEMENT

Well done there, lad, got him at last.
(to MARINES)
Keep your guns on him, make sure he is dead.

The surprised group are further taken aback when
BETTY appears.

BETTY

Hello, Dan. Hello, lambchop! Wonderful to see
you, pity about your Dad. On the other hand it

is the way what he always said he wanted to
go,
(pause)
     horribly.

CLEMENT strides over to them as YELLOWBEARD's
lifeless shape is given the thumbs down by MARINES.
He proudly introduces himself.

                    CLEMENT
          Commander Clement Royal Navy.

                    BETTY
(aside to LAMBOURN and GILPIN)
          I've tried bribin' him . . . so we'd better think of
          something fast.

GILPIN goes to CLEMENT and shakes him by the
hand.

                    GILPIN
          Ah Clement. Thank God you got here. We were
          press-ganged by that pirate Moon. Dan killed
          him and we got the treasure for you.

LAMBOURN and DAN are perplexed.

                    LAMBOURN
     Eh?

                    DAN
          Oh . . . er . . . yes . . . we did . . .

                    LAMBOURN
     Yes.

                    CLEMENT
       Good. Well, there should be a handsome reward
       in this for all of you.

All are cheerier. CLEMENT walks to treasure.

                    CLEMENT
(with ceremony)
       I claim this treasure . . .

                    TRIOLA
       He claims it?

                    CLEMENT
       . . . in the name of Her Majesty, Queen Anne.

                    TRIOLA
       Dan, darling. I don't think I love you anymore.

                    DAN
       You are right, you don't. Goodbye, Triola.

She goes.

                                              CUT TO

126   QUAYSIDE IN PORTSMOUTH

THE EDITH is docked. On the quayside crowds of
cheering people. The chests of treasure are standing
opened. Seated on a canopied throne on a dais is
QUEEN ANNE. Standing near her at an angle is
PRINCE GEORGE. LADY SARAH CHURCHILL is in
attendance. Standing before her, waiting to be
received, are DAN, GILPIN, BETTY, CLEMENT and

                      231

MANSELL. LAMBOURN is awkwardly re-united with
LADY LAMBOURN.

* *   A group of the QUEEN'S OWN GUARDS march down the
gangplank of the ship, having completed an exhaustive
search for any further valuables. Their 'SS'-like
CAPTAIN, the last to leave, holds up a small golden
coffee spoon. He shrugs, indicating that it was the only
article of value left on board. He nods to SARAH
CHURCHILL as he throws the spoon into an open chest.

CUT TO

SARAH
And now Her Majesty wishes to bestow her
gratitude on two loyal subjects. Lord Lambourn
of Lambourn and Dr Lupus Gilpin.

They step forward and bow.

SARAH
For their part in the recovery of Her Majesty's
bounty.

Gin-sodden QUEEN picks up sword. SARAH stops
firmly.

SARAH
No. They just get the signed portraits.

SARAH takes sword from QUEEN who dozes off.
SARAH takes two small portraits of the Queen and
places them in the QUEEN's hands for a moment then
removes them to give them to the gallant duo who
register disappointment but feign gratitude.

SARAH

They *are* signed 'Best Wishes, Anne R.'

They bow and return to their places.

LADY LAMBOURN

I was 'opin' for a Dukedom at least. Not to be
fobbed off with Royal bric-a-brac.

LAMBOURN

Shut up, woman!

GILPIN

Better than being hung.

LAMBOURN looks at his wife and isn't sure.

SARAH

Mr Daniel Beard.

DAN steps forward and bows.

SARAH

Who sacrificed even his own father for the sake
of his country
(Betty weeps)
Her gracious Majesty generously awards him
and his courageous mother one quarter share
of his father's treasure.

AN USHER hands them a slightly larger portrait each.
They rejoin group.

SARAH

Commander Clement Royal Navy. Who has
fulfilled everything exactly as promised

(then sotto voce to him)
        except for last night
(normal voice)
        a beautiful medal.

FLUNKIE steps forward and takes medal and briefly touches the hand of the QUEEN (who is now snoring) with it and places it over CLEMENT'S head. He retires crestfallen.

                    SARAH
        Lieutenant Orrick Mansell. For courage above and beyond the call of his duty as a treasury officer.

MANSELL smugly steps forward in civilian clothes.

                    CLEMENT
(to DAN)
        I knew he wasn't a Navy man.

                    SARAH
        The Dukedom of his choice.

*   *   CLEMENT and LAMBOURN are clearly upset by this. GILPIN stands by quite content with his now-complete volume of 'Bizarre Deaths'.

                    MANSELL
        Your Majesty, Lady Sarah. It is as a treasury official I feel bound to point out to Mr Beard that his recent windfall so graciously bestowed will be counted as unearned income and therefore subject to tax at the rate of ninety-nine point nine, nine, nine, nine per cent. I've

234

already made the calculations and herewith
present him with his point 0001 per cent.

MANSELL hands DAN a small jingly bag of coins.

MANSELL
Three cheers for Her Majesty.

As crowd cheer, the chests are closed and borne off.
QUEEN wakes up and is also borne off, with a satisfied
smile at MANSELL.

YELLOWBEARD

BASED ON A SCREENPLAY BY

GRAHAM CHAPMAN, PETER COOK

AND

BERNARD MCKENNA

CHAPTER 1

The Spanish Man-O'-War, the *Santa Huron*, a forty-four gun, three-masted square rigger of the Royal Fleet, lay at anchor in the bay of an uncharted island in the Southern Caribbean. It was early morning of November 12th, 1687.

The *Santa Huron* had been the flagship of a fleet of nine vessels sailing from what is now called the isthmus of Panama, heavily laden with gold and silver, precious gems and ornate Indian artifacts. The Spaniards felt that the native Indians rather undervalued their trinkets and that they would be better appreciated at the Court of their King, Carlos of Spain.

The *Santa Huron* became separated from the rest of the fleet in the high seas, lashing rains and driving wind at the tail end of an unseasonal hurricane. They had weathered the storm with difficulty, hampered by their heavy cargo. The Captain, Señor Bartolomé Rodriguez Juan-Julio San José de Sinsamilla the Second, known as El Segundo, had ordered his crew to put on sail and head northeast in the hope of rejoining the fleet but the Admiral of the Fleet was also on board. Generalissimo Sancho-Jerez Castilliano-Juan-Cedric Feliciano Burrito Frijoles Singas Ramon Costa del Mantequilla the Eighteenth, often called El Nebuloso, ordered his Captain to change course to bring them to the leeward side of the island where they spent the night safely at anchor celebrating their deliverance from the tempest. A hogshead of wine and a barrel of brandy were opened and

El Segundo allowed the women from the tiny flotilla of native Indian dug-out canoes which came out to investigate his ship to stay on board and indulge his crew. The Sinsamilla family motto was, after all, '*Dieu est Droit*' and 'Never risk a mutiny for a piece of tail'.

El Segundo hadn't felt like joining in the festivities. He was too busy keeping an eye on the horizon for any sign of ships, not only of their fleet but now that they were separated from it, for pirates. He had heard many reports of their ships attacking even the most heavily armed of Spanish galleons. He was not worried just because he might lose the gold, his ship or even his life, but he had heard horrifying tales of the pirates' bestial cruelty. He knew of one Spanish nobleman who fought bravely but in vain to save his ship only to have his heart torn out and eaten whole by a pirate captain to give his ghoulish crew a laugh.

El Nebuloso had not taken part in the celebrations either. He spent his time in the Grand Cabin weighing some of the finest Indian works-of-art to see how beautiful they really were. One gold casket and its contents alone proved to be more beautiful than seven and a quarter million pesos. He was pleased that his men were getting on so well with the native population; secretly he knew the island well. El Segundo's men would easily be persuaded to stay. On previous visits he had deposited what he considered to be a reasonable proportion of the King of Spain's wealth there for safekeeping. Paying the natives with pigs, glass beads and iron nails, he persuaded them to build an impressive fortress to guard his rapidly filling vaults.

According to his rough calculations, El Nebuloso could now consider himself truly the richest person in the world. Looking round the Grand Cabin he thought, 'Now I am the richest person in the world!' Checking that he was absolutely alone, the tall, imposing, wild-eyed figure allowed himself to strut a little and to admit out loud for the first time, 'Now *I* am the richest person in the world.' His even louder repetition of this claim was rapidly converted into a coughing fit as El Segundo entered the cabin.

'There's not another ship in sight, sir,' he said. Relieved at this himself, he could appreciate the gold for the first time. He thrust his hands into a chest full of coins. 'This should make King Carlos very happy!'

Less than fifty yards from the stern of the Spanish galleon there were no pirate ships. But instead, troubling the water less, though more disturbing to the soul, were eleven desperate men swimming silent and deadly as sharks, following their leader, the most infamous of pirates, the reckless yellow-maned, jagged-toothed, blood-ravening Yellowbeard.

The determined crew approached the stern of the *Santa Huron*. Yellowbeard tore his dagger from his teeth and plunged it into the hull of the ship. Heaving himself up on the bulwark he reached out above his head, grabbed the sternmost mizzen stay and climbed on upwards as the others followed.

Happily unaware of this, El Segundo enjoyed the sensation of pieces of eight trickling through his fingers. 'The King will be very grateful . . . he might even make me a . . .' He was interrupted.

'Who is more important to please,' snapped El Nebuloso, 'the King of Spain, or God?'

'Well, God of course . . .'

'And who is God's appointed representative in this vicinity?'

'You are, El Nebuloso, your Blessed Rectitude.'

'Well, God says he would like to keep it all.'

This startled El Segundo. It was treason. 'But. . .' he began.

'Those who "but" his Representative,' interrupted El Nebuloso, threateningly, 'get their heads pierced and go to meet God very quickly!'

Terrified that this familiar mood of his master might persist, Segundo hurriedly assented. 'That is more than they could reasonably hope for, Your Mercilessness,' he said, backing away from El Nebuloso with a placatory hint of a bow.

'Instead,' roared El Nebuloso, 'you may bang your head upon the floor until you are forgiven!'

'Oh, thank you,' gasped Segundo and immediately began to bang his head on the floor with gusto before His Mercilessness changed his mind and thought of something more fiendishly unpleasant, involving blood.

Choosing a moment when the sole Spanish guard on the poop-deck paced away from him, Yellowbeard scrambled up the ratlines to the head of the main mast. Skilfully, he dropped the noosed end of a rope round the guard's neck as he passed beneath him. Hurling himself instantly off the other side of the cross-beam and using the strangling guard as a grisly counterweight, he descended to the deck with practised ease. Then, immediately letting the rope slip from his grasp, he left the unfortunate guard to hurtle to the deck with a sickening thud.

The rest of Yellowbeard's men, led by his second-in-command, the muscular, mean and brooding Mr Moon, had edged their way along the side of the ship towards the bow. As soon as he heard the guard thud to the deck, Mr Moon peered cautiously over the gunwhale. Several of the Spanish crew lay sleeping off their excesses. Three of the men, awake but still drunk, sprawled in the middle of the deck amidst empty bottles and half-eaten food attended by naked native girls. One of them heard a noise from the stern of the ship and turned. Mr Moon, now standing on the gunwhale, hurled his knife with deadly accuracy into his back. The girls screamed. The Spaniards roused themselves and fled in terror as the pirate crew swarmed onto the deck. A brave Spanish lieutenant took a step towards Mr Moon, but before he could aim his firing-piece, it was kicked from his hand and Moon's sword flashed into his side. The other pirates were equally swift, silent and bloody about their business. Yellowbeard, at a sign from Moon, sitting on the front edge of the poop-deck, drummed on the door to the cabin with his heels. A helmeted guard emerged on deck. His eyes boggled at the carnage before him. Yellowbeard's boots clamped round his neck; his helmet clattered to the floor and in a continuous movement the pirate captain bludgeoned the guard's head with a belaying-pin as he dropped to the deck and ran through the doorway towards the Grand Cabin.

Below decks, outside the Grand Cabin, a guard started from his daydream as he heard the distant sound of a scuffle on deck. He tightened his grip on his pike staff and listened intently in the flickering light of a guttering lantern. There was a noise from the top of the stairway in front of him. He looked up. His jaw received the full force of Yellowbeard's right boot, his head jerking back violently, and his unconscious body slumped to the floor. Yellowbeard leaped to the foot of the stairway, grabbing the lantern to light lengths of gunners' matches, or 'fuses', he had tied into his wild straggly beard and hair.

Inside the Grand Cabin, El Nebuloso lay dozing on his cot, an empty silver goblet held loosely in his hand. From the floor came a rhythmic 'thump, thump' as Segundo dutifully continued his penance though now with less enthusiasm. Hoping that he was no longer the centre of his master's attention, he paused and looked up. There was a splintering crash behind him. The Cabin door, shattered at its hinges, fell onto him, knocking him flat. Yellowbeard charged over it into the Cabin with wild eyes, evilly grinning teeth and his yellow hair billowing smoke from glowing fuses.

Waking suddenly from a dream of more wealth than

anyone had ever been able to dream before, Nebuloso found the horrendous sight too alarming for rational thought and passed clean out in a faint. Mr Moon charged into the room with his bloody sword still drawn. His eyes widened at the sight of the gold.

'Congratulations, Captain Yellowbeard, my plan was a success.'

'Your plan, *my* gold,' said Yellowbeard coldly.

Moon picked up a handful of trinkets from a chest that stood open on the table.

'Hands off, Mr Moon!' thundered Yellowbeard.

But Moon was too engrossed. The pirate captain strode over and slammed the heavy iron lid of the chest shut tight. Moon winced in agony, then peered in horror at the stump where his hand had been.

'Do I have to do everything myself?' said Yellowbeard in mild exasperation. He opened the lid again and there in the chest, surrounded by the jewels, lay Moon's severed hand.

'Don't stand around gapin', man, go and get that stump dipped in some boiling pitch; and lay off the rum. We're going to divide this lot up equal . . . I don't want no squabblin' . . .'

The Spaniards' Indian plunder was carried ashore to be carefully weighed, measured and divided up amongst the pirates in strictly equal shares, according to the pirate code.

Mr Gilbert, Moon's closest ally, a furtive, tricky little man, tended Moon and made him as comfortable as he could in his bunk after the searing pain of the cauterisation by boiling pitch. Gilbert inwardly boiled too at Yellowbeard's treatment of his friend. He had been trying to rouse the crew against their captain since setting sail, seven long months ago. Above all else Mr Gilbert wanted to be a bosun. He dreamed of respectfully being called 'Mister' by the men who would be under his charge. He dreamed of authority –

but not too much. He was not so keen on responsibility – after all, his family had been thieves for generations. But far from making him a bosun, Yellowbeard had not even noticed him. Gilbert lost no time in giving the men skilfully enriched details of Yellowbeard's harsh treatment of his friend, who rightfully ought to be captain himself!

Some of the men were only too eager to pick a fight, readily seeing the advantage of thinning down their numbers. With very little further prompting by Gilbert a petty dispute on the sandy shore about whether or not to divide up a magnificent silk cloak was soon inflamed into a blazing riot of flashing swords and daggers; old scores were settled, long pent-up emotions unleashed, as pirate fought pirate in maniacal frenzy.

Yellowbeard emerged unscathed, restricting himself shrewdly to the tactic of self-defence. If someone struck at him, he struck back. To kill. Otherwise he stood by with masterly indifference to the mayhem around him. He knew there would be fewer left to share the spoils.

Only the barely conscious Mr Moon and a handful of drunken men were left on the ship. El Nebuloso and El Segundo had no difficulty reaching land and slipping into the jungle unseen.

Less than a dozen men survived the battle and Yellowbeard convinced them that it would be foolhardy to ship the treasure to England with so small a crew to defend it. Gilbert slid out from behind the rock where he had been hiding, slipped into the sea and swam off to inform Mr Moon.

Yellowbeard ordered half of the men back to the ship and the rest to follow him and bury the treasure in a spot he would show them. He told them fiercely that any man who did not do as he was ordered would be forced to eat his own lips. The men set off, dragging the chests along the beach, following their captain's every step. They knew him to be a man of his word when it came to cruelty.

One of the dying pirates, vicious to the last, threw a despairing dagger into the back of his retreating captain. Yellowbeard flinched, turned, but seeing that the man was already dead, staggered off uncaringly up the beach. The men followed, dragging their loads, after their insuperable leader. They dared do nothing but follow exactly the path he took.

It was curious that of the seven men who knew the exact burial place of the treasure, only Yellowbeard himself arrived back in England alive.

CHAPTER 2

Yellowbeard set out from the island and sailed a deliberately erratic course intended to confuse any pursuers and his crew. He further protected his knowledge by leaving deliberately misleading references to latitude and longitude for his crew to steal and he made sure that the secrets of no fewer than three helmsmen died with them before they reached the shores of England. He swore the rest of his crew to secrecy and promised them they would all get their share when they sailed with him again. But news of his buried wealth travelled quickly, even to the Court of His Majesty King William III of England who ordered his immediate capture. And so at the end of the year 1687 the infamous pirate Yellowbeard was secretly captured and imprisoned. But, despite years of torture and deprivation, he told them nothing.

Twenty years later, with King William long dead and Queen Anne ruling England, Yellowbeard still lived. So did the legend of his treasure . . .

Mr Moon (as soon as his health had recovered) tracked down and interrogated every survivor, he even had agents pose as prisoners, but still gained no useful information. He had sailed in search of the island several times to no avail.

Few people survived even a short stay in prison but, after twenty years, Yellowbeard had served his sentence and survived . . .

Shivering and miserable from the cold and driving rain, a petty thief stared mournfully through the bars of the prison-cart at his new home. Before the gates of the prison closed slowly behind them, he and the other new prisoners were dismayed to see an ominous cart loaded with five crude coffins being wheeled out. They arrived inside the main courtyard of the prison. Ugly, huge prison guards with batons stood at intervals around the perimeter: before them a sad line of prisoners slowly shuffled round in a circle. One of them stumbled and was beaten fiercely by a guard but he could not carry on and crumpled to the ground. The circle of prisoners continued to move, stepping over the fallen man. A very much older, more gaunt and, if possible, even more ferocious Yellowbeard watched from beneath grime-caked eyebrows like a dishevelled bird of prey. Nearby, putting the finishing touches to a wooden coffin, sat a wizened, scrawny fellow prisoner, a recent arrival who had been quick to ingratiate himself with the pirate. The captain's indifference to him and the ravages of twenty years at sea had made disguise unnecessary for Mr Gilbert.

Gilbert grumbled his way over to the fallen prisoner.

'Corpses, corpses, corpses. That's the fifth this morning.'

'Don't know what prisoners are coming to,' growled Yellowbeard in agreement, 'whimperin', snivelling weaklings that faint like virgins as soon as anyone so much as beats them about the head with a cudgel . . .'

Irritably they picked up the dead man's legs and dragged him over to the coffins.

'A couple of years being stretched on the rack and most of them start feeling queasy.'

They manhandled the poor wretch's body into a coffin and loaded it onto a waiting cart. Yellowbeard kicked the foot of the coffin and at this signal the cart trundled out of the gate.

'Pathetic!' shouted Yellowbeard after the disappearing coffins.

'What?' said Gilbert as he admired his new shoes 'borrowed' from the dead man.

'Pathetic,' repeated Yellowbeard staring at the cart as it disappeared through the prison gates, 'taking the easy way out like that.'

'How do you mean?' queried Gilbert.

'Dying. He'd only been in here fifteen years. You won't catch me dying. They'll have to kill me before I die.'

Gilbert stood up and walked over to an unfinished coffin. 'Many a man has tried, Captain Yellowbeard. But soon you'll be at large again.'

Yellowbeard joined him with the coffin's lid. 'Yes, I shall. With a hand-picked crew of the hardest buccaneers that ever stained the Seven Seas with Spanish blood.'

'It was most unjust,' observed Gilbert, 'locking you up for *merely* doing your duty.'

'It was. Twenty years for killing five thousand dagos and frogs.' Yellowbeard spat. 'Betrayed by my right-hand man, that bastard Moon. Blabbermouth!'

Gilbert flinched as Yellowbeard hammered a nail home in one blow.

'But he never found out where you hid the treasure, did he, Captain Yellowbeard?' Gilbert grinned conspiringly.

'No!' snapped Yellowbeard. 'Nor will he ever.'

Gilbert, nonchalantly tapping home a nail, attempted an air of indifference as he casually enquired, 'Where did you put it by the way?'

'You won't catch me with those trick questions,' rapped Yellowbeard.

A guard, approaching him from behind, caught Yellowbeard a terrible blow on the back with a heavy wooden cudgel. The pirate seemed not to notice and continued, 'What really pisses me off is . . .' An even heavier blow landed on his back. Yellowbeard turned to the guard as though irritated by a tap on the shoulder.

'What is it now?'

'You have a visitor,' leered the guard.

'What?'

'A woman.'

'Oh, I expect that'll be the Queen with my pardon!' Pushing the guard out of his way he strode purposefully off to the Visitor's Room.

The Visitor's Room was really a cold, damp, mossy corridor, running outside a small stone dungeon in which the prisoners were kept separated from their visitors by thick stone walls, with iron-barred windows through which they could talk.

A middle-aged lady, with more than a trace of her former voluptuousness, stood waiting, watched over by a guard. Betty called herself Betty Beard and liked to tell customers at the Maimed Fox, the inn she kept, that she was the wife of Yellowbeard the pirate. She had little claim to this in reality: the young Yellowbeard had visited her in his own speedily amorous way on a couple of occasions when the mood had taken him. She liked people to think of him as her 'husband' to help explain the existence of her son, Dan. Yellowbeard himself knew nothing of this but did recognise the barmaid from the inn.

'Hello, sugar-drawers,' cooed Betty.

'What! You again?' Yellowbeard was surprised.

'Again?' queried a startled Betty. 'I haven't seen you for fifteen years.'

'What is it this time?' asked Yellowbeard as though she'd been pestering him daily.

'Well, what with you being let out next week, I thought it was my duty as a wife . . .'

One of the pirate's eyebrows rose, but she continued, '. . .

250

to bring you up to date on a few things. Remember just before you were arrested we were having a cuddle . . .'

'I was rapin' you if that's what you mean.' The word 'cuddle' was not piratical . . .

'All right,' she agreed, 'sort of half cuddle, half rape . . . well something happened which I've been meaning to tell you for the past twenty years . . .'

'Get on with it, woman,' Yellowbeard glowered at her.

'Well, I haven't told you this before because I wanted him to be brought up like a gentleman and not a pirate.'

'*Who* are you talking about?'

'The fruit of your loins, sugar-drawers,' she simpered.

'Are you mad, woman? I haven't got fruit in my loins. *Lice*, yes, and proud of them.'

'It's a biblical phrase, sugar-drawers. Fruit of your loins means that we have spawned a son.'

'What!' He was losing patience.

Betty had to get to the point. Fast. 'You have just become the father of a one hundred and sixty pound, twenty-year-old, bouncing boy called Dan.' There, it was out.

The new father grunted in recognition. 'Ahhh. A son. Takes after me, does he?'

'Well, er,' Betty hesitated.

'By the time I was twenty I had killed five hundred men.'

'Well, he's not quite so *extroverted* as you, but he's . . . er . . .'

'A thief?' His eyes glinted.

'No.'

'A rapist?' He grinned.

'No.'

His face dropped. 'Oh bloody hell. I give up. What is he then?'

She took a deep breath. 'Well, he's sort of quiet.'

'Quiet! You've brought him up to be QUIET!!' His roar

251

echoed along the walls startling other visitors into silence. 'A Yellowbeard QUIET!'

Now it was Betty's turn to be indignant. 'Well, it's not all my fault.' Then she collected herself. 'You remember Lord Lambourn?' She smiled sweetly. 'You strangled his gardener.'

Yellowbeard scowled. 'Oh, that old loony.'

'Yes, he's been ever so good to Dan. He's even given him a job up at the Hall.'

Betty wisely took a step back from the bars.

'He's got a *job*?' he bellowed. 'No Yellowbeard ever had a job. Are you *sure* it was you I raped before I was arrested?'

'It *was* me, sugar-drawers.'

'What's this job he's got?'

'He's a gardener.' She had hoped it would not be this difficult, but help was at hand.

As her husband bellowed in disbelief, 'A gardener!' the guard delivered a crippling blow to his back. He did not feel it. 'I'll see about that when I'm out!'

The guard exerted himself a second time.

Yellowbeard turned to see what was interrupting his train of thought. 'What is it?'

'Time's up, sir,' and as the exhausted wife sank to a bench, the guard started to usher out the fuming pirate.

'So your son's a gardener, eh?' he mocked . . . and was clearly just about to make a meal of this piece of news when Yellowbeard grabbed his cudgel, bit it in half like a stick of celery, flung the pieces to the ground and strode back into the rain-sodden yard of St Victim's Prison for the Extremely Naughty.

Percy, Seventh Earl of Lambourn, and his Lady were receiving guests at Lambourn Hall. For the moment it was no longer their home as it had become the temporary resting-place of the Queen of England and her Court who were breaking their return journey from Portsmouth where Queen Anne had just attended a Review of Her Fleet.

The Hall, while magnificent and stately, had seen better days. It had been the impressive home of Lambourns for generations but Lord Lambourn was the last of his line and, except for what he believed to be an illegitimate son Dan, it seemed unlikely that he would have any heirs. His wife, who he had married for money, had also seen better days, but now was busying herself on the steps doing everything she could think of to restore some of the former grandeur to the house on this auspicious occasion. She'd decorated the trees with bunting and a banner draped above her over the porch read 'Welcome to 'Er Majesty!' As she scanned the lawns before her she noticed with satisfaction the jugglers, acrobats and the dancing bear she'd had sent up from London especially. Her smile soon changed to a grimace as she saw Dan, the lazy boy that Lambourn had taken on as a gardener, happily watching this spectacle instead of wheeling his barrow of manure out of sight.

She called out to him, 'Dan, I want the garden spic and span. We must h'ave an h'air of courtly dignity h'about the 'All.'

Dan looked puzzled. 'Don't you mean "Hall", your Ladyship?'

'I do not. The letter "H" is not being aspirated this season by 'Er Majesty 'oo 'ates it. Lambourn!'

Lord Lambourn started as she boomed out his name.

'Stop that man pissin' on the 'edge, it's imported!'

Before Lambourn could react she was chasing off the offending gardener with a broom.

Dan set down his wheelbarrow and whispered in Lord Lambourn's ear, 'How long is the Queen staying, your Lordship?'

'Forever if my wife has anything to do with it. The woman's mad!'

Another carriage was drawing up. Lady Lambourn dropped the broom and bustled back into position beside her husband just as the carriage stopped and out of it stepped Commander Clement of Her Majesty's Navy and his young lieutenant, Mansell.

'Welcome to Lambourn Hall, Commander Clement.' Lord Lambourn bowed.

His Lady rose from a curtsy and smiled up at the Commander. ''Er Majesty's temporary throne-room is in the 'uge with-drawin'-room!'

'Thank you, Lady Lambourn,' Clement replied, bemused at her eccentric language, and entered the Hall.

Mansell bowed awkwardly and followed after.

When the Queen of England travelled anywhere the entire Court went with her and this included her old friend and confidante Sarah Churchill, First Duchess of Marlborough, chief among her staff and very much the power behind the throne. Her Majesty was herself not a brilliant woman and preferred a game of cards and a glass or three of brandy to affairs of State which, for the most part, she gladly left to the ambitious Lady Sarah.

Since Lambourn Hall was now the Seat of Government, every corridor was filled with scurrying secretaries, emissaries and petitioning ambassadors fighting for precedence, and so Commander Clement was lucky to find a helpful but somewhat over-familiar flunkey who ushered him into the Great Hall. The huge room was full of people. A group of musicians played above in the minstrel's gallery. An artist painted a very flattering portrait of a youthful Queen Anne and a cartographer was busily engaged working on a large map of the world, shading the parts of it that were British, pink.

The flunkey advised the Commander: ''Er Majesty's the fat one on the throne. She's not too well this morning. I should kneel upwind of 'er if I was you. The skinny one's Lady Churchill, the brains of the outfit!'

254

Commander Clement stepped forward, knelt and waited for the Queen to speak. After an awkward silence, in which she did not, Commander Clement coughed politely. The Queen stared straight ahead of her and seemed in a daze but some royal sixth sense must have told her that the throne had been approached. 'State your business,' she declaimed to the room in general.

Commander Clement stood up and began, hesitantly at first, not being entirely sure to whom she was speaking. He glanced around him just to check before saying nervously, 'Your Majesty. We in the Naval Department, while being keenly aware of recent spirals in Defence expenditure, humbly submit . . .'

The Queen interrupted loudly: 'Are you the Prime Minister?'

Clement was taken aback and again looked round to make sure that he was being addressed. Then he took a step forward to disclose his identity with appropriate tact.

He shook his head, put a finger to his lips and whispered, 'Secret Service!'

'Oh Charades . . .' whooped the Queen, suddenly becoming animated. 'You're a beekeeper!'

Clement, who hoped things would have been more straightforward and had no wish to infringe some royal etiquette, was about to say 'no' but looked around for help.

'That's right!' said Lady Sarah. 'Very clever . . .' and applauded politely.

The Queen beamed contentedly.

'That'll do . . . for her.'

'Will it?' Clement enquired nervously.

The Queen's voice suddenly echoed round the room. 'What do you want?'

Commander Clement was not at ease and was relieved to see Lady Churchill gesturing him to continue. He did so.

'The pirate Yellowbeard is due to be released in two days,

Your Majesty, and despite years of unpleasantness he has told us nothing about the treasure he has hidden. However . . .' He took a scroll from under his arm. 'I have a detailed plan here.'

Lady Sarah pushed the scroll aside.

'I doubt if she could manage to read more than the label on a gin bottle this morning. Just tell us, Commander.'

'Well, Milady, we'd like you to increase his sentence so that he's bound to escape and make straight for the treasure. I shall need a fast ship to follow him . . .'

'A sensible request I think, Your Majesty,' said Lady Churchill.

'A plate full of steamed fish,' came the Queen's forceful reply.

Lady Sarah had had a difficult morning and this latest nonsense tried her patience. 'I sometimes think I'm running this soddin' country on my own. 'Owever, my 'usband, the Duke of Marlborough, needs that gold for his glorious slaughter of the French who are a load of bum-biting foreigners,' she confided. 'From what I've heard, there's enough to buy the whole of Bavaria *and* some nice pink bits for me map.'

'I didn't expect such bluntitude, Mrs Marlborough. Will Her Majesty agree to this?' he whispered, handing over the document for signature.

'In 'er state, of course she will.' She prodded the Queen with the rolled-up parchment and shouted with almost treasonable force, 'The beekeeper would like this signed.'

The Queen stirred, signed the document automatically with the proffered pen and said the word 'certainly!' so loudly that the hounds in the garden began to bay.

'Oh thank you, Ma'am, and thank *you*, Milady,' Clement said to Lady Churchill, thankful that his ordeal was at an end.

'Not at all. It was your flashin' blue eyes what done it. I'm only in this for the perks.'

Commander Clement bowed once more to the Queen.

'What's in this for you?' added Lady Churchill, fondling his bottom as he bowed.

'Pardon?' gulped Clement as his smile froze. 'Oh . . . er . . . well, since you mention it, Milady . . . my wife always hankered after me being . . . "Sir" someone or other.'

'If you get that loot pronto,' urged the Duchess of Marlborough, 'you'll be a duke like my husband what goes away a lot . . .'

Clement had to stoically accept another, even more intimate fondle before he could extricate himself from the Affairs of State . . .

CHAPTER 3

The rain stopped and it was now late on a sunny summer afternoon. Dan finished his morning's work at the Hall and set out for his home in the village. The fields and trees were lush and green and on the leafy narrow country lane leading from Lambourn Hall to the nearby village of Lambourn, the trees sparkled in the breeze. The gentle lowing of cows could be heard from a nearby elegy, bees buzzed and flies made the sort of noise one associates with contented flies on such an afternoon.

The tiny Hampshire fishing village of Lambourn was complacent in the sun and, apart from the scratching of chickens and the crunch-crunch of a browsing donkey, the only sounds of activity came from within the Village Inn. The Maimed Fox, a charming half-timbered Elizabethan inn, was not as charming as it appeared. Inside, the inn was smoke-filled and noisy and full of hard-drinking seafaring types.

A tall blind man dressed in black, Mr Pew, sat stiffly erect in the middle of the crowded bar, avidly listening to conversation around him. Men sitting at nearby tables flinched at his slightest sign of movement. From the deference they showed he was clearly regarded with considerable respect.

Betty finished pouring Pew a drink.

'There you are, Mr Pew.' Betty set the tankard down beside him.

'I said a *double*!'

'It is a double!'

'Come off it, Mrs Beard. I can hear a double when I hear one.'

Betty resignedly continued to pour.

'When!' said Pew. 'Are you trying to get me drunk or something?' Suddenly he stiffened and cocked his head on one side. 'Dan's coming,' he said, evenly.

No one else could have heard anything from outside through the hubbub created by the drunken seafarers in that room but Pew impressively added, '. . . reading as usual . . .' Correctly discerning Dan's preoccupation merely from the cadence of his steps, he took a satisfied gulp and licked his lips in triumph as Dan entered engrossed in his book.

'There you are, Dan,' Betty yelled out across the room. 'Have you got a moment?'

Dan mumbled, 'I'm reading something,' and walked automatically over to his favourite corner of the bar.

Betty rushed over to him, grabbed the book, closed it and thumped it down on the table in front of him. 'Read, read, read, read, read!' she nagged. 'There's more important things in life than reading, son. Oh, keep an ear on the bar, would you Mr Pew?'

Pew nodded in consent.

'If there's one thing I've learnt in life,' she continued, 'it's that learning things never taught me anything. And *books* are the worst.'

'All right, Mother,' said Dan making a mental note of his place in the book and resigning himself to one of his mother's 'little chats'.

'Last time I read a book,' she warned, 'I was raped, so let that be a lesson to you!'

Dan, who often wondered what on earth his mother was talking about, wished she would get to the point. 'What do you want?'

'Well, Dan, it's about your father.'

'What about him?'

'When I told you he was dead I was only trying to cushion the blow . . .'

'What blow?' Dan was curious.

'Well . . .' she paused dramatically, '. . . he's alive. He's alive and imprisoned as a pirate!'

'A pirate!' Dan was shocked. 'You mean . . . a pirate . . . like Yellowbeard?'

Pew sat bolt upright at this and cocked an ear in their direction.

'Very like Yellowbeard . . . in fact, he is Yellowbeard!'

Dan, stunned by this piece of news, sat in silent thought as all the implications sank in . . .

At St Victim's Prison, Yellowbeard himself, waiting for his second visitor in twenty years, stood impatiently at the bars. Commander Clement, holding a kerchief against his nose to minimise the foul stench of the prison, approached the prisoner.

'Ah, Mr Yellowbeard . . .'

'*Captain* to you, you scum,' roared Yellowbeard.

'Quite. Sorry, *Captain* Yellowbeard. Now let's see . . . twenty years ago today,' Commander Clement perused an official document, 'you were sentenced to twenty years in gaol!'

'Yes, and now I'm due to be released,' he menaced the bars.

'Yes . . . or rather no,' said Clement. 'Twenty years ago no man was really expected to live in gaol for twenty years in the filthy, horrendous conditions that existed then and, indeed, still exist today . . .'

Yellowbeard, sensing official trickery, moved closer to the bars to listen.

'So, when the judge sentenced you to twenty years he had

no idea that you would survive. In the light of these facts, Her Majesty the Queen has graciously agreed to extend your sentence a further one hundred and forty years. Case dismissed!'

Commander Clement reacted quickly and leaped back just in time as Yellowbeard's arms plunged through the bars, his strong hands grabbing for his throat. Yellowbeard, bellowing like a bull, was immediately set upon by four huge guards who dragged him away from the bars. One of the guards collapsed backwards as Yellowbeard's elbow thudded into the pit of his stomach. Yet another was sent flying to crash head first into the stone wall. The third and fourth were joined by other guards and they dragged Yellowbeard screaming and roaring from the room. They manhandled him across the prison courtyard and threw him towards a very curious Mr Gilbert working on an unfinished coffin.

'Went well with the Commander, did it?' enquired Gilbert, inappropriately.

'No!' was the terse reply.

'Oh,' said Gilbert, anxious to appear merely conversational, 'so you won't be leaving us then?'

'They broke their solemn word,' fumed Yellowbeard.

'That's governments for you, isn't it?' sympathised Gilbert, and then asked as casually as he could, 'I expect they wanted to know about the treasure?'

'Yes and that's one thing they'll never know!'

'Oh well, until you tell them about the treasure the only way you're going to leave here is feet first . . .'

As Gilbert continued unaware, Yellowbeard picked up an empty coffin and ran with enormous speed up to a cart which was about to leave the prison gate. In one move he threw the coffin onto the cart and himself into it, sliding the lid over himself. The cart trundled out into the gathering dusk and the gates clanged shut behind him.

Gilbert had noticed none of this as he tried cleverly to come to the point. 'I mean it must be an awful strain, being the only man in the world knowing where the treasure is. I once heard of a man who knew where a much, much smaller treasure was and the strain of knowing that made him pull all his own giblets out . . . why don't you share the burden, with a friend?' He turned to Yellowbeard. There was no Yellowbeard. He looked around the prison yard. No sign of him. Yellowbeard had escaped.

Just at that moment Gilbert heard a whistle. A signal, for him. He looked towards the appointed place on the prison wall. A rope had been lowered down to him. Gilbert looked round to make sure he was unobserved and ran quickly towards the rope.

'Mr Moon, is that you?'

'Get a move on, Gilbert,' said the gruff voice of Mr Moon from the other side of the wall. The agile figure of Gilbert lost no time in scaling the wall and was soon outside the prison.

Mr Moon, twenty years older, looked more formidable than ever. He wore an evil-looking iron hook in place of his right hand.

'Did you get any information out of the mad old fool yet?' he rasped.

'No. He's gone!'

'Gone!' said Moon exasperated, pushing his accomplice to the ground in disgust. 'You let him escape without you! All right, Gilbert, go to the village. He might be mad enough to go to the pub. It's been a few years since he visited Betty . . .'

Betty surveyed the bar of the Maimed Fox checking that the potwoman had lit all the lamps and that the fire was well stoked, then went upstairs to tidy herself in preparation for the evening's business. Many of the customers had been there all day and one or two of them lay where they had fallen in the beer-sodden sawdust. Mr Beast was drunk, as usual, a massive wart-ridden toad of a man. He sat hunched over his tankard talking with his unfortunate stutter to the beer it contained. In stark contrast to him, on his shoulder sat a proud and beautiful giant blue and yellow macaw, a prize trophy from one of his exotic travels.

Another very large gentleman, Mr Baggot, tiring of Mr Beast's company, stood up and began to heave his ponderous weight towards the bar, pushing the potwoman out of his way as he did so. Blind Pew sat at his usual seat in the middle of the room listening to a conversation in the house next door. He'd become so engrossed in their conversation – they'd just started a story about Blind Pew – that he had only just noticed the sound from outside of someone in a hurry approaching the inn. He was just about to say, 'Here's Yellowbeard,' when Yellowbeard burst in through the door.

Mr Baggot was about to yell, 'Close that door!' when Yellowbeard's forehead crashed into the bridge of his nose. Yellowbeard had little time for conversation. As Mr Baggot's head reeled, Yellowbeard snatched a couple of daggers from his ample belt and dashed straight past the questing nose of the alert Blind Pew, straight up the stairs to Betty's bedroom.

'That's Yellowbeard,' nodded Blind Pew to himself and he sat listening for developments.

As soon as Betty heard someone on the stairs she hid her cash box in the chest at the foot of her bed and sat calmly upon it. Yellowbeard dashed in and ran immediately to a corner of the bedroom and began to hack away at the wall with his daggers. Betty provocatively hitched her skirts up to her knees and, as she leaned backwards, said, 'I do wish it didn't have to be such a rush every time!'

'What?' said Yellowbeard, pausing for a moment. Then

realising what Betty was anticipating, added, 'I haven't got time for that now.' He carried on demolishing the plaster work.

'It's been twenty years,' said Betty, 'since we had a little cuddle and what do you do? Come in here and give me a kiss? No, you rush in and hack a hole in the wall!'

Yellowbeard stopped hacking. 'Where's the map?' he demanded.

'What map?'

'If you say you don't know where it is,' he said, advancing on her with the daggers, 'I'll nail your tits to the table,' and on this he plunged the knives into the table which stood between them.

Betty rose quickly and backed away a little. 'Oh, I know where it is,' and at a safer distance she added, 'I burnt it.'

'You burnt my map!' He ran at her, daggers raised.

'. . . But only after I'd copied it,' she screamed.

Yellowbeard was relieved but still menaced her. 'Where's the copy?'

'Well,' smiled Betty nervously, 'when little Dan came along . . .'

'Who's Dan?'

Fierce or not, Betty was still angered by Yellowbeard's inattentiveness. 'My and probably your son,' she said defiantly. 'When he was only two minutes old I tattooed it on his head.'

'Does he know about this?' He was in deadly earnest.

'Oh, no, no . . . nor no one else, neither. That's why I kept him in a cupboard for three years. That may be why he's a bit odd with all those books and stuff.'

'Where is he now?' Yellowbeard's eyes burned fiercely.

'He's up at Lambourn Hall,' she smiled weakly.

'Right, I'll go and cut his head off.' He strode over to a cupboard and began to undress.

'Oh, how nice,' cooed Betty, beginning to unlace her bodice, 'you've still got time for a cuddle before you kill your son.'

Yellowbeard wrenched open the cupboard and was surprised to find a large array of frocks and dresses.

'Where's my piratin' outfit?' he yelled. 'And *where* did you get all those frocks?'

'Well,' Betty began her explanation, 'you know the one I said has been ever so kind to Dan – well he's been ever so kind to me.'

Yellowbeard hurriedly put on his brilliant scarlet coat with the deep cuffs and gold braid over his favourite gold suede waistcoat with cut-steel buttons and pulled on his boots, and he began once again to take on the true stature of the famed pirate Yellowbeard.

Downstairs the atmosphere was even more smoke-filled and booze-laden as the bar now had its full complement of evening customers. Swarthy seafarers – a man with only one eye, another with an arm missing, two with wooden legs, one with two wooden legs – all thugs – men with sinister eye patches and even one with a tin nose.

Mr Beast, who had somehow managed to recover for another bout of drinking, roared with laughter as a friend's wooden leg caught in a knot-hole in the floor and snapped as he fell drunkenly backwards. His macaw shrilly echoed his laughter, causing another convulsion of mirth during which his false eye dropped out and landed with a plop in his drink. Still wheezing with laughter, he fished it out of his drink, wiped it on grubby trousers and popped it back into the socket. At that moment the tavern door opened and in came Commander Clement and Lieutenant Mansell.

'Royal Navy here,' announced the Commander over the hubbub.

A chorus of catcalls and moans greeted this news from around the bar. The customers were obviously not

266

impressed. Wolf whistles greeted the sight of naval uniforms at this establishment.

Unperturbed, Clement asked to the room in general, 'Where's Yellowbeard?'

At the mention of this name the bar fell suddenly silent, broken only by the macaw's echoing squawk, 'Yellowbeard!'

This was greeted with much laughter. Clement, ignoring the laughter and the parrot, closed in on its owner and demanded, 'Where's Yellowbeard?'

'He's g . . . g . . . g . . . he's g . . . g . . . g . . .' stammered Mr Beast.

Clement raised an enquiring eyebrow at the parrot, angrily challenging it to reply.

'He's g . . . g . . . g . . . he's g . . . g . . . g . . .' repeated the parrot to a gale of laughter.

Clement banged his gloves down sharply on the table in front of Mr Beast and stared fixedly at him.

'. . . gone!' said Mr Beast.

'Gone!' echoed the parrot.

'Well if he's *gone*,' Clement said to the assembled crowd, 'you must have seen him.'

There was a chorus of 'no's and they all shook their heads except the parrot. Clement, exasperated, stared in mock expectation at the bird.

The macaw cocked his head to one side as though deep in thought and then suddenly squawked, 'Who's a pretty boy then?'

The unsavoury customers laughed raucously.

Upstairs in Betty's bedroom Yellowbeard, searching for his swordbelt, came across a suit of fine gentleman's clothing. 'What's this?' he asked of a now more composed Betty.

'Oh that's Lord Lambourn's as well. He's *such* a kind man, he left those here in case you escaped and needed a change of clothing. Wasn't that nice?'

'I'm sure *I killed* the last one I raped, it can't have been you,' mused Yellowbeard suspiciously.

'The afterplay was a bit on the rough side,' agreed Betty, 'but not fatal.'

Neither Yellowbeard nor Betty were aware that their conversation was by now being overheard by Mr Gilbert, a second eavesdropper, who had hauled himself up to the window outside and stood on top of a couple of empty beer barrels.

'What does this Dan, or whatever you call him, look like?' asked Yellowbeard.

'Well, a little bit like Lord Lambourn,' began Betty, but then realising her error quickly added, 'but a bit more like *you*, much more like you in fact.'

Yellowbeard dashed out of the room and down the stairs, but before entering the bar saw Clement and Mansell, turned and dashed back up the stairs. He ran across Betty's bedroom and, without hesitation, dived straight through her window. A surprised Gilbert fell to the ground with a thud as Yellowbeard landed surrounded by shattered glass and woodwork. The pirate sprang to his feet and dashed off into the night leaving a dazed Gilbert to wonder what had happened.

Inside the bar, as soon as the laughter at the parrot's last utterance had subsided, Clement asked, 'So not one of you has seen Yellowbeard?'

'No!' came the unanimous reply.

Commander Clement cursed under his breath and left angrily, followed closely by Lieutenant Mansell who stopped and wagged a finger at those lacking respect for Her Majesty's Navy. He received none.

Mansell joined the Commander in the street outside the inn. A sudden noise made them stop.

'Pssstt!' came again from the murky shadows at the side of the inn.

268

'I think that's our agent, sir,' said Mansell, stepping in that direction.

They walked past a coachman standing beside his waiting coach and there in the shadows stood their agent. It was Blind Pew.

Clement began to question him. 'Did you see . . .' – then he realised and turned to Mansell. 'He's blind, you silly sod!'

'I may be blind,' said Pew, 'but I 'ave acute 'earing.'

'I'm not interested in your jewellery, cloth-eyes,' snapped Clement, 'I'm trying . . .'

'Yellowbeard was 'ere,' Pew interrupted.

'How do you know?' asked Clement.

Pew explained. 'He sounded about forty-seven years old and his clothing gave off the unmistakeable sound of the eighty per cent hemp . . .'

'Where did he go?' Clement repeated impatiently.

Pew continued, '. . . twenty per cent hessian mixture used in prison uniforms . . .'

Clement interrupted again. 'Where did he go?'

But Pew was determined to finish. '. . . while the deafening rustle of his beard indicated a length of not less than . . .'

Commander Clement grabbed Pew by the throat and yelled, 'Where did he go?'

Pew, quite unaffected by the physical assault, took out a purse which he held open in front of him. Mansell looked at his superior officer and, after getting an impatient but approving look, dropped a coin into the purse.

Pew spoke. 'Upstairs . . . and then . . .'

Clement and Mansell immediately dashed back into the inn.

Pew cupped his hand to his mouth and called loudly after them, '. . . and then Yellowbeard shouted something very loud indeed . . .'

Clement and Mansell paused in their dash.

'. . . but I didn't quite catch that.'

Exasperated, they resumed their headlong flight back into the inn.

'People's attention spans are getting shorter and shorter,' mumbled Pew to himself as he tapped his way down the street past the waiting coachman. Here he paused, sniffed and listened, and said in an offhand manner, 'Evening, Gilbert,' and tapped his way back to the bar. This infuriated Gilbert who had taken great pains over his disguise.

Betty was tidying up her room after her 'husband's' visit; clothes still littered the floor. Clement and Mansell crashed in and were immediately aware of the odour given off by the pirate's discarded garments.

'Where's Yellowbeard?' demanded Clement.

'He's in prison, isn't he?' said Betty innocently.

'Mrs Beard, your husband escaped this evening and we have reason to believe that he came straight to see you.'

'Oh yes, come to think of it,' Betty thought quickly, 'someone did come in here a while back but I don't think it was my husband.'

'These are his clothes,' observed Mansell, holding up a stinking prison shirt on his sword at arm's length.

'Oh wait a minute, someone did just pop in and rape me,' she explained. 'These must be his clothes . . .'

'That *was* Yellowbeard,' Commander Clement stated.

'Well, prison has reformed him then. He never used to take his clothes off in the old days . . .'

'Where did he go, Mrs Beard?' asked Clement.

'I've no idea,' she replied.

'Come on, bring those clothes, Mansell, we'll need a scent for the dogs.'

Clement left the room and Mansell followed still carrying the shirt on the end of his sword.

Betty made one final attempt to confuse them and

shouted from the doorway, 'If it was my hubby who raped me, I imagine he's dashed off to rape someone else. He was never satisfied with just the one . . .' She began to undress while saying this but the Royal Navy was not to be so easily distracted.

CHAPTER 4

Gilbert ran off to dispose of his disguise and quickly returned to the bar of the Maimed Fox. He rushed straight over to Blind Pew. 'How did you know it was me out there?' he asked.

'Your side whiskers,' replied Pew mysteriously.

'What?' said the incredulous Gilbert.

'They make a high-pitched slightly metallic rustling sound that's quite unmistakeable,' explained Pew. 'Also your bodily odour is uniquely unforgettable . . .'

'Now listen to me, Pew,' Gilbert warned.

'I'm all ears,' interrupted Pew.

'Listen, Pew, you didn't tell everything you heard to those two naval gentlemen, did you, shipmate?'

'What gentlemen,' said Pew innocently.

Gilbert was not put off. 'I didn't hear you mention much about a map?'

'What map?' Pew was playing his part.

'Yellowbeard's map,' snarled Gilbert, '. . . what any pirate worth his salt would give both his arms to get hold of . . .'

Pew stood up, towering over Gilbert. 'You're drunk, Gilbert, your mind's wandering.'

'My hands will be wandering towards your throat, Pew,' threatened Gilbert. His hands reached up, '. . . unless you tell me what you 'eard.'

'So you can pass the information on to Mr Moon, so he can find the treasure? Over my dead body!' spat Pew.

'Very well,' said Gilbert, 'if those are your conditions.' He turned and addressed the entire room. 'My Hearties! This dear old blind man . . . is a government agent!'

Everyone in the bar suddenly became attentive. They all had reasons for disliking agents of the government. They murmured angrily.

' 'Tis true,' expanded Gilbert, 'I saw him talking to those two naval officers outside . . .'

Pew knew this could go badly for him. ' 'Tis a lie!' he shouted, and turned so that his back was towards a pillar.

The cut-throat crew began to advance on him. Someone shouted, 'Kill him!'

'Informing on a shipmate,' added Gilbert, stoking the fire.

'Death! Kill him now,' they shouted, closing in.

Two burly seafarers grabbed Pew from behind while another held a glinting blade at his throat. Gilbert slunk outside, laughing to himself evilly.

Pew, with a knife pressing on his windpipe, thought quickly. 'I only told them one thing . . .' his voice cut through the ugly crowd's mutterings '. . . about *treasure*,' he added with special emphasis. There was a sudden silence as this word worked on their greedy minds. He now had their full attention. 'But it is very, very secret.'

'Well te . . . te . . . te . . .' stammered Mr Beast excitedly, 'te . . . te . . . tell us, Pe . . . Pe . . . Pew.'

' 'Tis too secret,' said Pew. The knife blade moved closer to his throat again but he was in control.

'All right,' he said, 'lock that door.' The door was quickly locked. 'Draw them curtains and put those other lights out.' The men released their grip on him, anxious to hear the news. Pew leaned towards the only remaining candle in the room and surreptitiously drew a sword out of his white cane. 'Now listen carefully,' he whispered, as they crowded closely round him. In a flash, he flailed his sword, cleanly cutting the flame from the candle. Pew had manoeuvred himself a terrible advantage. There was complete darkness and a moment of silence, then a scream of pain, then another. The swishing of Pew's evil blade was followed by ominous gurgles and horrible cries of agony.

Grinning with satisfaction at the screams behind him, Gilbert crept stealthily around the side of the inn. A hook through his collar suddenly pulled him into an upright position. The hook was that replacing the right hand of the vengeful Mr Moon.

'Where's Yellowbeard?' he hissed.

It was Gilbert's turn to be terrified. 'Oh Mr Moon, sir. I tried to follow him, but I thought I was being followed . . . if you follow me.'

'Who'd follow you?' said Moon, twisting the hook a little, almost lifting him off the ground.

'Some stupid blind man,' Gilbert explained.

'Well, Gilbert, we've got to follow Yellowbeard and make sure that no one else is following him.' He twisted again. 'Do you follow me?'

There was a deathly scream from within and an abrupt silence followed. Moon's grip loosened.

'What's going on in there?' They both ran towards the bar.

On entering the inn it was pitch dark. A flint was struck and a candle in the middle of the room flickered into life. The door swung closed behind Gilbert to reveal Mr Beast stuck to the back of it, impaled on his own sword. The room was a total and bloody wreck. Every single customer that had been in that bar lay bleeding and unconscious or dead.

Pew, the innocent, harmless blind man, slowly tapped his way out, saying as he passed the silent Mr Moon, 'Evening. Sounded as though there was a bit of a squabble.'

'Squabble?' said Moon astounded. 'They're all dead.'

'Must have been more of a tiff then,' observed the

blameless Pew adding, '*Mr* Moon', in mock deference. He downed the last drop of his drink and tapped his way out of the bar.

The next morning at Lambourn Hall, Lord Lambourn, who had spent the entire night having a couple of drinks, was wandering in the garden, still anxious to avoid his royalty-besotted wife. He chatted amiably to a Rear-Admiral – part of the Queen's entourage – in whom he'd found a kindred spirit. He loved an early morning starter. They ambled amongst the dewy bushes taking occasional sips from Lambourn's flask of brandy.

'I only drink when I'm working,' Lambourn was confiding in his friend when Lady Lambourn's voice shrilled in interruption.

'There you are, Lambourn. I'd like some advice on a matter of etiquette . . .' She hurried over to them, dressed in all her finery even at this hour.

Lambourn hid his hip flask under his coat and his eyes looked heavenward.

'Does one curtsy while saying "'ello"?' said Lady Lambourn, 'or does one go down while speakin' . . . ?' She demonstrated a curtsy, displaying her ample bosom as she dipped down low.

Just at that moment Yellowbeard, searching for Dan, burst through from the bushes where he'd spent the night. He caught sight of Lady Lambourn as she practised. After twenty years in prison the sight was too much for him. He ran to her and hauled her bodily back into the bushes. Lady Lambourn should have been outraged but, somewhat flattered, she was courteous to the last.

'Excuse me, Admiral while I just 'ave a word with this gentleman . . .' She disappeared into the undergrowth.

Loud screams of fear gradually turning more to delight made to sound like fear, combined with Yellowbeardic bellows, sounds of clothes being ripped and articles of finery flying out of bushes, made quite an entertainment for the two friends to observe as they once more sipped away at the flask.

'Who was that chap who just dashed up and seized hold of the wife?' asked Lambourn.

A petticoat flew out of the bushes.

'Don't know,' replied the Admiral. 'He seems to have taken a bit of a shine to Lady L.'

Suddenly the figure of the pirate dashed out of the foliage and disappeared across the lawn. Lady Lambourn extricated herself from the undergrowth very much on her dignity, adjusting her dishevelled dress as she tottered towards them. The two of them stared at her and both involuntarily held up kerchieves to their noses as they caught a strong whiff of Yellowbeard.

'Should you be wonderin' 'oo that was,' warbled a flushed Lady Lambourn, 'it were one of 'Er Majesty's emissaries apologisin' and saying I'm needed up the bathroom – urgent.' With that she gathered up her remaining garments and bustled off into the Hall.

Dan sat on the edge of his wheelbarrow reading a book in the kitchen garden. The bushes behind him parted and out rushed Yellowbeard with his cutlass drawn. 'Is your name Dan?' he growled.

Dan looked up, startled at the wild apparition. 'Yes,' he said.

'I need your head, my lad,' continued the crazed figure.

Dan had never seen such an horrendous apparition and came to his own conclusion. 'You're my father.'

'So your mother says,' snorted Yellowbeard, 'but that's no reason to believe it. Never trust a woman or a government.'

'Pleased to meet you.' Dan held his hand out in as polite a greeting as he could muster.

'I haven't got time for idle chit chat. I need your head.'

'That makes a change,' he joked. 'Mother seems to disapprove of me using it at all . . .'

There was no trace of filial affection, however, from Yellowbeard. 'You're not going to use it, you're going to lose it, lad . . .'

Dan backed away as his father raised his cutlass and advanced.

' . . . I'm going to use it. Right, put your head over the end of that wheelbarrow, it'll be cleaner that way . . .' His sword arm reached back as he prepared to strike.

Now Dan needed to think quickly. 'You want to cut my head off? What for?'

'I don't want to lug your body half way round the world, do I? Your 'ead's got a map on it that I need.'

Yellowbeard brought his cutlass down, splintering into the woodwork of the wheelbarrow, narrowly missing Dan's scalp. Dan ducked down in time and sprang out of the way. He managed to keep his distance successfully as Yellowbeard chased him around the garden lopping the tops off bushes and small trees as the cutlass slashed. Yellowbeard took another fierce lunge at his head. Dan dodged behind an ornamental urn. The pirate feinted to the right and lunged out with his left arm instead and caught Dan by the neck.

'You don't need to kill me for it,' pleaded Dan, now very fearful, but his mind was working faster than ever. 'Why don't you copy it?'

'What!' yelled the pirate. '. . . and have *two* maps!'

Yellowbeard now forced his head back pulling on his hair.

'If you cut my head off,' Dan said hurriedly, 'it will start to putrefy . . .'

'Do what?' Yellowbeard paused momentarily.

Dan explained quickly, '. . . putrefy, go rotten.'

'Yes,' agreed the pirate, intrigued, but not loosening his grip, 'it would ooze a lot. Heads do, but I can live with that . . .' He raised his sword again to strike.

'Stop!' yelled Dan. 'I could help you, Dad. Everyone will be following you: the Navy, rival pirates. If they catch you *they'll* have the map.'

'Bugger them, I'll eat it first. It won't be the first head I've eaten.'

Seeing those jagged teeth, Dan could well believe this.

'But then you'll have lost it forever. Wouldn't it be better to leave it where it's safe?'

'What! And take you along?' Yellowbeard was appalled by this suggestion. 'You're not pirate material, you wouldn't fit in . . .'

At this moment Lord Lambourn, who had just left the Admiral happily inspecting his beehives, walked up to them. He was now feeling the benefit of half a pint of brandy and was not really aware of the gravity of the situation. 'Hello, Dan,' he greeted him cheerily, 'been doing some gardening?' Focusing on Yellowbeard properly for the first time he blinked in surprise. 'Have we been introduced?'

Yellowbeard grabbed the newcomer by the waistcoat and pushed him forcibly to the ground and raised his cutlass.

'All right, Dan. If you're my son, prove it.' He offered Dan his sword. 'Kill this stupid old bugger.'

'Oh, hold your horses . . .' burbled Lambourn, unprepared for this kind of thing.

'I can't kill *him*,' Dan reasoned. 'He brought me up . . . just like a father . . .'

'Oh,' roared Yellowbeard, '. . . you mean he's beaten you and kicked you and smashed you in the teeth?'

'No!' said Dan. 'He's been kind and gentle . . .'

'What kind of father is that?' replied Yellowbeard in disgust. 'Kill him now.' He raised his cutlass once more.

'No!' yelled Dan and gripped the pirate's forearm in both hands, holding him back a moment.

'All right, *I'll* do it . . .' 'Yellowbeard's strong sword arm swung back and he began his lunge.

Dan, not knowing what to do next, played for time. 'Don't! Don't! He could be useful . . .'

'Could I?' queried Lambourn, but now fully realising his danger rapidly agreed. 'Oh. Yes, yes, I could. Why not? I could . . . er . . .' Unfortunately he had not the faintest idea what he could do. 'I could . . . I could . . . what could I do?' But then from behind the hedgerow at the bottom of the garden came the baying of a pack of hounds and Dan could see the plumed hats of Clement and Mansell in the distance.

'The Navy,' said Dan urgently to his father, 'they've followed you here.'

Yellowbeard released his grip on a thankful Lambourn and turned, cutlass at the ready to meet his foe. 'I'll kill 'em all.'

Dan looked around for an escape route and then gestured at the wheelbarrow full of manure. 'Quick, hide in here.'

After his years in St Victim's, the manure looked quite homely to Yellowbeard and he was tempted.

'There's a lot of them,' Dan urged, 'quickly, hide in here, we'll go to Dr Gilpin's. He always knows what to do . . .'

'. . . and then kill everybody . . .' said Yellowbeard as he buried himself eagerly under the manure and straw.

'Whatever you like, Dad.'

'Dad? Him?' asked Lambourn. 'I'm not your father then?'

'No,' answered Dan, 'Mother says he is . . .' he pointed at the ordure, 'but you're still my father to me.'

'And I'm still my father to you, son,' added Lambourn, mystifyingly.

Dan began to push the wheelbarrow out of the garden.

'Look,' he explained. He was very fond of his loopy, loving 'father' too. 'You brought me up . . . you are my father. I don't even know him . . .'

Lady Lambourn's ample voice could be heard from the rose garden. 'Lambourn?'

'I'll come with you, son,' said Lambourn, becoming suddenly animated, and helped Dan to push the load.

'This Dr Gilpin . . .' added Lambourn, suddenly befogged, 'do I know him?'

'He's your best friend, Father.'

'I . . . well, I look forward to meeting him,' said Lambourn, still finding things just a little blurred.

They barely managed to get out of sight before the hounds in full cry ran into the garden. With noses to the ground they had followed Yellowbeard's route through the bushes but then came to a halt where the wheelbarrow had been. A confusion of scents disrupted the momentum of the chase and, when Clement and Mansell arrived panting at the spot, the dogs were scattered around the garden pursuing their own fancy, pirates forgotten.

Blind Pew had heard the hounds at the Hall long before Dan and paused, on his way to the Maimed Fox, to listen and sniff. He detected the change as the baying beasts seemed to find something, but from the cacophony of human voices shouting he clearly detected Clement's displeased tones. 'They haven't found him then,' he concluded suddenly, his nostrils twitched in the breeze. 'Mmm,' he thought, 'Yellowbeard . . . moving rather quickly.' He tapped his way hastily to the lane leading from Lambourn Hall. The scent was fresh here and easily followed.

CHAPTER 5

Dr Gilpin's house was more like a laboratory than a home. His study walls were lined with books, jars containing specimens; chemicals and herbs were everywhere. There were benches full of chemists' equipment: scales, retorts, crucibles and glass flasks with weird liquids, shelves held a multitude of deep blue tightly stoppered glass jars with inscriptions in Latin. Examples of animal species stood or hung amongst a botanical collection that could have formed a museum.

Dan, Lambourn and Yellowbeard had left the wheelbarrow in the road outside. Dr Gilpin, an erudite, sprightly old man, came to live in this particular back-water in order to rid himself of the fierce criticism with which the conservative scientific establishment had greeted most of his worthwhile discoveries. But it was the men of the Church in London who had finally insisted on an end to his scientific enquiry – he narrowly escaped with his life after being labelled a necromancer because of his experimental demonstrations of electrical stimulation of the muscles in a frog's leg.

Dr Gilpin, a good doctor, was doing his best to improve Yellowbeard's appearance. The manure-covered outfit had been brushed down but now it was his wild hair and beard which received attention. The Doctor spoke to Dan and Lambourn as he brushed and combed.

'Look, if you go with him you'd be criminals and never be

able to return to England.' Then he added, '. . . on the other hand, if the Government gets the treasure,' he had no love for the Government, 'they'll only waste it on warmongering in Europe.' Britain was at this very time at war with France. 'There you are,' he said, as he gave the pirate a mirror with which to admire his handiwork.

Yellowbeard stared at himself. 'That looks nothing like me.' He stood up and slammed the mirror down.

'That's the whole idea,' said the Doctor. 'A disguise.' But Yellowbeard was more interested in a collection of surgical knives he'd seen.

Lambourn was perusing a shelf of bottles wondering if there was anything like brandy in any of them.

As Dan drew the Doctor aside, he was unaware of the shadowy figure of Pew, lurking outside the window. 'I've got to go with him . . . er . . . my father, to get the treasure,' he explained. 'I've got the map of the island.'

'It'll be dangerous,' said Lambourn as he sniffed at a flask.

'Oh it'll be dangerous,' added Yellowbeard, '. . . do the boy good to get a bit of senseless violence into his life.'

'You will come with us too, Doctor,' coaxed Dan. 'Think of all the new plants and medicines you could discover.'

Lambourn took a slurp from the flask he was holding, quite liked the taste and asked, 'What's this?'

'Stop!' Gilpin made a grab for the flask – too late. 'It's a precious extract from a rare tropical tree. One drop of it paralyses a man instantly . . .'

Lambourn stood dazedly considering himself. They all waited anxiously for him to collapse. He peered curiously at his limbs. 'Perhaps it wears off instantly,' he concluded, as the Doctor corked the flask and put it in his pocket thoughtfully.

'Mmm, well obviously it's ineffective when taken by mouth. Mmm, interesting . . . Now look, if we really were going on a botanical expedition . . .' He stopped abruptly. There was a loud knock on the door. 'Good God, the Navy! They're here. Let's hide.'

'Kill!' suggested Yellowbeard, drawing his cutlass.

'There's no need to,' said Dan, 'you look quite different.'

'We'd better give him a name,' Gilpin sensibly suggested. 'How about Professor . . . er Professor . . .'

'Professor Flask?' offered Lambourn.

'Professor Death?' said Yellowbeard keenly. This did not meet with general approval.

'Professor Table?' was his Lordship's next ill-received offering.

'Professor Rape,' enthused the pirate, enjoying himself.

Lambourn's 'Professor Clock?' and 'Professor Floorboard?' were politely ignored.

'How about Professor Anthrax?' suggested Gilpin. Yellowbeard obviously liked the unpleasant sound of this word and so it was hurriedly agreed and the Doctor opened the door.

It was Betty. She was yelling at the eavesdropping Pew outside. 'Bugger off, you evil git!' She became polite and sweet as she saw the Doctor. 'Oh, evening, Doctor, I was just sayin' good day to Mr Pew.' She walked into the room and looked around. Everyone had assumed nonchalant poses. 'Oh hello, Lord Lambourn – oh and Dan and . . .' she paused as she stared uneasily at Yellowbeard.

'This is Professor Anthrax,' Gilpin introduced the stranger hidden behind a huge open tome.

'That's Yellowbeard,' said Betty.

'I'm in disguise, you stupid tart . . .' grumbled Yellowbeard. The pirate, tiring already of his disguise, went to investigate some vaguely edible-looking exhibits on a table by the window.

'We've got some exciting news . . .' Dan began to tell his mother.

'You're all going after the treasure,' she said.

A chorus of 'no's and shaking heads greeted this remark.

'We're going on an expedition,' explained Lambourn.

'Botanical . . .' enlarged Dr Gilpin.

'Killin' plants,' added Yellowbeard, biting clean through the stem of a specimen shrub.

Betty ignored their elaborations. 'Well I'm entitled to my share, what with all the lying and cheating and tattooing I've done over the years.'

Dan assured his mother she had nothing to worry about, she would get her share.

'I don't ask for much,' said Betty. 'I'd just like to make a few of my little dreams come true.' She became almost wistful. 'Do you know I've always wanted to buy Denmark and be richer than the Queen?'

Dan put his arm round his mother. 'If you do your job covering up for us, Mother, that will all come true.' He joined Dr Gilpin who was consulting a book of tides and prevailing weather conditions.

Lambourn took Betty to one side. 'Why did you tell me he was my son?'

'I didn't,' said Betty. 'You were so sure he was I didn't have the heart to tell you.'

'Oh was I? Hope I didn't tell Lady Lambourn . . . Oh, yes, do tell the wife that I'm . . .' there was a pause, '. . . dead,' he added succinctly.

'Oh yes, don't you worry, lambchop,' Betty grinned.

Yellowbeard, at this point, was just considering trying a quick nibble from some animal foetus he'd found in a jar of liquid when Gilpin closed his book and announced, 'We'll find a ship for Jamaica at Portsmouth. I think we'd better leave at once.'

As they hurriedly finalised their arrangements for departure, Betty returned to the Maimed Fox. She'd spent quite a time tidying the inn after the 'squabble'. Now a heap of dead bodies lay on the cobbles in front of the pub. She found Blind Pew who'd arrived before her, already going through the dead customers' pockets. Just across the street in the nearby churchyard, Moon and Gilbert kept a careful watch posing as grave-diggers as they did so.

Betty grabbed Pew's stick and belaboured him about the head with it shouting, 'Stop that, you thief!' She threw his white stick back at him and he scurried off. Alone at last, she started to go through the pockets herself. She'd just come across a rather nice silver half-hunter watch when she heard a cough from behind her. It was Commander Clement with his lieutenant. 'I'm only taking what's my due, to cover expenses,' she explained. 'You should see the mess they made,' she whined.

Clement stared in disbelief at the pile of bodies. 'What happened?' he demanded.

'Plague,' answered Betty quickly.

Clement and Mansell both took an involuntary step back. 'Plague!' Clement was astonished.

'All of a sudden, like,' moaned Betty. 'Lucky I was out!'

'That man's got a sword in him,' observed Mansell.

'He fell on it,' Betty replied instantly.

The Commander eyed her suspiciously. 'Has Yellow-beard been around here?'

'He's dead too, and Lord Lambourn,' wailed Betty, 'and Dr Gilpin . . . oh and my son Dan . . . all gone . . . Oooohhh . . .' Betty howled in a creditably convincing display of grief. She sobbed her way to the door of the inn.

'Oh hell, sir,' cursed Mansell. 'If they're all dead, what will you tell the Queen, I mean we're supposed to follow Yellowbeard to the treas—' His speech broke off in mid-sentence as he received a crippling blow to the groin from his superior's right knee.

Clement caught sight of a black figure lurking suspiciously behind a cart. 'Halt! In the name of the law!' he shouted.

Pew's head appeared. 'All right, I'm not deaf,' he replied.

'Have you heard anything?' Clement asked their spy.

Pew, who was never a spy for nothing, immediately offered his purse to them. Clement, more than a match for Pew's greed, produced a sovereign on a piece of string. He dropped the coin in and pulled it straight out as Pew, satisfied at the clink, closed his purse.

'Little did Yellowbeard surmise,' started Pew, 'as he presented himself to his prospective travelling companions, that the details of the engagements that would arise shortly to occupy the forthcoming month were being overheard by an elderly blind man of impressive bearing . . .'

The Commander grew impatient. 'Cut the purple prose, Pew, just give us the facts.'

'You Secret Service clods wouldn't recognise superior prose if it bit you in the buttocks . . .'

'Where's Yellowbeard gone?' Clement demanded.

Again Blind Pew purposefully opened his purse. Clement dropped his coin in again and whipped it out.

'Portsmouth,' said Pew.

'With whom?' asked Clement.

'Three people,' replied Pew, opening his purse. Clink went the coin. 'Lambourn,' said Pew. Clink went the coin again. 'Dan,' clink, 'and Gilpin.'

Having the three names, Clement laughed and snatched the purse away and handed it to Mansell in triumph. 'Right, Mansell, we'll be needing that frigate.' He walked off.

Mansell laughed in imitation of his superior and mistakenly handed the purse back to Pew with his final guffaw. He ran off to join Clement leaving Pew shaking his purse, trying to work out what had occurred financially.

Gilbert and Moon, who had heard the whole of this conversation, had long decided that Pew knew too much to remain alive. They were now absolutely certain that he should wait no longer for his demise. Gilbert, hiding behind the cart, leaped out as Pew passed and trumpeted loud blasts through a cow's horn directly into Pew's ear. Pew, who'd been tapping his way along the wall of the inn, became disorientated and did not realise that his stick had tapped his way onto a gravestone, held as though it were a direct continuation of the wall by the burly Mr Moon. Moon, carrying the stone slab, cleverly led Pew to tap his way into an outhouse at the side of the inn. Once inside, Moon and Gilbert barred the door and scurried off to hide behind the church wall. There was an enormous explosion as the outhouse and Mr Pew disintegrated. A handful of gold coins rained around the two pirates.

Portsmouth was fewer than twenty miles from the village of Lambourn but it was a new and different world for Dan. He dawdled behind Lambourn, Dr Gilpin and Yellowbeard through the cobbled streets, marvelling at the sheer size of the place and its maze of busy streets. He found himself staring almost rudely at the fascinating people who filled the bustling thoroughfares. Finely dressed ladies and important-looking gentlemen, overdressed 'dandies', under-dressed tarts, sailors everywhere. On doorsteps and in gutters there were drunks and exceptionally poor beggars to be seen at every turn. Dan marvelled how unafraid even the tiny children seemed in the complexity of this maritime metropolis.

They were walking towards the quayside looking for a boat called the *Lady Edith* on which Lord Lambourn had managed to purchase rights of passage to Jamaica for them. Lambourn blinked and took another sip from his replenished flask as he wondered whether they were being followed by a very pretty, blue-eyed, fair-haired, eight-year-old girl. Perhaps he'd become obsessed with being followed? he thought. He noticed that the girl was dressed very poorly. She carried a basket on her arm and was really sweet and orphanic. He dismissed her as a possible threat and walked on down the street. Staring about them as they walked, Dan saw a group of ladies standing in a shop front which had a sign on it reading:

Travel Agents
Have a good time in:
Barbados
Port au Prince
Jamaica
Martinique
Tobago with whips extra.

Dan walked on.

Unseen by the others, Yellowbeard dashed into this dubious establishment grabbing a 'lady' under each arm. Squeals, giggles and female shouts of alarm announced his entry.

Dan, oblivious to this, had become fascinated by a stall claiming to belong to E. B. Bradshaw, 'purveyor of crutches, wooden legs and hooks to the gentry'.

The sweet little orphanic girl carrying the basket tugged at Dan's coat tails. 'Oh Mister,' she pleaded sweetly, 'give us three farthings for a lump of shit.'

Dan, scarcely able to believe his ears, bent down to her and said, 'I beg your pardon.'

'I said give us three farthings for a lump of shit,' she repeated.

'No,' said Dan, firmly but tolerantly, and the little girl hurled a wet handful straight into his face before running away. Dan's pride was hurt.

'Society's to blame,' observed Dr Gilpin philosophically.

Lord Lambourn, who took a more practical view of society, approached the little girl at the far side of the street. 'Here's three farthings for you, little lady,' he said. He dropped three farthings to the ground behind her. As she bent to pick them up, Lambourn violently kicked her down some steps into a cellar. 'Tell that to society,' he called after her with satisfaction and went back to join the others.

Sounds of a scuffle broke out behind Dan. A panicky man ran past shouting 'press-gang, press-gang', at the top of his voice.

Dan and Gilpin turned to see a violent struggle. Unconscious men were being dragged out of an inn, the Stoned Crow, by some very unsavoury, large men led by a huge ship's bosun. Their victims were being manhandled onto a cart like sacks of potatoes.

'What's a press-gang?' Dan asked the doctor.

'They persuade drunks and vagrants to become sailors.'

'But what happens when they sober up?'

'They're at sea,' smiled Gilpin.

Moon and Gilbert were in Portsmouth too and at this moment standing hidden behind the press-gang's cart. As the huge bosun walked round the cart with a club, deftly thumping at any protruding arms and legs, he suddenly froze, feeling the point of a sharpened hook at his throat. The nimble Gilbert wielded the man's own club and the bosun fell unconscious. Moon swiftly exchanged jacket and hat with him and strode out in front of the cart. The huge, oafish press-gang men were too busy to question the authority of their new bosun.

Lambourn returned to join Dan and Gilpin. 'I'm sure I just saw Commander Clement. He was heading the other way though . . . Where's Yellowbeard, er . . . er . . . Professor Anthrax?' They looked round in alarm, suddenly realising that they had been too preoccupied with the sights of Portsmouth to notice that Yellowbeard was no longer with them.

'He can't be far away.' Dr Gilpin felt confident. 'He'll find us. He needs that map.'

The ubiquitous Gilbert, on overhearing this, scurried back to 'bosun' Moon.

Dan did not share the doctor's optimism. 'I hope he finds us before they find him. It's not long before we sail . . .'

They all looked around for Yellowbeard but it seemed hopeless in that crowded street.

'It's no use,' said Dan, 'he's run out on us, he's the worst father anyone ever had . . .'

'Well he isn't dull,' Lambourn told them in between swigs from his flask, 'he gave me the best day of my life . . .'

'If we have lost him,' said Dan, 'we know that it's an island close to Jamaica and we've got the map of it but, without him to tell us which island, we might as well go home.' Dan tried to hide his disappointment.

Bosun Moon's loud voice boomed out above the hubbub of the street as he slowly ambled towards them, enjoying his new role. 'Now I'm sure some of you gentlemen,' he beamed, sounding reassuringly polite, 'would like to volunteer for a well-paid, well-fed adventure holiday such as youths dream of, upon a modern, rat-free, leak-proof ship. Any volunteers lie down on the ground with your eyes shut . . .'

The naval psychopaths hardly let this sink in before laying about innocent standers-by and drunks with their clubs and loading them onto the cart.

Our three heroes looked on at this, thankful that they were not drunks or vagrants.

'. . . ample opportunities to kill foreigners, limp-wristed perverts and Hottentots,' continued Moon, 'free training for a new career.' He took a step towards Lambourn and asked politely, 'Excuse me, sir, would you gentlemen be looking for a ship?'

'Well,' began Lambourn, 'we do have tickets as a matter of fact, for . . .'

All three of them were swiftly clubbed from behind.

Unconscious, their bodies were loaded onto the cart by the psychopaths. That same moment a couple of devastated ladies of the night stumbled out of the Travel Agent's Establishment, exhausted and clutching remnants of clothing. They were followed closely by Yellowbeard who grabbed another wench and was about to carry her screaming inside when he saw Gilbert across the street, frisking Dan's unconscious form. He dropped the wench unceremoniously into a horse trough and ran off to follow the cart. It trundled off with its cargo of 'recruits' towards the quayside.

The *Lady Edith*, a one-hundred-and-twenty-foot armed merchant man, was being loaded with cargo and provisions for her voyage to Jamaica. The three-masted, square-rigged vessel had some twenty rather old cannons to protect her from marauding pirates. She was not a fighting ship, the weapons were intended more as a deterrent. The main function of this once proud vessel was now to ferry cargoes of luxury goods and highly valued farming 'equipment', the latter an euphemism for manacles and chains used by the colonists. It was late evening and already dark but the quayside was still bursting with activity as the ship was loaded ready for sail. Crowds of opportunist vendors cluttered the wharf selling liquor, chewing tobacco and snuff, medicaments for maritime ailments, patent seasickness and scurvy remedies, tin whistles, squeeze boxes and similar bric-a-brac.

The Master of the *Edith*, Captain Hughes, a tall, imposing figure, stood behind an ill-attended signing-on table near a gangplank at the stern of the ship. A rather stupid-looking volunteer, Mr Askey, concluded naïvely that life at sea could not be worse than his life on land and walked up and made his mark in Captain Hughes' book. The Captain gave Askey a shilling and he climbed thankfully aboard, not realising the grim significance of the two burly sailors who immediately blocked the gangplank behind him.

At the forward gangplank more provisions were being loaded and it was here that the press-gang's cart halted. Bosun Moon began supervising the loading of press-gangees – our three unconscious heroes among them – as if they were cargo. Captain Hughes peered curiously at the bosun and remarked to his first officer, Lieutenant Martin, 'I didn't notice that hook when the bosun signed on . . .'

The officer was about to agree when Gilbert, who hovered ever watchful nearby, interjected, 'He's right-handed, sir.' The Captain seemed to accept this explanation.

From the shadows of the quayside buildings, Yellowbeard saw Dan being carried aboard. He also saw seven or eight pigs about to be hoisted up on deck in a huge rope net. He dashed out and slipped unseen into the enveloping net just as it left the ground. The net was lowered into a pig pen fixed near the prow of the ship. He quickly made himself comfortable in the straw with the pigs and settled down for a pleasant sleep.

Captain Hughes watched as another of his officers, Mr Crisp, stepped onto the gangplank, followed by a cabin boy carrying his box of belongings. He noted that the cabin boy had a rather ample pair of breasts.

'Mr Crisp,' he barked.

'Yes, sir!' replied Crisp, saluting smartly.

'What is that Mr Crisp?'

'My box, sir.'

'No, no,' said Hughes drily, '. . . carrying your box . . .'

'Oh, er . . .' Mr Crisp tried to look innocent. 'Er . . . cabin boy Smith, sir.'

The Captain glanced at him. 'Smith's got tits.'

'Er, well,' stammered Crisp, 'he's been a bit ill, sir.'

'Get her off, Crisp,' said Hughes with quiet menace. He'd seen it all before.

'Yes, sir,' he agreed immediately and swiftly taking his

box from 'Smith' walked smartly up on deck as she reluctantly turned to go.

'The ancient superstition,' Captain Hughes announced authoritatively, 'that a woman brings bad luck is nowadays a proven scientific fact . . . Just a minute!' He saw two sailors, accompanied by Gilbert, carrying a large stuffed crocodile towards the gangplank. 'What is that?'

'It's a croc-o-dile, sir,' explained Gilbert.

'What's it for?'

'Each sailor is by tradition allowed a pet, sir.'

'One pet per sailor,' recited Hughes, 'parrots preferred.'

'Oh well . . . er . . . we like clubbed together, if you get my drift, sir.'

'That's bigger than three parrots.'

'Not if they're in cages,' Gilbert patiently pointed out.

'Open it up,' Hughes ordered.

'Open it up, sir?' Gilbert blinked.

'Yes,' said the Captain, 'it's got buttons down the side.'

'So it has . . .' Gilbert feigned astonishment but reluctantly the sailors lowered the crocodile and undid the buttons. An attractive wench stepped out.

'Good try, Doris,' one of the sailors called out as she walked down the gangplank.

Reaching the quayside she passed a sailor about to carry an enormous woolly sheep on board. She stopped and tapped the confused animal on the head as she said, as though to someone inside it, 'I shouldn't bother, love, they're fairly strict on this one.' The sheep bleated as a mystified sailor carried it aboard.

Shortly before midnight at high tide the *Lady Edith* set sail.

CHAPTER 6

Lambourn woke bleary-eyed. This was not unusual for him. Before making the effort to focus on anything he automatically reached for his hip flask. It had gone and his waistcoat was wet, in fact he was wet and cold. There was a loud and constant creaking sound and water dripped and sloshed all around him. He sat up and cracked his head on a beam just above him. He'd just started to try and piece together, as he did almost every morning, the events leading up to his falling unconscious the night before when, in the dim flickering orange light of a single swinging lantern, he saw a rat swim past his shackled feet. He looked around the bilges of the *Edith* and saw rows of forlorn, shackled men also aware of their predicament. Dan and Gilpin sat close by and stared blankly back at him. He looked at his shackles and shifted uneasily.

'You know, I've just been thinking. If this cabin cost us three hundred guineas, thank God we didn't fall for one of the cheaper ones.'

A particularly gloomy-looking man chained by both hands and feet to a roof beam spoke with a strange Scandinavian accent. 'It's all right for you English with your well-known laughing-in-adversity type behaviour. We Finns prefer to face the stark reality of the wretchedness of life. Why turn it into happiness? What we have here is high quality misery . . .'

This did little to cheer anyone up but Gilpin had already

made friends with a rat and had removed his wig to make a nest for it.

Suddenly a hatch opened and Mr Crisp's harsh voice sent a shiver of fear through them. 'Right, gentlemen, I'm afraid I shall have to interrupt your morning bath. On your knees and crawl up here on the double . . .'

Wet and shivering with cold they shuffled along and climbed the stairs as best they could on their knees and then on up to the orlop deck.

'When you've successfully survived your training as able-bodied seamen, you'll be permitted to crouch freely on this deck. Wait here.' He ran up a companionway onto the main deck and disappeared. The orlop deck was comparatively dry and our three friends looked around them.

Two men were working frantically at a pump; one, amiable and paunchy, called Tarbuck and the other a weasel of a man called Gilbert. Lambourn spoke to Tarbuck. 'What did you do to deserve this?'

'We were the first to stow our hammocks,' he explained over his shoulder.

'Is that wrong?' asked Dan.

Tarbuck became indignant. 'No! Pumping is an honour, all the rest got sent up the rigging . . .'

There was a scream of horror terminating in a heavy thud from above them. 'Was Mike in the rigging? Sounded like Mike,' Tarbuck observed, routinely.

Gilbert considered this for a moment, then agreed, 'Yes, it did.'

Dan signalled to the others to close up to him. 'Listen, things aren't as bad as they seem. All right, we've been press-ganged but that means that nobody knows where we are.'

'Including ourselves,' Lambourn pointed out.

'We do,' Dan assured them, 'this ship *is* going to Jamaica, that's a start and we've got the map, even though we've lost Yellowbeard . . .'

Gilbert had stopped pumping and was now casually eavesdropping and eyeing Dr Gilpin's bag suspiciously.

'I shall go discreetly to the Captain,' Lambourn said somewhat pompously, 'and tell him who I am and demand a cabin . . .'

'No, no,' cautioned the Doctor, 'we're safer if no one knows who we are. All we have to do is keep out of trouble until we reach Jamaica . . .' He felt his bag tug on his shoulder and looked down to see Gilbert's arm disappearing into it. 'Can I help you?'

'Oh sorry,' Gilbert effused, 'my arm must have somehow dropped into your bag . . . I do apologise . . .'

Crisp returned and yelled down from the top of the companionway at the conspirators. 'Right! I shall be keeping a very close watch on you there. Up here on the double!'

They hurriedly clanked their way up to the main deck.

The ship was in full sail and there was no land in sight. The press-gangees were unshackled and herded into a line on deck by the sailors. The whole ship's company was assembled on deck. A chaplain was finishing a prayer over a corpse. The body was under a flag on a plank which jutted over the side of the ship. Mr Moon stood by the mizzen mast at attention and shouted, 'All hands present on deck, Mr Crisp, sir!'

'Thank you, Bosun,' said Crisp, and marched off to stand beside Mr Martin and another officer. This happened to be an absolutely ravishing blonde, in an officer's uniform, with huge tits, pouting lips, a retroussé nose and an obviously drawn-on black moustache. Mr Crisp nodded to a nearby sailor who put a bosun's whistle to his lips and blew a salute. All the enlisted men and officers came smartly to attention. The press-gangees raggedly followed suit.

Captain Hughes, looking impressive in his gold-braided blue and red uniform and plumed hat, walked imperiously onto the deck and mounted a raised podium from which he stared down on his crew. 'My name is Captain Hughes. These are my officers. This is Lieutenant Martin,' he indicated Martin, 'who is responsible for discipline. And this is Lieutenant Crisp who is responsible for discipline,' he gestured again, 'and this is Mr Prostitute who is responsible for . . .'

There was a snigger from Mr Tarbuck who could contain his amusement no longer.

'. . . nail that man's foot to the deck,' said Captain Hughes with quiet authority and continued his speech unperturbed, '. . . discipline.'

No one dared move as Mr Crisp saw to it that the order was carried out. As soon as the sound of nailing and screaming ceased, the Captain continued. 'Now in fairness to you all, I'm honour bound to ask the question, is there anyone here who does not wish to be a member of Her Majesty's Navy?'

Every man on deck stood silent in fear but for Mr Askey who stepped smartly forward. 'Me, sir,' he said honestly.

A shot rang out and Askey fell to the deck clutching his chest as Captain Hughes handed a still-smoking firing-piece to Mr Martin. 'Chaplain!' shouted Hughes, and the Chaplain rushed forward with two sailors who carried Askey to the plank hastily and placed a flag over him.

The Chaplain was well-practised and swift. 'Oh Lord, we hereby commit the body of our dear departed,' at which the body was tipped into the sea, 'into the sea, Amen.'

Captain Hughes resumed his address to the ship's company fingering another flintlock.

'Is there anyone else unwilling to serve?' There was no reply. 'Right. At first some of you may find the discipline on this ship slightly on the harsh side of strict. But I would remind you that it is our solemn duty to seek out and destroy Her Majesty's enemies, the foul and most foreign French. While sooner or later the entire world is bound to be of this opinion, in the meantime it is our most urgent task to push things on a little . . . Carry on, Mr Crisp . . . Mr Prostitute, Mr Martin, luncheon duty!' And with that he retired to the Captain's cabin.

Lord Lambourn yelped involuntarily as he was lashed behind the knees with a length of knotted rope carried by Mr Crisp. He fell to the deck and was set to work along with the others scrubbing the deck with sanding-stones and water. The fearsome Mr Crisp warned the press-gangees: 'If you haven't finished by the time I get back you'll get more of this.' To emphasise his point he whacked the deck with his knotted rope. They began scrubbing, furiously.

After a night of extreme discomfort, they were again ordered to scrub the decks. Dan was completing the section of deck which had poor Mr Tarbuck nailed to it. Accommodatingly, Tarbuck raised his unnailed foot for Dan to scrub beneath it.

Mr Prostitute was taking a stroll around the deck. Under other circumstances Mr Prostitute's presence would have evoked leers and catcalls from members of the crew but they were too fearful of their Captain. As Mr Prostitute walked past the pig pen, Yellowbeard's hand reached out, grabbed her and pulled her in amongst the pigs whose snorts and squeals muffled her screams.

A press-gangee, a few yards away from Dan, yelled out in pain as Mr Crisp lashed him with his rope for poor scrubbing. Dan was worried about Lord Lambourn as the poor man, bereft of brandy, sat in a daze having completed less than a square foot of deck. Quickly Dan swapped places with him and scrubbed frantically. Unfortunately Mr Crisp came his way and, assuming that he had completed very little compared with Lambourn, put his foot down on one of Dan's outstretched hands and ground it into the deck. Dan had to summon up all his strength not to cry out in pain.

The somewhat dazed and very dishevelled Mr Prostitute

hauled herself out of the pig pen. There was the hint of a smile about her lips. She spruced herself up as best she could and continued her walk on deck as though nothing had happened.

The following days of the voyage were some of the worst in Dan's memory. Working under extremely harsh conditions they suffered the utmost deprivation. Captain Hughes had even halved their rations in order to conserve provisions for the latter part of their journey. Meanwhile he himself lived in great style.

Less than a day behind the *Lady Edith* and on the same course was the Royal Navy's newest and fastest frigate, HMS *Pompey*. Commander Clement was proud of his new ship but paced its poop-deck uneasily. Their course had been set based on too little information for his liking. He desperately needed to know exactly the whereabouts of the island. A sprightly Lieutenant Mansell, enjoying only his second sea voyage, saluted him smartly.

'I think the prisoner may be ready to talk, sir.'

'Good. Hoist her up, Mansell.'

Mansell signalled and promptly sailors began to push the capstan round. Hoisted up from the cold, forbidding sea on a pulley from the mizzen-tops, a very miserable and bedraggled Betty appeared dripping wet over the starboard gunwhale.

'Are you ready to talk yet, Mrs Beard?' asked Clement, impatiently.

'No,' said Betty, stubbornly.

'Lower her away, Mansell.' Mrs Beard returned to the sea.

Many leagues away, Captain Hughes strode onto the deck of the *Edith*. 'Mr Martin,' he called out behind him, 'I'm taking Mr Prostitute on an inspection of the ship, him being new to it or should I have said "he" being new to it?'

'I don't think it matters these days, sir,' was Mr Martin's considered reply.

While acknowledging a salute from the fiercely efficient Mr Crisp, he noticed an exhausted sailor leaning against the gunwhale attempting to stifle a yawn. 'That man over there yawned!' barked Hughes. 'Give him a swimming lesson!'

A burly bosun's mate grabbed the man and threw him screaming bodily into the sea before quietly resuming his duties.

Captain Hughes and Mr Prostitute passed the Finn and another poor sailor who were stripped to the waist and lashed either side of the main mast. Mr Crisp whipped each of their already raw backs in turn with a knotted rope's end.

The Finn was taking his punishment philosophically as the man beside him screamed in agony. 'Oh you English,' the Finn deprecated, 'you always complain. Where I come from we are stripped nude, beaten with logs and thrown into the snow for fun.'

Dan, Lambourn and Gilpin were beginning to wonder whether they would survive the journey to Jamaica. A fierce hatred of the cruel Captain Hughes began to well up inside Dan, but Dr Gilpin wisely counselled patience. To make any move or even a complaint against the Captain would be certain death.

That night was the most uncomfortable yet as the ship weathered a ferocious storm. Our unhappy trio, cold and sick from the constant buffeting, squatted miserably below on the orlop deck which was itself frequently awash. The pumps had to be manned all night. Lashed by the driving rain and biting wind, Mr Tarbuck, still nailed to the spot, was left to face the storm alone. The most comfortable aboard was Yellowbeard. Well-sheltered in the pig pen, he lay fast asleep curled up warmly with the pigs . . .

The next day the storm had passed and the skies were a cloudless blue. In his cabin aboard the *Pompey*, Commander

Clement was dictating a report to Lieutenant Mansell. 'And so, Your Majesty, I am very pleased to report, that after several brave and expensive battles . . .' Mansell looked up from his dictation registering disapproval then immediately thought better of it and returned to his task, '. . . the pirate Yellowbeard is now well and truly in our grasp.'

'*Is* that strictly accurate, sir?'

'Mansell, that is what we in the Royal Navy call a lie. Now get that off right away.' He sat down at his table to begin a well-earned lunch.

'Ah . . . a lie. But that's treason, sir!'

Clement did not wish to know this. 'Shut up. Deliver it to the Queen at once.'

Mansell hurriedly left the cabin, only to re-enter immediately, nervously fingering the missive . . . 'Er, *how*, sir?'

'Pigeon, Mansell.' Clement lifted the cover of the silver dish in front of him. Mansell paused, fidgeted guiltily and, looking ill at ease, pointed hesitantly at the Commander's plate. Clement looked down. There on his plate was a beautifully garnished pigeon. Clement buried his head in his hands and moaned. 'Just send it, Mansell.'

No sooner had Mansell left than there was a loud knocking on the cabin door. 'Come in!' yelled Clement impatiently, expecting Mansell yet again, but in came Henson, a handsome young sailor, with Betty Beard. They were both soaking wet, with traces of seaweed about their hair and clothing. Betty looked miserable.

'I think she might be ready to talk now, sir,' Henson told his Captain.

'Yes,' said the unhappy Betty, 'being underwater must have reminded me. I do seem to recall something about an island . . .'

'Good work, Henson.' Clement was pleased.

'Thank you, sir.' Henson smiled. As he turned to leave, a

large black shark's fin sewn onto the back of his shirt became visible. Betty did not see this but Clement winked his appreciation. 'Oh,' said Henson, about to close the door, 'shall I see you in the pump room later, sir?'

The Commander quickly gesticulated for discretion. Henson left, closing the door behind him.

'Now then, Mrs Beard, do sit down and tell me everything you know about this island.'

On the *Edith*, Dan had decided that Captain Hughes' cruelty had gone far enough. As he walked along the deck looking for Mr Crisp for permission to speak to the Captain, he passed sailors who were scrubbing the deck clean of blood from some further act of barbarism by their Captain. He nodded politely to Mr Tarbuck, who stood looking bored, idly tapping his unnailed foot. As he approached the stern he passed the Chaplain who was finishing yet another last-rites ceremony. 'Where can I find Mr Crisp?' he asked.

The Chaplain pointed further to the stern and Dan found Mr Crisp beside the mizzen mast, placing a couple of live lobsters into a sack which contained a man struggling helplessly inside. The man, though fast tiring, was complaining vigorously.

'Yes?' Crisp asked Dan, expectantly.

Dan did his best to control his temper. 'Do you know that you have three paying passengers on board this ship who are being treated as abominably as the rest of the crew?'

'Oh,' said Mr Crisp while knocking out the man in the sack with a belaying pin, '. . . really?' he added in mock surprise.

Dan pressed on. 'I think once the Captain realises who we are, we'll get an easier passage.'

Suddenly Crisp thrust out his hand and gave Dan a tremendous shove which threw him to the floor. Mr Moon and Gilbert were observing all this with satisfaction from their vantage point behind some cargo. Content that their plan was working, they went below.

Dan's progress along the deck had also been watched keenly by Yellowbeard who had clambered his way along the outside of the ship. He did not want to lose his map. Dan, in a daze, raised himself up on one elbow and quickly resolved what he should do. Noticing a heavy wooden bucket left over from deck-scrubbing, he said, calmly but coldly as he stood up, 'I can see there's only one thing you'll understand.'

'Oh yes,' leered Crisp, 'and what pray . . .'

Quickly Dan grabbed the bucket from the deck and smashed Crisp hard in the face with it, but the huge Crisp continued his speech unaffected, '. . . might that be?'

Mr Crisp swung back his right arm and then let fly, hitting Dan a terrible blow. He was sent sprawling yards away. Mr Crisp cracked his knuckles and strode towards the unconscious Dan saying, 'Right, let's finish it.' Suddenly he was wrenched into an upright position by a furious Yellowbeard. Before he could react, Yellowbeard's forehead smashed into his face. Yellowbeard gripped the tottering Crisp's nose like a vice and dragged him to the stern.

Below decks Mr Moon, hearing no reply to his knock, rushed into the Captain's cabin. He was astonished to see Captain Hughes sitting up in bed with the scantily clad Mr Prostitute. She was lazily puffing on a cigar with one leg draped over the Captain's shoulder.

'Oh I'm sorry, sir,' mumbled Moon, embarrassed.

'What for?' said Hughes, turning.

'. . . er, interrupting you . . .'

'Oh? I was only smoking a cigar,' explained the Captain calmly.

'Oh, quite so, sir . . . I just came to tell you that the son of Yellowbeard the pirate is on this ship.'

Captain Hughes leaped up throwing Mr Prostitute to the floor in a flurry of bedding and pillows. 'The son of Yellowbeard!' he cried in amazement. There was a crashing sound from the deck above them and they caught sight of a dangling Mr Crisp, outside the cabin window, momentarily suspended by the nose. 'What is that?' said Hughes.

There was a scream and a splash as a hand gripping Crisp's nose released its hold. 'That was Mr Crisp,' explained Mr Moon.

Up on deck, Dan recovered consciousness. Mr Crisp was nowhere to be seen. Suddenly the bosun's whistle sounded and a sailor drummed 'action-stations'. Men rushed to their strategic positions, side arms were issued, swivel guns were positioned and Dan was grabbed firmly by two enormous seamen who bound him and carried him off bodily to stand beside the confused and similarly tied Gilpin and Lambourn.

Mr Moon, amazed to see Dan unscathed after his encounter with Mr Crisp, stood to attention as Captain Hughes, with a thunderous expression, mounted his podium. 'Officers and men of the *Edith*,' he pointed at the well-trussed trio, 'these three people posing as pressees, are stowaways. The perspicacity of Mr Moon has led to a discovery of a conspiracy against the Crown.' The excited crew gasped and Hughes continued. 'There is no doubt in my mind that the one in the middle is the son of the evil *Yellowbeard* who has just now despatched dear Mr Crisp to the deep, his purpose clearly being to take over the ship. We must deliver these traitors to the authorities. Set course for Portsmouth, Mr Moon, you know what to do.'

Mr Moon nodded in agreement and then signalled to Gilbert. He and four of the largest men on board closely surrounded the Captain. 'Mutiny!' hissed Hughes. Gilbert grinned and nodded. Hughes became apoplectic with rage but he was quickly gagged and bound and hauled upside down to the to' gallant of the main mast.

'Oh dear,' yelled out Mr Moon, 'the Captain would appear to be out of sorts.' This was greeted by a gleeful chorus of mock concern. Moon told his men to untie Dan and the others. 'Right,' said Moon, 'so who do you want for your new Captain?'

The excited crew all shouted at once in their enthusiasm.

'Me!' suggested one sailor who was promptly hit.

'Mr Prostitute,' shouted another, causing a raucous cheer.

Gilbert busily weaved in and out of the crowd and shouted 'him!' pointing at Dan then, from a different position, calling 'Dan for Captain!' and then wearing a different hat shouting, 'We want Dan!' The excited sailors soon found themselves with one voice calling for Dan to be their Captain.

'It's unanimous then, the ship's yours, Captain.' Pausing, Moon looked at Dan, 'To take where you will.'

Lambourn and Gilpin were delighted. Dan was not so sure but as Moon and Gilbert lifted him up on their shoulders and the men cheered, he began to realise that it would be very much to their advantage. A barrel of rum was brought out, the skull and crossbones flag of piracy fluttered from the main mast and men cheered and shouted as Tarbuck was unnailed from the deck.

As they walked off towards the Captain's cabin, Moon asked Dan, 'I hope you didn't mind us tying up Captain Hughes like that, sir?'

'No, not at all,' agreed the new Captain.

'I was only following your lead,' explained Mr Moon, 'you killin' Mr Crisp was an example to us all . . .'

'I only hit him with a bucket and then everything went black . . .'

'It's like that, killin',' said Moon, philosophically.

Dan's first act as Captain was to order a long-boat with supplies to be made ready for Captain Hughes and his officers. Lord Lambourn's first act with Dan as Captain was to help himself to a new flask of brandy from the Captain's private store . . .

The whole crew lined up on deck to watch the long-boat depart. Captain Hughes, Mr Martin and Mr Prostitute sat patiently in the boat thankful to Dan for having spared their lives.

'Couldn't Mr Prostitute stay?' suggested Lambourn. 'I'm sure we wouldn't have any trouble from him.'

'I don't know,' said Gilpin looking at the crew ogling her, 'there's something about that lad . . .'

Mr Gilbert, having finished preparing the long-boat, nodded to Mr Moon as he swung back on board. 'The long-boat's ready to put away, sir!' Moon shouted.

Dan called down to them, 'No hard feelings, Captain Hughes?'

'I'll take note of your consideration,' replied the ever-confident Hughes.

'Now, Bosun,' shouted Dan loudly enough for Hughes to overhear, 'set course for Madagascar.'

'Eh?' queried Moon. Dan winked at him knowingly.

'Oh yes . . . you heard what the Captain said! So it's Madagascar!'

'I gave them the lamp, sir,' said Gilbert quietly to Moon, and winked conspiratorially. Dan was quietly impressed at the new spirit of kindliness on his ship.

Later that evening as night was falling the long-boat was alone in an empty sea.

'Pass that big lamp, Mr Prostitute,' said Captain Hughes.

'Aye, aye, sir!'

'Get a flint ready, Mr Martin.'

'Yes, sir,' replied Mr Martin.

The sound of a flint being struck was followed by an enormous explosion.

CHAPTER 7

The *Edith* sailed on, serene through the cool night air. The days began to get hotter as they reached more southerly latitudes. The helmsman checked the lie of the wheel and lashed it in position. He stepped up to the hourglass at the foot of the mizzen mast. As the last few grains of sand ran through, he upended it and tapped it once to check that the sand was flowing freely. He then stood cupping his hands to his mouth and, in a cadence comforting and familiar to the rest of the crew, called, 'Aa . . . ll's we . . . ll.' He returned to his position at the wheel. There was nothing to be heard save the creaking of the ship's timbers and the straining of the sheets as the light breeze gently filled her sails.

Yellowbeard, since the change in captaincy, no longer received such exotic leftovers from the Captain's table. Determined to keep his presence on board a secret, he indulged in a little night-time fishing from the cradling beneath the bowsprit. He pulled in his line and tucked it temporarily inside his shirt. He had more important work to do. With his experience of stellar navigation and estimates of their travel-time, and speed, he calculated that now was the moment to adjust their course by a few degrees to take them more directly due southeast of Jamaica to the island. Nimbly he climbed up onto the gunwhale and, barefoot, silently ran along its length to the stern of the ship. He dropped off the outboard side of the gunwhale to a stance by the scuppers. He looked up, checking that he had not been seen by the helmsman, reached down to the deck over the gunwhale and grabbed a wooden bucket. He filled it from the dark waters swirling past beneath him.

The helmsman checked his course with a compass and, satisfied that it needed no correction, stood idly behind the wheel resting his hands on the spokes, dreaming of exotic lands they would discover. He was cruelly woken from this reverie suddenly drenched by a bucketful of cold sea-water. A sound from the direction of the port-side scuppers told him that was the location of the prankster. Angrily he tied off the wheel and ran over to investigate. Yellowbeard stood, a rope from the mizzen-tops in his hand, on the starboard gunwhale. The helmsman bent over the port-side looking for the cause of his discomfort. Yellowbeard leaped and swung across the breadth of the ship catching the helmsman full in the back with both feet, sending him headlong into the sea. 'Aaaaaaa . . . !!!' he screamed. Some of the crew below decks sat up in alarm but Yellowbeard finished off the helmsman's cry as he yelled, 'Aaa . . . ll's we . . . ell . . .' with appropriate cadence. The startled crew settled down again, content. Yellowbeard scurried to the wheel, unlashed it and, checking his course with both compass and stars, stayed at the wheel until he was sure that it was properly maintained. Then he relashed the wheel, stole the helmsman's bread and cheese and returned happily to his fishing.

Early the next morning, Dr Gilpin stood on the deck near the wheel-housing lining up his sextant with the sun. The new Captain stood nearby making notes in the ship's log. Mr Moon and Gilbert were also on deck, making their observations, Gilbert using a rather old-fashioned navigational cross-staff.

'We went ten degrees east off-course overnight. Did you notice that, Mr Moon?' called the Doctor suspiciously.

'Indeed I did, sir,' replied Moon, equally suspicious and asked quietly of Gilbert at his side, 'Our Captain didn't bump the helmsman off last night, did he?'

'No,' confirmed Gilbert, 'didn't leave his cabin.' They both looked knowingly towards the Captain.

Drawing Dan to one side Gilpin asked him discreetly, 'Did you order a change of course?'

'No,' said Dan.

'Well,' continued Gilpin under his breath, 'I think someone,' he nodded in Moon's direction, 'knows where the island is.'

Mr Moon whispered an aside to Gilbert, 'See, they're leading us to it,' and then shouted aloud to Dan, 'Shall I maintain this course, Captain?'

'Well,' called Dan, winking at Gilpin, 'it's a pretty good course, isn't it?'

'Aye, aye, sir,' agreed Moon with enthusiasm.

Both groups were very pleased with themselves.

On board HMS *Pompey*, Betty Beard was seated at Commander Clement's desk in his cabin. Spread out in front of her were dozens of drawings of island outlines. Clement had assembled sketches of every known island in the Caribbean. Betty had found nothing to her liking. The nearest she had got was a compromise using pieces of no fewer than three other islands as a composite. Clement stood over her as she moaned, 'No, it still doesn't look right.'

The Commander was exasperated. 'I don't think you're being as helpful as you promised. Would you like some more "shark" treatment?'

'I'm doin' my best,' complained the harassed Betty.

There was a knock and Mansell came down the companionway from the deck above.

'Nothing in sight sir, absolutely nothing at all. Nothing,

sir. Nothing . . . talk about clear horizons . . . this is it. We've been weeks without sighting anything, let alone the *Edith* . . .'

'Sail ahoy!' came the urgent cry from a look-out. Clement and Mansell dashed up the companionway and onto the deck.

Mansell arrived first and began to scour the horizon ahead of him through his telescope. 'There you are, sir, nothing again. Nothing whatsoever . . .'

Clement, without his telescope, spotting something on the horizon behind them, called over his shoulder, 'Behind you, Mansell.'

'Ah, so you are, sir,' said Mansell without turning.

'A *ship* is behind you.' Clement's patience was being stretched to the limit. Then Mansell spun round, hitting him a terrible crack on the back of the head and knocked him sprawling.

Mansell, excited at his sighting, was unaware of this and said, 'Good Lord, sir, it's the *Edith*!' He looked round. He couldn't see Clement anywhere. As he lowered his telescope it crashed straight onto the head of the furious Clement.

'It's the *Edith* all right,' said Clement angrily, between clenched teeth.

'If we're supposed to be following it, sir . . . and it's behind us . . . er . . . how can we be?'

Clement's patience finally snapped and he gave Mansell an enormous shove. He fell to the deck, bewildered, as Clement sprang into action. 'Strike the colours, Mr Beamish,' he shouted. 'Hoist the French flag and hard about!'

'Aye, aye, sir!' the officer of the watch replied.

On the deck of the *Edith*, Dan questioned Mr Moon, 'What sort of ship is it?'

314

'Some kind of frigate,' Moon answered, peering through his telescope.

'We wouldn't have come across it if we'd kept our course,' observed Dan.

'No, no, we wouldn't,' said Moon. They both eyed each other suspiciously.

'It's not flying a flag,' Dan observed.

'Perhaps we'd better take ours down,' said Gilpin, 'they've got twice as many guns, we don't want to appear too aggressive.'

'Wait a minute,' shouted Moon, 'there is a flag! They're French, and they're rounding on us!'

Dan acted as dramatically as he imagined his father would. 'Ready the port guns for action, Mr Moon, and as soon as they're in range – fire!'

On the *Pompey*, Clement explained things to his aide. 'They mustn't know we're after them, Mansell. If we can convince them that we're French we can avoid them and then perhaps we can return to following them discreetly.'

There was an enormous explosion and a cannon-ball from the *Edith* smashed into the deck of the *Pompey*, splintering the woodwork near them. Injured sailors were helped and carried below.

'Are you all right, Mansell?' asked Clement, cutting himself free from a tangle of fallen ropes.

'Yes, thank you, sir,' called Mansell cheerily as he stepped unscathed from under a pile of debris.

The Commander grunted in disappointment. 'What do the fools think they're doing? We out-gun them, we've got more men and we're faster.'

'I think it's that French flag of yours, sir,' Mansell pointed out.

Clement sighed wearily, then shouted at his gunners, 'To

avoid suspicion, we will appear to retaliate by firing at them a bit and missing them a lot.'

'That's a *much* better idea, sir,' said the eager Mansell.

On the *Edith*, everyone dived for cover as the frigate fired. The first salvo fell short, into the sea. The second whistled over their heads. The main deck of the *Edith* bustled with activity as, amidst acrid smoke and explosive recoils, they returned fire. Yellowbeard, dissatisfied with the speed and accuracy of their aggression, leaped from his hiding place in one of the long-boats down to a gun whose crew were ready to fire. With enormous strength he knocked the two gunners aside, altered the firing angle of the piece and, expertly checking its trajectory, grabbed a gunner's fuse and fired.

The ball hurtled straight to its mark. It thudded deep into the wood of the frigate's mizzen mast. Slowly at first, the top half of the mast bent, there was a cracking sound as the wood splintered, then it plummeted to the deck. Clement and Mansell were completely enveloped by the descending sail . . .

On the *Edith*, the other gunners turned to congratulate the mystery marksman but he was nowhere to be seen. A great cheer rose up from the men on the *Edith* as the smoke cleared and they saw what havoc their gunnery had caused.

Aboard the *Pompey*, Clement with his drawn sword cut his way to daylight through the sail.

'Jettison some ballast, Mr Beamish. We must sail as light as we can without our mizzen mast.'

Mansell joined him. 'Gunnery like that makes you proud to be English, doesn't it, sir?'

'Shit!' thought Clement.

The crew of the *Edith* stood cheering on deck watching Clement's distressed frigate disappear in the distance.

Moon's hook rested heavily on Dan's shoulder. 'Well done, lad, this calls for a celebration.'

'Well done, *Captain*,' corrected Lord Lambourn.

'Oh yes . . .' Moon shrugged. 'No disrespect intended, your Lordship.'

Soon the frigate was below the horizon behind them and the *Edith* cleared its way unhindered through the deep blue of the tropical ocean. Lambourn stood savouring a mouthful of brandy in the Captain's cabin. Gilpin sat writing up his journal at the desk, while Dan practised his swordsmanship with one of Captain Hughes' finer swords.

'Straight back, that's it, head up, son . . . er . . . Captain,' Lambourn instructed Dan. As he reached down into the drinks chest to refill his glass he thought he saw Yellowbeard's face at the cabin window. He rubbed his eyes, took another swig and the apparition had thankfully disappeared. 'I was just thinking,' he confided to his old friend.

'Yes?' replied Gilpin.

'Can brandy make you see things?'

'If you drink enough of it, yes.'

'Ah, that's what it was then, that island that I thought was over there.' He pointed lazily at the window. Dan and Gilpin rushed over.

'It *is* an island!' shouted Dan and they all scrambled to get on deck.

Yellowbeard had long since seen the island and now threw himself from his perch beneath the bowsprit and swam off vigorously towards land.

As Dan, Gilpin and Lambourn erupted onto the deck, a general shout of 'land ho' broke out amongst the excited crew as they rushed to get a better view of their landfall.

Dan stood at the prow and addressed the crew as the shore party prepared to leave.

'Now, men, a group of us are going to put ashore here, for provisions . . .' Moon exchanged a knowing glance with Gilbert who was secretly stowing shovels aboard a long-boat.

317

'Provisions . . . oh yes, of course, sir,' murmured Moon, sarcastically. He knew, even if most of Dan's crew didn't, the real purpose of their voyage to this island.

'It could be a mirage,' said Lambourn thoughtfully, staring at the island. 'I think I saw one once . . . looks rather like what I saw – if I saw it.'

Dan discreetly questioned the Doctor. 'Is it anything like the map on my head?'

Gilpin could tell already from the island's topography that it coincided exactly. 'This *is* the island,' he reassured Dan and as the long-boats were being lowered confided in his friend, Lambourn, 'You know it's amazing, with the progress of modern science to think that we can now travel from England to Jamaica in less than three and a half months and we still can't find a cure for the common cold . . .'

Less than an hour later they were all standing on the shore on the fine soft warm sand of an idyllic tropical beach. The less experienced sailors amongst them were amazed to find that the beach and the thick lush deep green jungle-covered hills of the island above it swayed gently, just as the boat had, beneath their feet.

Dr Gilpin explained this temporary phenomenon.

'Well,' announced Captain Dan, 'we could all do with some good food and clean water. Ready a hunting party, Mr Moon!'

'Aye, aye, Sir!' he nodded to Gilbert who selected the men. 'Why don't you go ahead and forage, sir, and me and a few of the lads will stay behind and guard the boat?'

'A good suggestion, Mr Moon,' Dan agreed readily. He moved over to Dr Gilpin who had something important to tell him.

Moon and his party were some distance away. The Doctor sneaked a look at Dan's head. It confirmed his opinion. 'What we're looking for is a beach like this which ought to be on the other side of the island. We'll cover more ground if we separate.'

Moon and Gilbert watched the conspirators. 'We'll have every gun ready for them when they return, *Bosun* Gilbert.' Moon took off his bosun's hat and placed it on Gilbert's head.

'Aye, aye, *Captain* Moon,' said Gilbert, ecstatic.

Lambourn and Gilpin took some of the men with them and set off, soon disappearing into the jungle. Dan and Tarbuck, his foot still bandaged, led the other party off the beach.

Further into the interior of the island stood the long completed fortress of El Nebuloso. In the brilliant tropical sun the stone work of the palace shimmered against the vibrant greens of the life-teeming jungle beyond.

In the grandest room of his palace, El Nebuloso, the self-appointed Redeemer and Emperor of the island, dressed lavishly in orange silk robes with a magnificent headdress of gold and turquoise in the form of a striking snake, sat on his ornate throne. He idly fingered a chain of small solid golden skulls around his neck, symbolic of his power over life and death.

Near naked, pert-breasted Indian girls cooled him with fans and caressed his feet. Triola, his beautiful daughter, dressed in a simple, white, but silken and sensuous variation of a nun's habit, complete with its own rosary of tiny solid gold skulls at her waist, was also tended by handmaidens.

El Verdugo entered. An eccentrically moustached mechanical genius of a Frenchman with a passion for torture, he had been dubbed El Verdugo (literally 'the torture') by his Spanish employers.

Verdugo, daintily lifting the front of his robes, flitted down the marble stairs from the main hall, passing guards dressed according to El Nebuloso's concept of soldier priests. These Inquisition-style soldiers-of-the-Lord wore cowls, breastplates and swordbelts over monk's habits. The crosses which hung from their belts also saw temporal service as lethal daggers. Reaching the bottom, Verdugo glided across the gold-veined mosaic floor, falling to his knees before the throne and holding one of his Redeemer's feet to his nose said, bowing low, 'I gladly moisten your feet with my nostril, Your Barbarity. I 'ave a some-a-thing to show you . . .'

'Excellent, excellent,' enthused El Nebuloso, rising. He followed Verdugo towards his favourite room, the torture chamber. Triola followed them. Her handmaidens followed her.

Verdugo's workmen had just redesigned his latest torture chamber. 'I 'ave added a pool,' he began to explain as they walked. He was quick to react to El Nebuloso's look of concern. 'Oh, do not worry, Your Monstrosity, a pool of *acid*!' El Nebuloso smiled.

They entered the chamber. From the balcony on which they stood, they saw and smelt a deep, forty-foot-square pool of acid thirty feet beneath them at the bottom of the chamber. They passed by the usual racks and torture wheels as they descended the stone staircase to the poolside. A complicated mechanical chair-like device was set on an island in the middle of the pool.

'Explain to me, Señor Verdugo, the intricacies of this most Holy Instrument of Confession.' He turned. 'Triola, I don't think you should see this, my daughter.'

'But it's only another torture machine.' She was unable to hide her girlish excitement.

'No, I want it to be a surprise for you. Later, my sweet.'

'Oh all right, Daddy,' she pouted, turned and left the room. Her attendants followed obediently.

'Now,' her father said to Verdugo, 'your new confessional . . .'

'Ah yes,' said Verdugo in his outrageous French accent, as they reached the poolside, 'but first you will see, Your Severity, the instrument is surrounded by this acid which will destroy anything thrown into it – except gold and precious stones. But flesh and bone and iron . . .' At this point he dipped a long thin iron rod into the pool. It immediately became surrounded by a tumult of acrid gas bubbles. There was a hissing sound as the acid bit into the metal. He withdrew the still sizzling and now smaller rod.

'Impressive!' said El Nebuloso and, as he stepped onto the narrow gangway leading to the chair on the island, added, 'And it doesn't destroy gold, you say?'

'Oh no, Your Vapidity – even if they've swallowed their valuables there'll be no need for any more of those messy searches we used to 'ave . . . Your Horridity.'

'Unless we want one,' insisted El Nebuloso, his eyes gleaming.

'Of course, Your Outrageousness.'

El Nebuloso reached the tiny island with the chair. 'And this is the new confessional.' El Nebuloso pointed to the chair.

'Oh yes,' said El Verdugo proudly, climbing into the chair to demonstrate. 'It works this way. The prisoner is totally restrained by means of this iron banding.'

'Excellent! Excellent,' the Emperor congratulated him.

'But there is more to it than that, Oh Blizzard of the Wrong. By means of these ratchets and screws we can place any part of him in any position we want for as long as we want and do anything to it. You can break every bone in his hand, one at a time.'

'And feet?' asked El Nebuloso.

'Oh yes, and feet.'

'And back?'

'And back!'

'And slowly crush them *and* break them?' El Nebuloso was warming to the device.

321

'Oh yes, it is very effective, Your Acute Horrendousness.'

'People will be even more frightened of me when they hear I have this.' The Emperor began to salivate.

'Oh yes, definitely, Your Blind Stupidity.'

'Even you – Señor Verdugo?'

'Well, not me, obviously. I mean, I made it . . . it's my baby . . .'

'Let's see if it works,' roared El Nebuloso, suddenly motioning to a guard who clamped the iron bands tight round Verdugo's limbs. 'If it does not I shall have to despatch you with heavenly force.' Nebuloso heard his daughter calling from the throne-room. 'Excuse me a moment.'

He left smiling, as a terrified scream from Verdugo rang around the vault.

Dan's party of men were now in the thick of the jungle in the middle of the island. They moved forward stealthily. The alien vegetation and unfamiliar noises of the jungle added to their sense of unease. The harsh metallic sounds of insects, the shrill cries as multi-coloured birds shrieked out from the undergrowth, the very vegetation seemed to be closing in on them, almost totally cutting out the sun's friendly light. The air here hung hot and humid. There was no breeze to dry the rivulets of sweat which poured from their mosquito-plagued bodies.

Dan heard a rustling in the bushes and motioned silence to those behind him. 'Could be wild boar,' he whispered hopefully. They crept towards their anticipated prey. Suddenly there was a blood-curdling scream and out of the trees and bushes came an attacking horde of soldier priests, armed with sword-like crosses, heavy chain-like rosaries and weighted thuribles which they swung wildly and lethally. More soldier priests screaming horribly swung in on lianas. It was a massacre. Dan fought bravely and skilfully but round him sailors were strangled with rosaries and stabbed with crucifixes and when despatched were received into the bosom of the Lord in a multitude of rapid Extreme Unctions. Tarbuck was one of those killed, but only after a most heroic fight for his new Captain.

Dan, still fighting bravely, was at last overwhelmed and felt the point of a dagger press into his throat. He heard a cry from above him. The priests lowered their weapons as El Segundo barked further commands to them. Dan, the sole survivor, was soon tightly bound hand and foot and carried off into the jungle, trussed beneath a pole like a captured animal.

On the far side of the island Lambourn, walking ahead of Gilpin and the others, using his sword, hacked through a few final strands of undergrowth before emerging onto a beautiful beach. It looked deserted, but he thought it wise to take out his telescope and check it thoroughly. Behind him, Dr Gilpin came scurrying out of the dense foliage, busily working with a pestle, holding the mortar in his other hand. Over his shoulder his bag brimmed with herbs and leaves and roots. Excitedly, even as he walked, he dipped a quill into the mixture in the mortar and pricked some of it into his arm.

'I think I may have found the stuff which the Indians use to knock beasts out with . . .'

'Which what?' said Lambourn. He looked round from his telescope and was surprised not to see Gilpin. Then he spotted him lying, lifeless, on the ground. He rushed over to him.

Though still unable to rise, Gilpin was overjoyed. 'I've found it! The juice from the tree! It paralyses . . . instantly . . . though temporarily,' he added as power returned to his limbs.

Lambourn was more excited by what he had just seen through his telescope far off in the jungle behind them.

'They've captured Dan!' he shouted.

'Who?' said Gilpin groggily, stumbling towards him, pulling out his telescope.

'Shall we get reinforcements?' said Lambourn excitedly. 'Or try and catch them now?'

Gilpin had just brought his telescope up to his eye when he saw someone else, further up the beach. 'Wait a moment! What's that over there? *There's* our reinforcement!' he added mysteriously.

'What?' said Lambourn and then looked in the same direction. 'Good Lord, how did *he* get *here*?'

At the far end of the beach he could see Yellowbeard. He was rolling around on the sand. Then he stood up for a moment and began lurching from side to side, intent on some inexplicable business. Suddenly he turned and drew his sword. Then they saw three soldier priests wielding swords come running out of the jungle to attack. Yellowbeard, with enormous strength, parried the lunges of the first two priests and sent them sprawling. He ducked as the third priest leaped upon him and smartly threw him clean over his head. One of the first priests ran at him with his sword. Yellowbeard neatly dodged the blow and knocked the man flying with a jaw-splintering punch using the hilt of his sword.

'He seems to have taken a mild dislike to the priests,' observed Lambourn drily.

Yellowbeard's sword sliced into the sword-arm of the second priest. He turned immediately and almost in one movement kicked him in the face. He picked the man up and hurled him at a rock. The other two priests now kept their distance and were clearly wary of another assault. Yellowbeard strode over to the rock, picked up the semi-conscious man and threw him bodily at the other two. Then he stood his ground and glared at them. Suddenly he ran towards them with a mighty roar. All three ran off into the

324

distance. Yellowbeard turned his back on them in disgust and continued with his previous bizarre behaviour as though nothing had occurred.

'Let's get Yellowbeard, he'll help us rescue Dan,' said Gilpin.

'Yes, come on, men,' shouted Lambourn at the rest of their tired party. 'We must save Captain Dan.' They did not move.

'And the treasure . . .' added Gilpin pointedly and the men's enthusiasm quickly returned.

CHAPTER 8

El Segundo marched in front of his men; like a returning hunting party they entered El Nebuloso's throne-room. Dan hung, firmly trussed, under the pole carried by two giant priests.

'Greetings, Your Vehemence,' saluted El Segundo. 'Your mission is accomplished. Eight heathen souls by the Grace of God and Heavenly Force have attained eternal serenity.'

'Only eight!' said the Grand Emperor. 'Any money?'

'On the paltry side, Your Brutality,' confessed Segundo.

El Nebuloso swept down from his throne. 'So . . . your mission was as so much fart gas.'

'Oh no, Your Offensiveness,' El Segundo explained. 'The ship they came from is after Yellowbeard's treasure . . .'

At the sound of Yellowbeard's name El Nebuloso yelped in fear.

'He's not *here*,' El Segundo rapidly assured him, 'just some men looking for his treasure, and this . . .' indicating Dan, '. . . is one of their officers, Your Molestation . . .'

'Ah! The treasure of Yellowbeard!' El Nebuloso gloated . . . 'and now I am the . . .' he snapped out of his reverie. 'We must find out all he knows. I've got *just* the thing . . .'

El Segundo led them out towards the torture chamber. Gilbert, who had been following Dan, had managed in the confusion of the ambush to steal some robes from a fallen 'cleric' and fell in at the rear of their column. Having seen and heard enough he shrewdly made his exit . . .

327

In the torture chamber a stiff and aching Verdugo was released and dragged out of his machine in a state of collapse. 'This is very effective,' Nebuloso promised.

'I can confirm that,' moaned Verdugo feebly.

Dan was thrust roughly into the machine and the iron bands tightened. 'You may torture me,' said Dan bravely, 'but it will avail you nothing.'

'We'll see about that, sailor!' threatened Nebuloso.

El Nebuloso stood by on a parapet as El Segundo peered through his telescope at the jungle beneath him.

'Excuse me, Your Monstrosity. That prisoner of ours must be very important . . . there's quite a little army assembling down there.'

'Could he be their leader?' asked Nebuloso.

'No. There's a man of very high rank giving orders.'

'He must know where the treasure is,' Nebuloso pointed out, '*he's* the one we must capture.'

'That'll be difficult, Oh Berserk One, he'd be the last in the attack and the first to escape . . . that's leaders for you . . .'

'What did you say!' thundered El Nebuloso.

El Segundo realised his mistake. 'Oh, except for *you*, oh Great and Mindless Slaughterer . . .'

El Nebuloso let out an enormous roar. Fearing the worst, El Segundo began to bang his head repeatedly against the battlements.

'That's the answer!' he concluded in a flash of inspiration. 'We shall lure their leader to the front by allowing their assault to succeed.' He paced up and down excitedly. 'We will pretend to resist and feign injury and death when they attack.' He paused, suddenly noticing El Segundo's bizarre behaviour. 'What *are* you doing, banging your head like that?'

'Was I?' said Segundo, innocently.

'We all saw you, you silly man . . .' He quickly returned to his throne. 'Once the invaders have reached the throne-room my men will rise up and despatch them all with maximum Heavenly Force.'

'A magnificent strategy, Your Arrogance,' said El Segundo with genuine enthusiasm.

'It must look realistic,' warned El Nebuloso. 'Anyone caught over-acting I shall personally frighten to death.'

It took Gilbert most of the afternoon to find his way back to the camp on the shore near the *Edith*. Moon sat barbequeing a fish on his hook when Gilbert, still in soldier-priest garb, rushed up to him. 'They've captured Dan,' said Gilbert breathlessly, 'and the others are going to attack the fortress to rescue him . . .'

'Excellent.' Moon calmly pulled the fish off his hook. 'They're making it easy for us. Well done, Gilbert!' He shook Gilbert's hand firmly in both of his. There was a hissing sound as Gilbert's hand singed on the still scalding hook . . .

Triola liked Dan a lot. She was beginning to think that she was in love, but she was a practical girl and preferred to fall in love with people she knew a little about. So she decided that as soon as El Verdugo took his supper-break she would pop down to the torture chamber.

Even as she walked across the gangway to the chair she decided that he was definitely the most attractive young man she'd ever seen tortured. 'Is it too cold for you?' she asked, kindly.

'I'm all right,' said Dan, bearing his painful position bravely.

'You *must* tell my father where the treasure is or you will surely die.' There was genuine concern in her voice.

'I'll tell him nothing.' His upper lip stiffened.

'But he only wants it for the grace and glory of God.'

'What kind of God is it,' asked Dan, 'that kills and tortures men?'

'My father's only purpose is to enable heathen souls to enter Heaven more rapidly than they would of their own accord. Please tell him, it hurts me to see you hurt.'

The iron bands and pressure screws were really biting now. Dan somehow kept his composure.

'It hurts me to see you be hurt by me being hurt,' he said.

Triola moved closer. 'I think I love you.'

'You're right, you do and I love you,' he said through gritted teeth, 'and when I am rescued I want you to come with me.'

'To come with you would mean leaving here. Are you taking the treasure?' She inspected her nails casually.

'That's right,' said Dan. Triola smiled warmly. 'Triola, you realise your father may be killed?'

'Oh, Daddy won't mind,' she bubbled with girlish glee, 'he's a bit odd about things like that. I must pack my things,' and with that she blew him a kiss and skipped off happily.

It was shortly before sunrise.

In the jungle, on the slopes below El Nebuloso's palace, Lambourn and Gilpin were assembling the men ready for their attack. Yellowbeard was still nowhere to be seen. They could wait no longer. At a signal from Lambourn they moved quickly and cautiously through the undergrowth up the hillside.

Out of sight behind the parapet, El Segundo completed his final check on the positions of his men. As the thin first light of dawn caught the leaves of the forest below, El Segundo cackled to himself in anticipation.

Lambourn, with Dr Gilpin close behind, inched forward into position behind a bush which was their last piece of cover before the gates of the stronghold. He checked that his men were all in position below him and was about to tell them to attack when he saw Yellowbeard carrying a keg of gunpowder with a lighted fuse sticking out of it stride uncaringly past his concealed men with as much caution as someone out for an early morning stroll.

Pushing a gesticulating Lambourn aside, Yellowbeard strode straight up to the massive oak doors of the main gate, placed his fizzing keg in front of them and then walked back a few yards waiting unconcernedly for the explosion. As the fuse sparkled closer to the top of the keg, Lambourn and his men shielded themselves as best they could. There was a tremendous explosion.

Lambourn thought he shouted 'attack', though deafened by the blast not even he heard it. Looking up at the walls he saw a series of soldier priests fall spectacularly from the battlements, one or two of which Lambourn thought were rather too far away from the explosion.

As the smoke cleared in the gateway it became obvious that the huge doors were completely shattered.

Behind the battlements El Segundo was annoyed with his men for dying so far from the explosion. As a priest staggered past him with full drama, a sword stuck dramatically underneath his arm, Segundo grabbed the sword and replaced it in the man's scabbard. 'That wouldn't fool anybody,' he complained. Then he noticed something odd about the man standing next to him. Despairingly his eyes rolled heavenwards. He bent down and picked up the soldier's additional leg complete with painted-on blood and threw it at the man. 'Pathetic!' he hissed in disgust.

'What about this, sir?' An eager priest tapped him on the shoulder, then pumped his arm up and down and stroked his neck lightly with his sword. Red liquid spurted out from his neck far too vigorously, spattering El Segundo.

'If you don't get closer before you die,' he warned them all angrily, 'I'll kill you.'

Before the last pieces of debris from the explosion had reached the ground, Yellowbeard, cutlass in hand, charged the gateway. Several soldier priests staggered out through the archway giving great performances as they writhed and fell as though mortally wounded. Yellowbeard roared his way through into the stronghold slashing viciously at those who got in his way. Behind him he left a gory trail of really dead and wounded men. The wounded complained bitterly and loudly that they had not expected it to be like this.

Yellowbeard fought his way destructively through to a courtyard. Biting the right ear of one soldier priest who got in his way, he ran off, his cutlass dripping blood, into the palace.

El Segundo unknowingly congratulated two really dead men on their performance but became annoyed at the incredible wailing and groaning coming from the soldier with the missing ear. 'Don't overdo it, Vasquez,' yelled Segundo, angered by the man's performance. He wandered off to look at the next group.

Lambourn, encouraged by Yellowbeard's advance and the enormous carnage already achieved, unsheathed his sword and waved his party into the attack. 'This way, men.'

As they ran through into the courtyard many more of the enemy fell to their swords or actually, Gilpin thought, 'sometimes slightly before their swords . . .' but it was difficult to be sure in the heat of battle. Lambourn was almost overcome by his own bravery. He waved his men on. Gilpin's firing-piece went off accidentally. Behind him four more men fell from the battlements. Lambourn grinned. 'Well done Doctor!' and ran on. Gilpin did not. He paused thoughtfully and walked over to the men he had 'killed' . . .

El Segundo was inspecting his guards in an inner court-yard and became apoplectically enraged when one man fell over backwards throwing two false legs into the air.

'I will have no more bad acting . . .' he screamed. At that

precise moment he turned and impaled himself on Lambourn's sword as the men from the *Edith* ran into the courtyard. El Segundo staggered round the courtyard gasping, gaping, tottering, stumbling, moaning, falling, staggering up again, shuddering and then, with a final scream, fell down flat on his back with Lambourn's sword still embedded in his chest.

Segundo's men, thinking this was yet another performance, gave him an enthusiastic round of applause. As soon as Gilpin pronounced that El Segundo was indeed dead, Lambourn retrieved his sword and led his men off.

With Mrs Beard's information at his disposal, Clement had no difficulty finding the island. He, Mansell and Betty were now being rowed ashore in one of the frigate's long-boats. Clement peered through his telescope.

'There's no one on board the *Edith* as far as I can see and there's some kind of battle at a fortress over there, Mansell.'

'I expect they'll be fighting over the treasure, sir, won't they? They usually do, sir, don't they, sir?'

'*Do* they, Mansell?'

They continued their journey to the shore followed by two more long-boats full of scarlet-uniformed marines.

The now incredibly brave Lambourn stood with a whole room full of 'injured' and 'dead' priests behind him. Several of them had gone too far with axes in their heads, swords through throats and even one or two yet more unrealistic dismemberments. Gilpin was at the other end of the room apparently examining the fallen men.

Lambourn ran through into the torture chamber and below him saw Dan in the chair. On the steps beside the pool stood El Nebuloso.

'Release that man!' Lambourn shouted.

'Ha ha!' laughed the Emperor. 'You have fallen for one of my less likely plans.'

Two 'dead' guards near Lambourn stood up, grinning. 'Ah, I see,' said Lambourn, though not doing so.

El Nebuloso strode triumphantly to the stop of the steps and raised his arms. 'Stand up, men!' There was no reaction. 'Stand up!!' he repeated.

'I administered a dose of this to them all, just as a precaution,' called Gilpin from the entrance to the chamber, holding up his quill and a flask of liquid. One of the two guards who had 'recovered' went to attack him but Gilpin stabbed him with his quill, giving the second guard another jab. Immediately they both slumped to the ground paralysed.

Realising he was on his own, El Nebuloso decided on a change of plan. 'Very well then, you fools,' he said dramatically. 'You have left me no choice, I shall have to . . . give in completely. Sorry, sorry, everyone . . . so sorry. I'll just go and set your friend free then, shall I then?'

Lambourn and Gilpin were amazed at this and turned to exchange views. As they did so El Nebuloso made a sudden dash and then stood his ground on the gangway over the acid pool. 'I'm much too fiendish for the likes of you white-faced persons. Your friend who you value so highly is in my power . . .'

Something on the far side of the chamber above and behind El Nebuloso caught Gilpin's attention. He nudged Lambourn. There descending the wall on a rope was Yellowbeard.

'What sort of power?' said Gilpin, now anxious to keep the conversation flowing at all costs.

El Nebuloso was intrigued. 'What?'

Lambourn, catching on, joined in. 'What sort of power do you have?'

'My divine right to command over life and death,' replied El Nebuloso.

'Oh,' said Gilpin, 'I thought you meant power . . . mechanical energy . . . that sort of thing . . .'

'Yes, I thought he meant that,' agreed Lambourn.

'As Ruler, my Supremacy is Absolute on this island.' He began to turn towards Dan.

Quickly Lambourn added a distraction. 'I thought this was an atoll . . .'

'An atoll?' Gilpin helped. 'Not atoll, I mean not at all. An atoll has a central lagoon. I thought this was an isthmus.'

'Yes.' Other sailors who had joined them began to agree or disagree.

'Silence!' the Emperor screamed. 'And obey or I will kill your Captain. I have despatched many souls to Heaven and God is on my side.'

At that moment Yellowbeard swung over the acid pool on a chain hanging from a torture cage high in the ceiling. He landed at the chair end of the gangway. El Nebuloso turned around as he roared ferociously.

'Yellowbeard!' El Nebuloso screamed in horror and he reeled backwards into the pool. The pool became a heaving mass of bubbles as the Emperor El Nebuloso started to disintegrate.

Lord Lambourn ran to release the astonished Dan.

'Father! We thought you were dead!'

'Us Yellowbeards are never more dangerous than when we're dead. How are you getting on piratin', lad?'

'Er, well . . . er,' began Dan.

'How many men have you killed so far?' the pirate-father grinned.

'Er, one . . . two, I think.'

'You think! You'll never kill anyone if you go around thinking.'

At that moment Dan saw Triola arrive at the far side of the gangway. Behind her were two handmaidens with her luggage.

'Ah Triola, I'd like you to meet my father,' said Dan, glad to be free of that dreadful chair.

'Ah,' said Yellowbeard, eyeing her lasciviously, 'been out rapin', lad? Nice work.'

'No, I haven't raped her!' Dan was indignant.

'No you wouldn't 'ave, you poncy little git. You're not the prawn of my loins. Your mother's a bloody liar, that's what I liked about her. She couldn't be your mother, no woman ever slept with me and lived.'

'What happened to my father?' asked Triola urgently.

'I killed him.' Yellowbeard was proud.

'He's gone to Heaven,' explained Dan gently.

'Oh that's nice,' Triola looked relieved, 'he's sent all his friends there . . .'

'She's yours then, is she, Dan?' Yellowbeard advanced on her. 'Let me have a bit of a prod at her first.'

'Father!' yelled Dan, appalled.

There was a cry from the stairway. It was one of the men from the *Edith* with a dagger through his chest.

'Captain Dan, Captain Dan, sir!' he called as he fell. 'It's . . . it's . . .' and, with his last gasp, whispered, '. . . Mr Moon.'

'Moon!' yelled Yellowbeard. 'That shithead Moon. It's time I got rid of him,' and he began to flail wildly with his cutlass.

'Dad, Dad, stop that!' shouted Dan. 'We'll all fight Mr Moon.'

'Oh good, another battle,' beamed Lambourn. 'Well done, son, Captain, Dan.'

Above, in the throne room, Moon assembled his men. 'Right, lads, we shouldn't have much trouble mopping up this little lot. Come on, men, let's get what we came for . . .'

Lambourn and Gilpin each stood behind a pillar either side of the doorway which led to the balcony above the acid pool. They held a chain loosely between them. Dan and the

336

other three or four of his surviving sailors placed themselves strategically around the entrance and waited. Yellowbeard had disappeared again.

The doors burst open as Moon, Gilbert and his men raced in. Lambourn and Gilpin jerked their chain taut and Gilbert, his momentum carrying him on, his legs caught by the chain, sailed clean over the balcony and fell screaming into the acid pool below.

'So long, mate, I'll look after your share . . .' Moon called after him.

'No you won't, Mr Moon,' said Dan leaping out in front of him.

'Oh it's little Dan,' grinned Moon as he advanced on the retreating Dan.

With a roar, swinging in on a rope, Yellowbeard landed between them. 'Moon, you bastard what betrayed me!' He lunged at him with his cutlass and drove him back to the wall with a series of sword thrusts. 'I'm going to make you eat both your own buttocks . . .'

A general fight broke out, Dan taking on two of Moon's men in a fine display of swordsmanship.

Lambourn, somehow sensing a little more realism in this fresh outbreak of violence around him, hid behind a torture wheel and took a few sips of brandy.

Triola bravely laid out one of Moon's men with the ball from a ball-and-chain she'd found lying in a corner. Gilpin accounted for anyone that passed with his poisonous quill.

After the fiercest of fights Yellowbeard had Moon at bay with his cutlass to his windpipe and a pillar behind him and, seeing that Dan had successfully dealt with two of Moon's men, yelled, 'He's all yours, lad!' and ran out of the room, anxious to get to his treasure.

Moon's strength soon rallied and his mouth watered at the sight of young Dan. He advanced on him. Easily parrying his first two blows he then drove him down the stairs towards the acid pool with a series of vicious thrusts. Dan was cornered by a balustrade. Moon, parrying a thrust from Dan, continued his movement with a flick of his wrist, enveloping Dan's sword and disarming him. Dan's sword flew towards the pool but landed safely on the gangway. Just as Moon was about to make his final lunge, Dan leaped out and down onto the gangway beneath. As he picked up his sword, Moon ran to join him on the gangway. A desperate fight to the death ensued above the still fuming pool of acid. What Dan lacked in strength he made up for with speed and skill. Finally Dan disarmed Moon who, momentarily off balance, was knocked from the gangway by a bucket thrown at him from the pool's edge by the anxious Triola. He fell helplessly and horribly to an acid pool death.

'Good shot, young lady,' called Lambourn.

Triola ran to embrace Dan. 'Later, Triola, I must find my father.'

'He ran down to the beach,' said Lambourn.

Dan ran off.

From the end of the beach Dan saw his father in the distance crawling, staggering, holding his back as though he'd been stabbed, falling to the ground, then staggering on again. Dan ran up to him.

'Stagger, stagger, crawl, crawl, stagger, stagger, crawl,' mumbled Yellowbeard.

'Are you all right, Father?'

'Oh bugger me, I've forgotten where I was, you stupid little sod.'

'Well what were you doing?' asked Dan, perplexed.

'Shut up,' said Yellowbeard. 'Now did I just say stagger or was it crawl?'

'I don't know,' admitted Dan, wondering how that could be significant.

'It was crawl – but was it crawl to the right, crawl to the left or crawl crawl then right and then a stagger, or was it, oh bugger, you've sodded the whole thing up like the stupid little twerp that you are. I was recreating what happened twenty years ago, man and boy . . .'

'Oh I see,' said Dan uncertainly. 'Why didn't you say?'

'Because I wanted to betray you.'

'But why?'

'I had to, betrayal is all part of piratin'. If you don't know that you're not even close to bein' a pirate. Prawn of my loins my foot . . .'

'What?' said Dan, not really understanding his father.

'You're either born a pirate or not. It's in the blood, Dan, and it's not in yours or you'd have betrayed me long ago.'

'All right. I may not be a pirate,' agreed Dan, 'but at least I've got a brain in my head so why don't we just follow the instructions . . .'

'Right!' said Yellowbeard and, with a single swipe of his cutlass, shaved the top of Dan's hair clean off. He examined the newly revealed scalp.

'Four crawls north, east at the rock, crawl twice, then dig.' Yellowbeard paced out the ground. 'Come on, lad, give us a hand,' he shouted. They both began digging away energetically at the sand near the edge of the jungle with their swords.

'The way you was fightin' back there, Dan, there may be some pirate blood in you after all . . .'

'I tricked Moon's man into falling into the acid . . .'

'With your head on my shoulders we could wreck civilisation.' Yellowbeard burrowed away happily . . .

Further down the beach, at present out of sight, Clement and Mansell and a long line of Marines followed Betty's lead.

'Well, Commander Clement, I had high hopes you'd split half the loot with me . . . I wouldn't tell anybody . . .' she sighed.

'Just lead me to Yellowbeard, that's all I want . . .' said Clement patiently.

Lord Lambourn, Dr Gilpin and Triola arrived in time to help Yellowbeard and Dan unearth four large chests. Yellowbeard allowed Dan the privilege of prying open the first chest with his dagger. The ancient lid creaked open and there revealed were vast quantities of gold and gems, pieces of eight and ingots of silver. The whole group rejoiced wildly, hugging each other and cavorting around dancing with joy. Yellowbeard frenziedly hugged his son Dan, then, with a startled look, he staggered backwards, pointing to Dan's dagger which was now embedded in his stomach. Dan was horrified at the enormity of the tragedy.

'But I didn't . . . it's . . .'

But Yellowbeard's startled look transformed into a delighted smile as he fell to the ground, oozing blood. 'You *are* a Yellowbeard . . . killing your father as I killed my father before me . . .'

'Dad, the blood . . .' Dan cradled him in his arms . . .

'Blood,' said Yellowbeard as he dipped his finger in his wound, put it to his dying lips and licked it ghoulishly. 'Blood, that's what I like to hear. You *are* my son.' He died, happily . . .

This sad and bewildered tableau around the treasure was interrupted by the arrival of Clement, Mansell and Betty, followed by the Marines with guns ready.

'Well done there, lad, got him at last . . .' Clement congratulated Dan.

'Hello, Dan, hello, lambchop,' Betty greeted them. 'Wonderful to see you . . . pity about your Dad . . . on the other hand it is the way what he said he wanted to go . . .' She paused. 'Horribly,' she added.

'I claim this treasure . . .' announced Clement with due pomp . . .

'He claims it?' queried Triola.

Clement continued . . . 'in the name of Her Majesty, Queen Anne . . .'

'Dan darling,' simpered Triola, 'I don't think I love you any more.'

'You're right, you don't. Goodbye, Triola . . .' Dan walked quickly away and ran off into the jungle.

Triola, sensing a change in fortune, sidled up to Clement. 'You have a lovely bottom, blue-eyes,' she said winningly . . . 'I've fallen in love with you . . .'

'What?' Clement was startled.

Mansell explained. 'She said you have a lovely bottom, sir and that she's . . .'

'Shut up, Mansell.' Clement blushed.

Triola nuzzled up to Clement who didn't object.

'Mansell! Clap that lot in irons for piracy on the High Seas! Where's that damned so-called son of Yellowbeard?'

Triola's sudden affection for him had momentarily made him forgetful.

'He ran off all upset because he killed his Daddy . . .' Betty whined.

'Shall I send a search party, sir?' asked Mansell.

'No, don't bother.'

'Poor little mite,' wailed Betty.

'Right, let's get this lot loaded onto the ship, Mansell.'

Lambourn protested. 'You're just going to leave him here?'

'He'll be better off than you,' said Clement, and added sarcastically, '. . . your Lordship.'

Two marines stood guard over Lambourn, Gilpin and Betty as they sat in chains on the deck. In the Captain's cabin, Clement and Mansell and Triola were relaxing after a fine dinner, examining their exotic gems.

'I was thinking,' reflected Mansell, 'Her Majesty can have no idea how much treasure she's got, can she, sir?'

'No, she can't,' Clement concurred, while gracefully accepting a jewel-encrusted crown offered to him by Triola, '. . . or even where we are, Mansell . . .'

'Oh I say, sir . . .' Mansell was awed by the implications of Clement's remark.

'Mansell, are you thinking what I think you're thinking?'

'I'll think whatever you say, sir . . .'

'Well, Mansell, have you ever been to the Americas?'

There was a crash of shattering glass and splintering woodwork as the fearsome spectres of Dan and Yellowbeard, both with smoke billowing from their glowing manes, hurtled, swords drawn, to the middle of the cabin.

'Us Yellowbeards are never more dangerous than when we're dead,' roared Dan.

Lambourn, Gilpin and Betty, released from their bonds, all burst into the room armed to the teeth. Triola leaped back to Dan's side. 'Oh Dan, I think I love you.' She smiled triumphantly. He moved to embrace her.

'Come on, lad . . .' bellowed Yellowbeard, finishing off a goblet of wine torn from the startled Clement's hand, '. . . there's piratin' to be done . . .'

The skull and crossbones fluttered to the top of the frigate's main mast as she sailed into the setting sun which is, as we all know, westward . . .